RENEGADE
Arts Entertainment

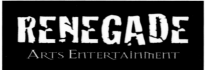

Presents

FRANK

Story & Art by
Ben Rankel

Letters by
Ryan Ferrier

Cover Design by
Ben Rankel & Ryan Ferrier

Editor
Alexander Finbow

Frank conceived, written and drawn by Ben Rankel.
Published by Renegade Arts Canmore Ltd trading as Renegade Arts Entertainment Ltd.

Hard Cover ISBN: 9781987825503 Soft Cover ISBN: 9781988903354

Office of Publication 25 Prospect Heights, Canmore, Alberta T1W 2S2 Canada
Renegade Arts Entertainment Ltd and logos are TM and copyright Renegade Arts Canmore Ltd.

Renegade Arts Entertainment is
Alexander Finbow Doug Bradley Alan Grant John Finbow Luisa Harkins
Emily Pomeroy Sean Tonelli.

Printed May 2018 in Canada by Friesens.

Check out more titles from Renegade Arts Entertainment at our website.

RenegadeArtsEntertainment.com

Made with the support of the Alberta Government through the Alberta Media Fund

FSC
www.fsc.org
MIX
Paper from
responsible sources
FSC® C016245

Alberta
Government

ENVIRONMENTAL BENEFITS STATEMENT
Renegade Arts Canmore Ltd saved the following
resources by printing the pages of this book on
chlorine free paper made with 10% post-consumer
waste.

TREES	WATER	ENERGY	SOLID WASTE	GREENHOUSE GASES
1	557	1	38	103
FULLY GROWN	GALLONS	MILLION BTUs	POUNDS	POUNDS

Environmental impact estimates were made using the Environmental Paper Network
Paper Calculator 3.2. For more information visit www.papercalculator.org.

By
Ben Rankel

Letters by
Ryan Ferrier

My deepest thanks to my partner, Fiona. It is not hyperbole to say that without your support this book couldn't exist.

Special thanks to Alexander Finbow and Ryan Ferrier for working with me and to absolutely anyone who ever liked a FRANK related image that I posted on Instagram.

You kept me going.

Ben Rankel - April 2nd 2018

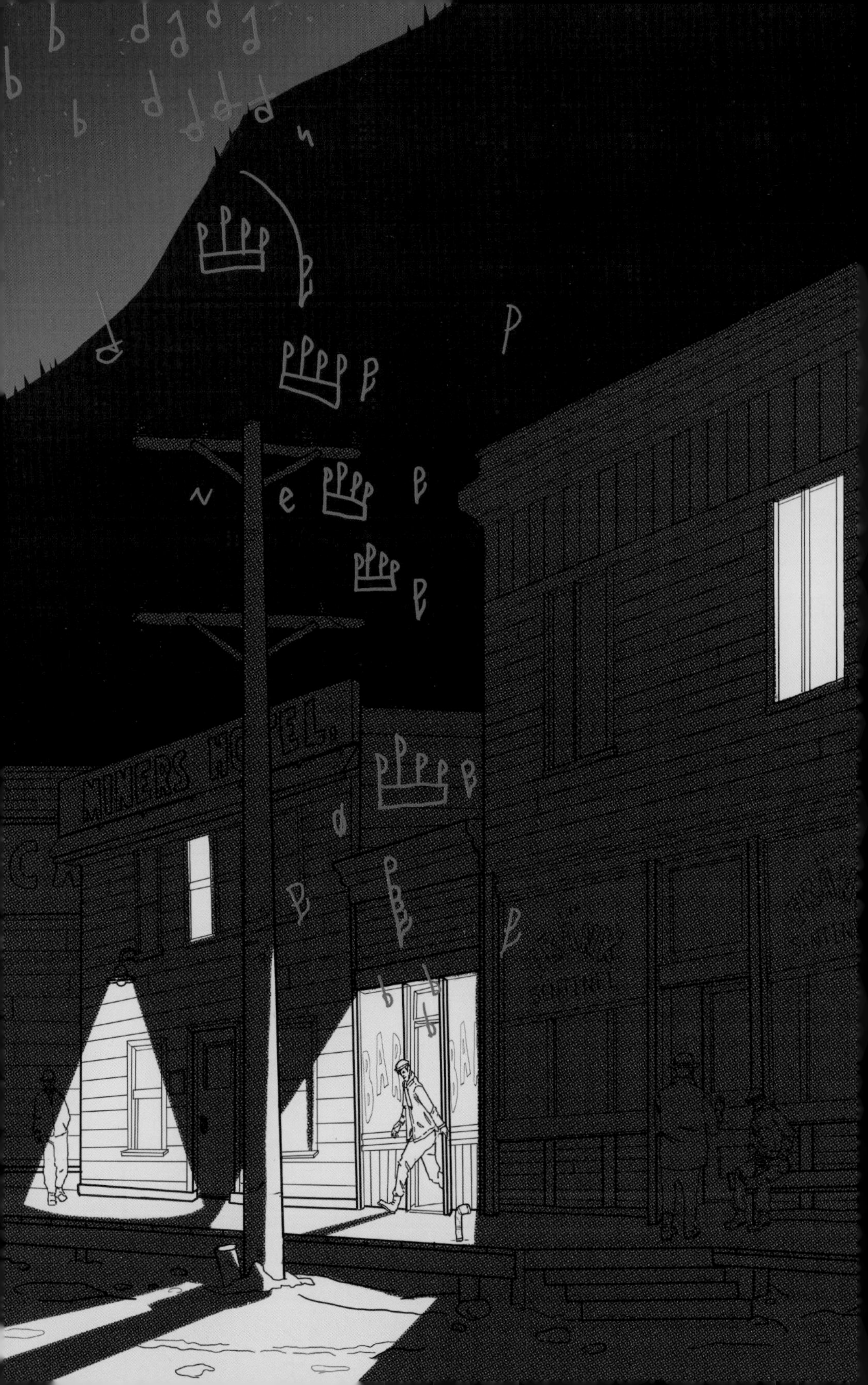
MINERS HOTEL
BAR

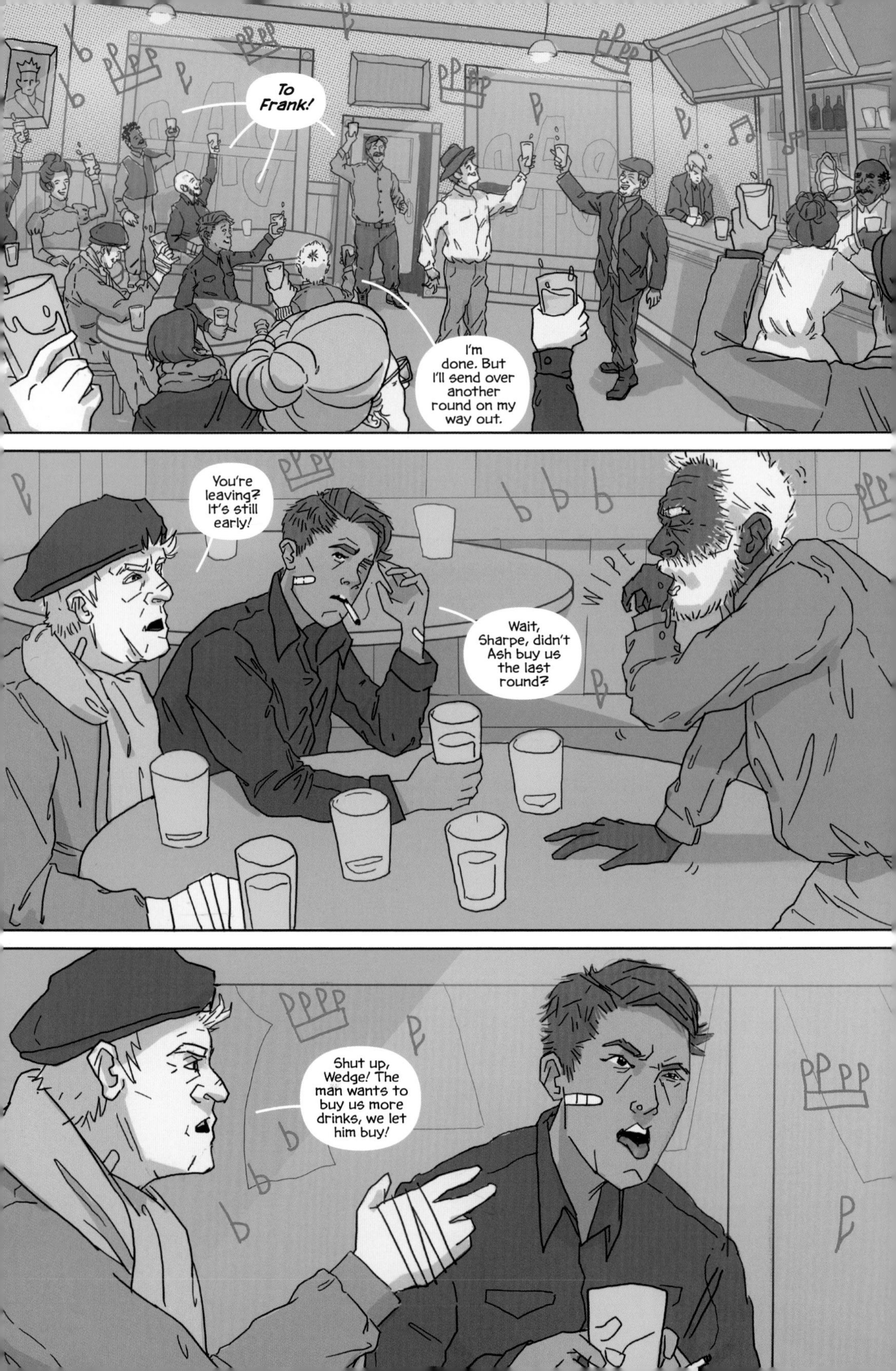

To Frank!
I'm done. But I'll send over another round on my way out.
You're leaving? It's still early!
WIPE
Wait, Sharpe, didn't Ash buy us the last round?
Shut up, Wedge! The man wants to buy us more drinks, we let him buy!

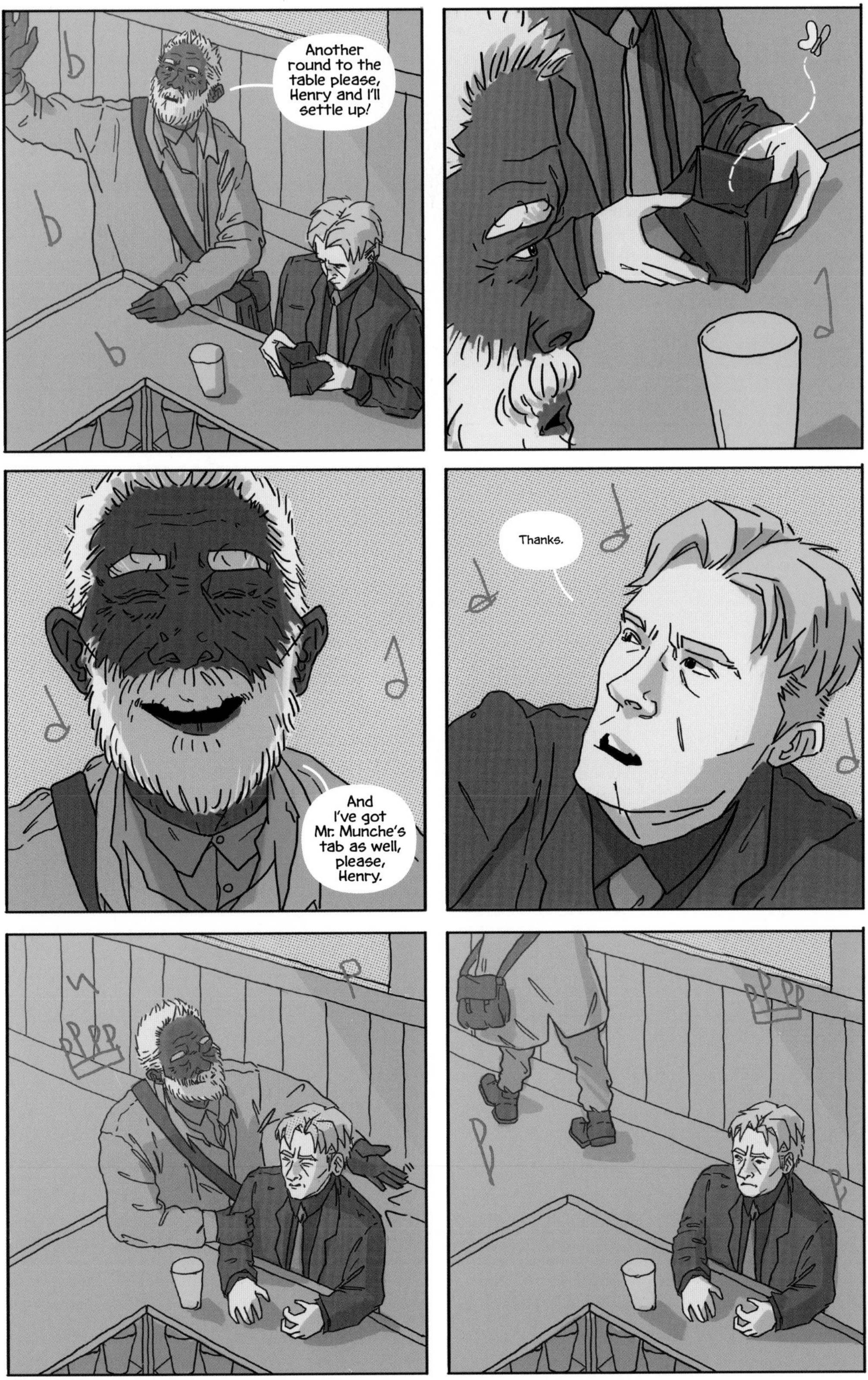
Another round to the table please, Henry and I'll settle up!
And I've got Mr. Munche's tab as well, please, Henry.
Thanks.

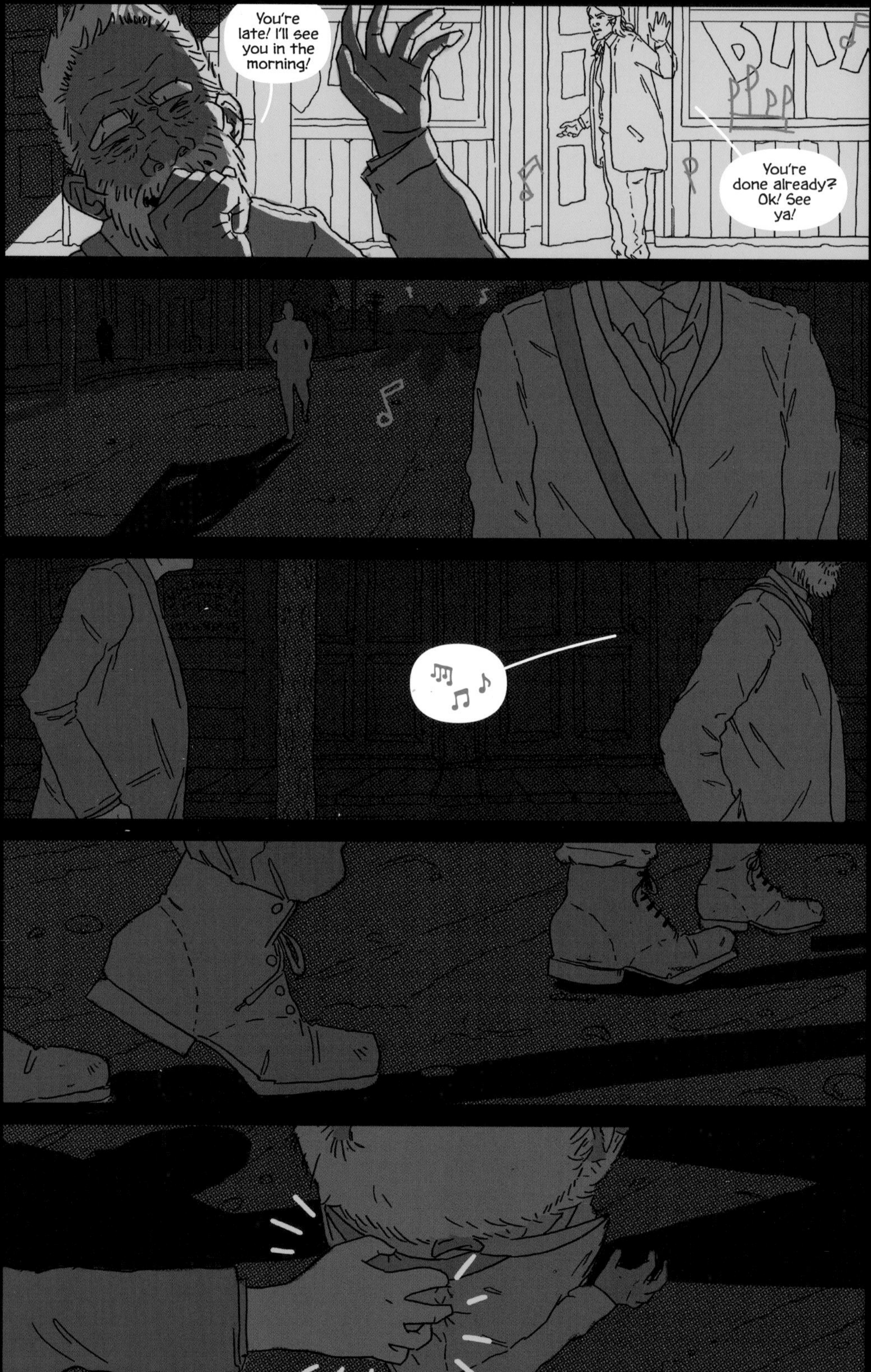
You're late! I'll see you in the morning!
You're done already? Ok! See ya!
♬ ♫ ♪

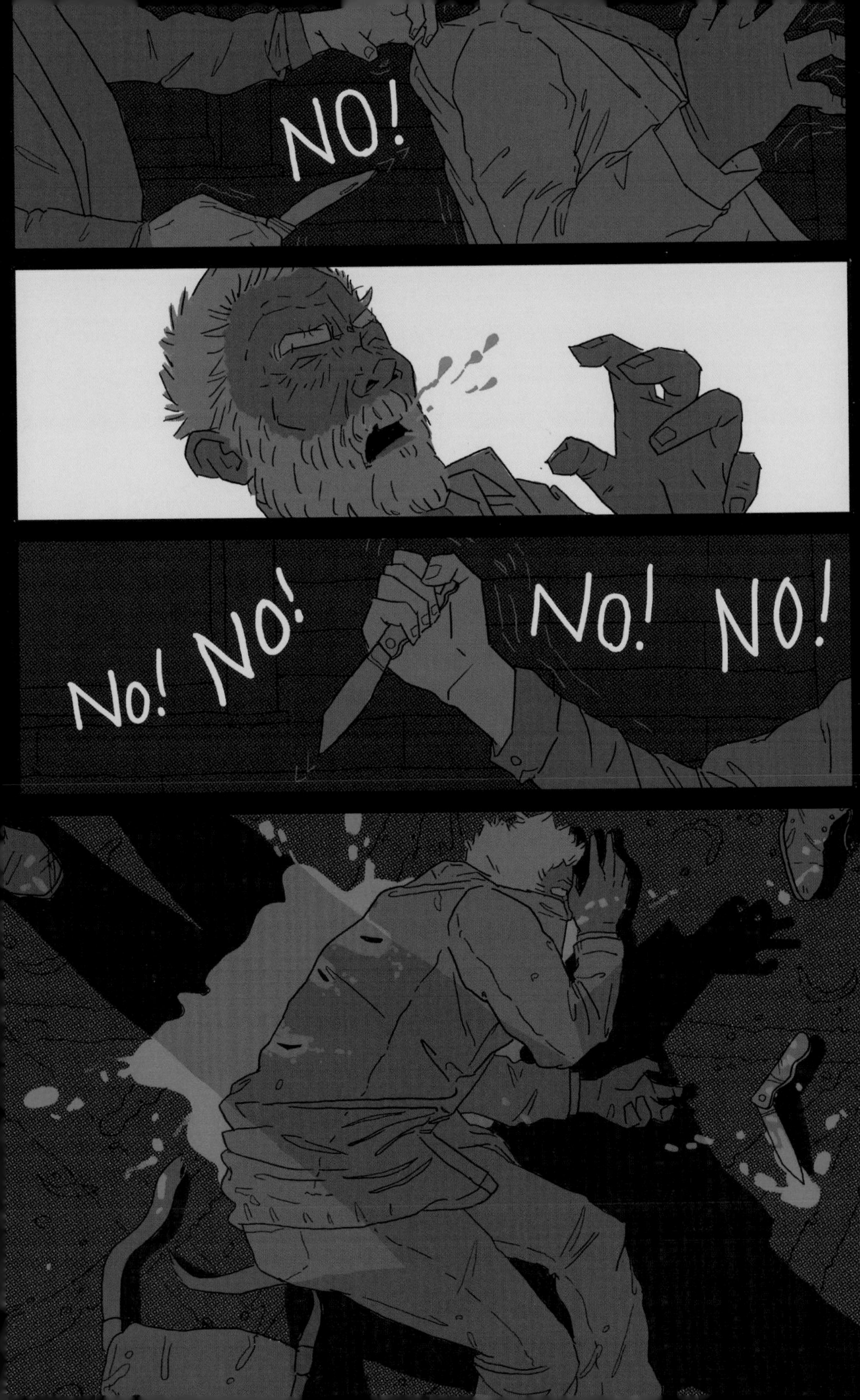
NO!
No!
NO!
No!
NO!

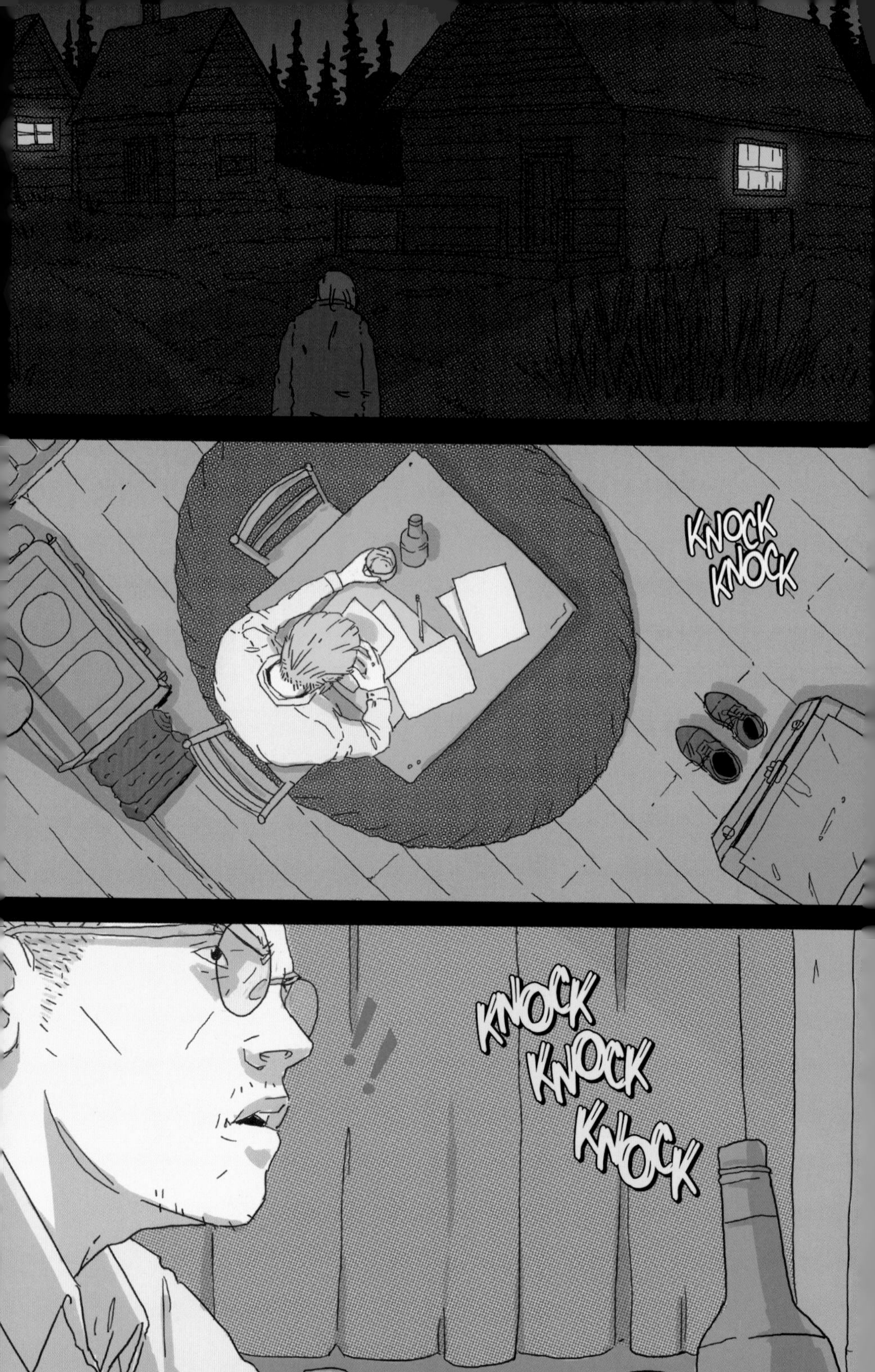
KNOCK KNOCK
!!
KNOCK KNOCK KNOCK

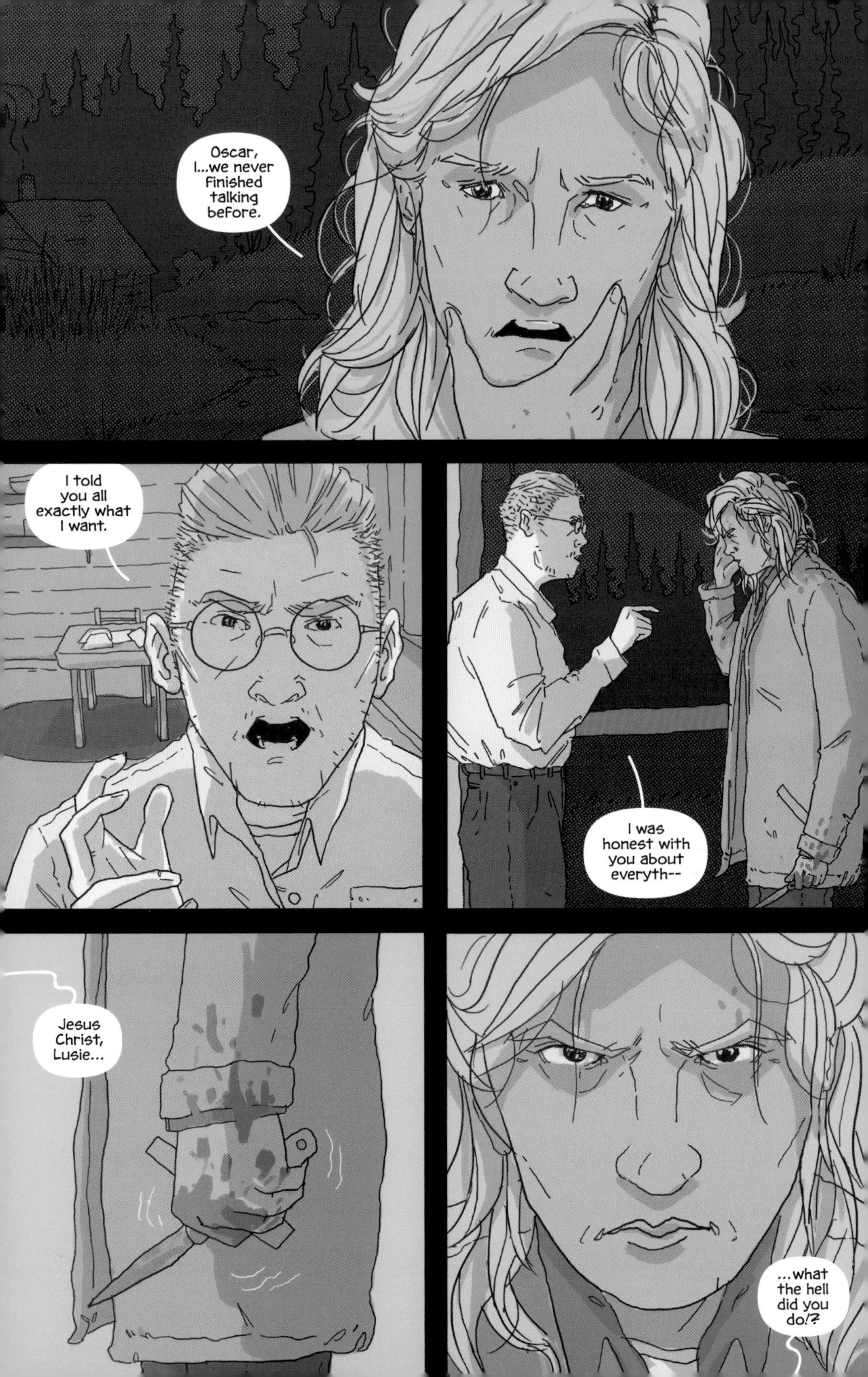
Oscar, I...we never finished talking before.
I told you all exactly what I want.
I was honest with you about everyth--
Jesus Christ, Lusie...
...what the hell did you do!?

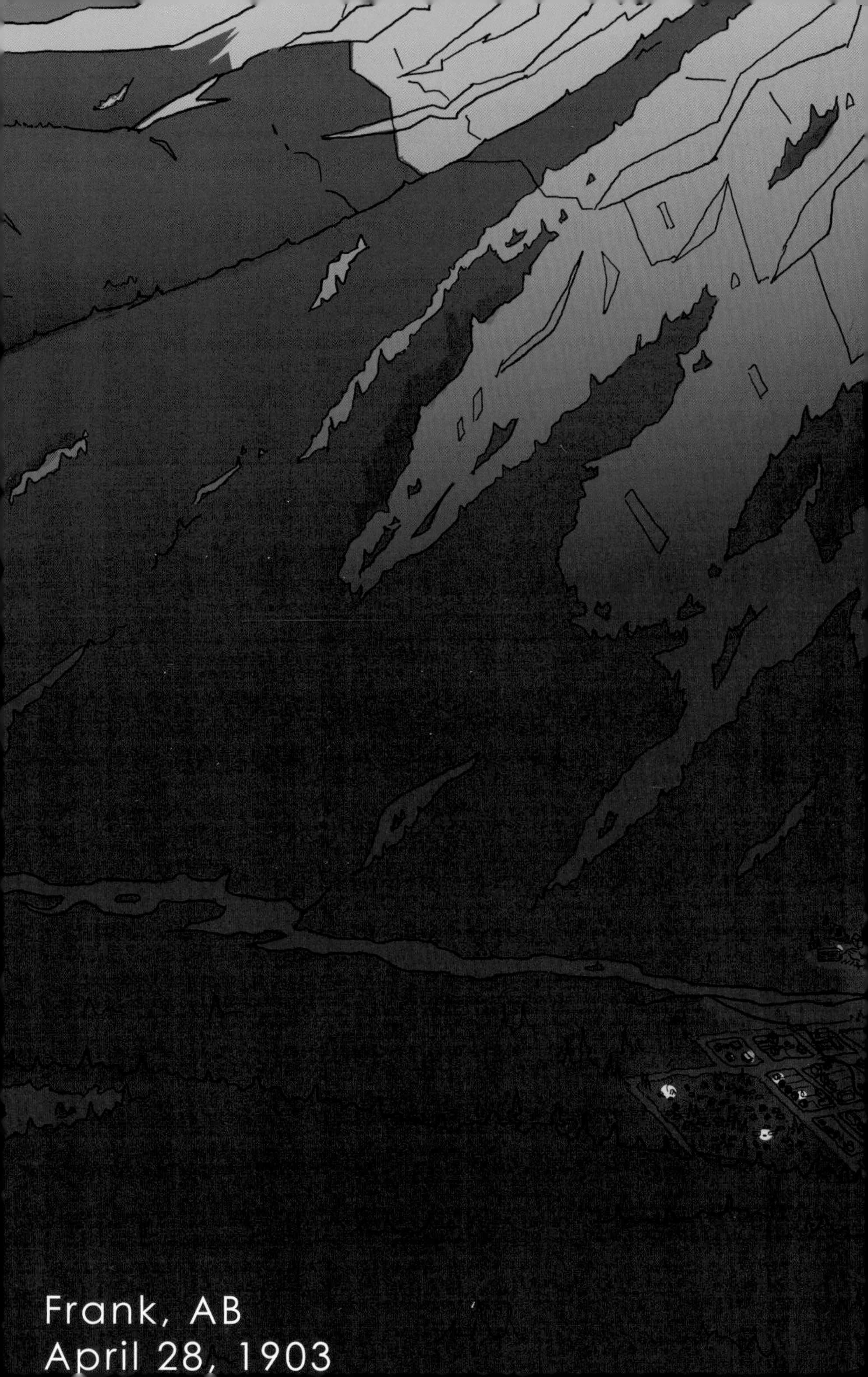
Frank, AB
April 28, 1903

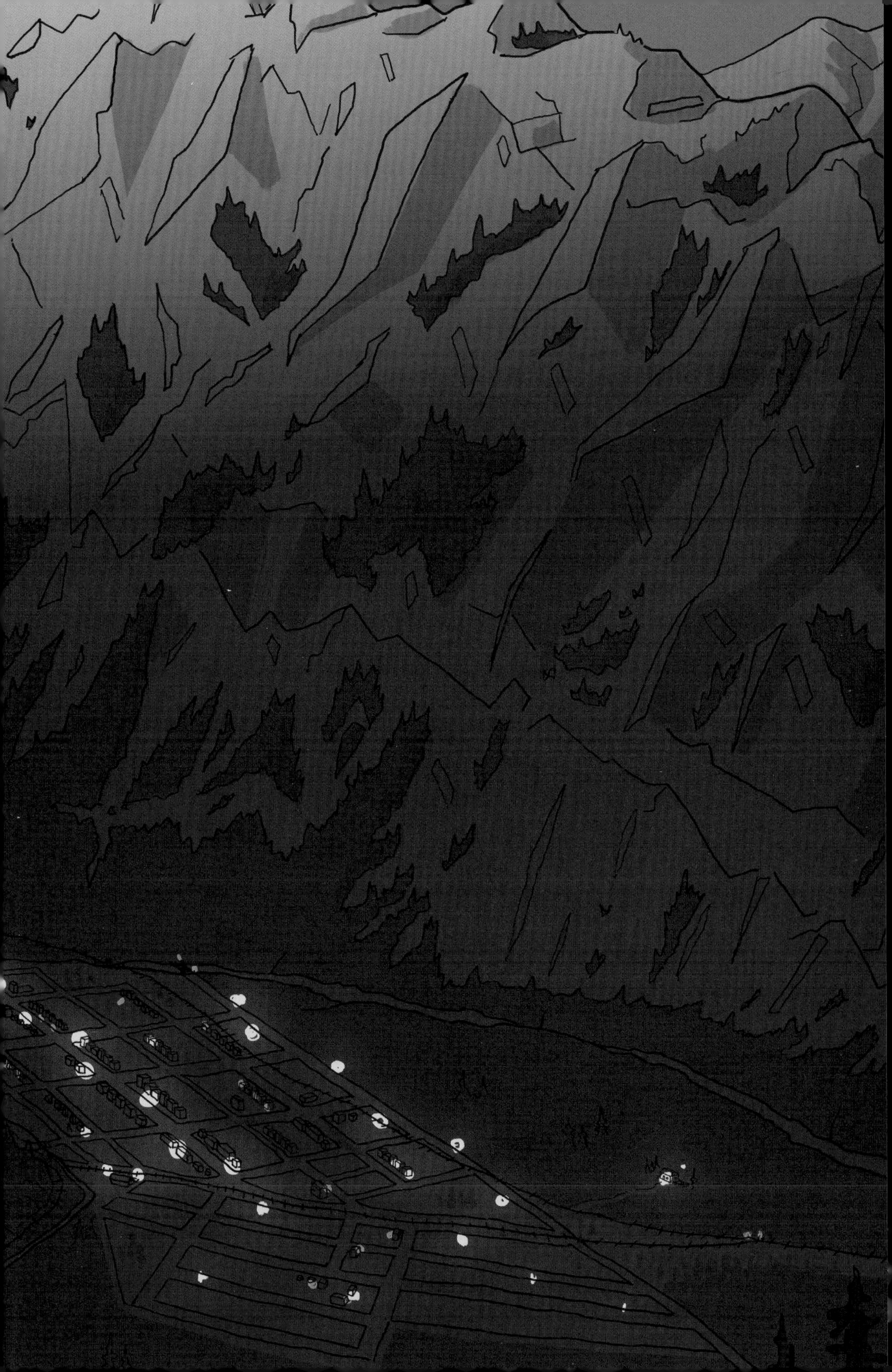

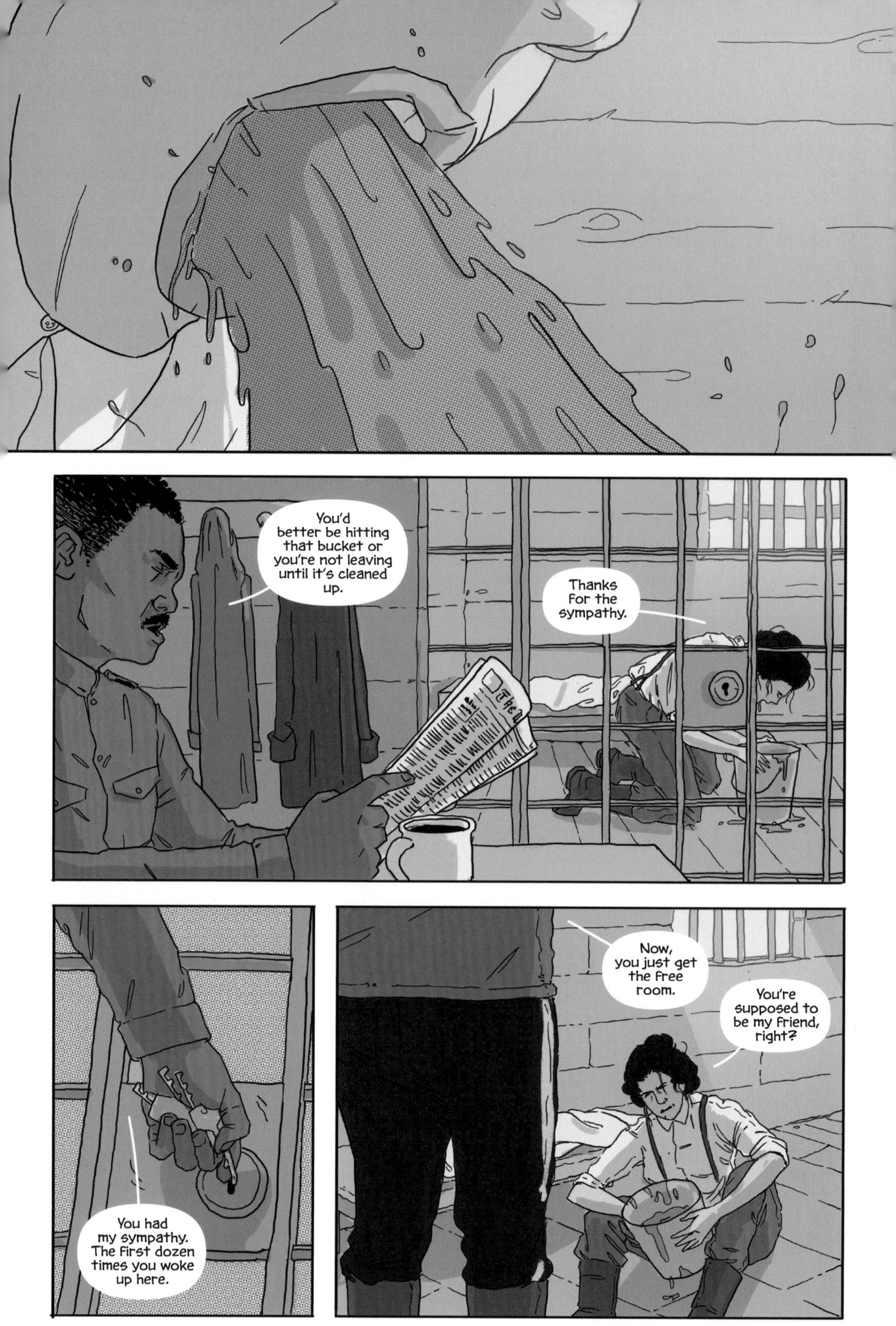
You'd better be hitting that bucket or you're not leaving until it's cleaned up.
Thanks for the sympathy.
You had my sympathy. The first dozen times you woke up here.
Now, you just get the free room.
You're supposed to be my friend, right?

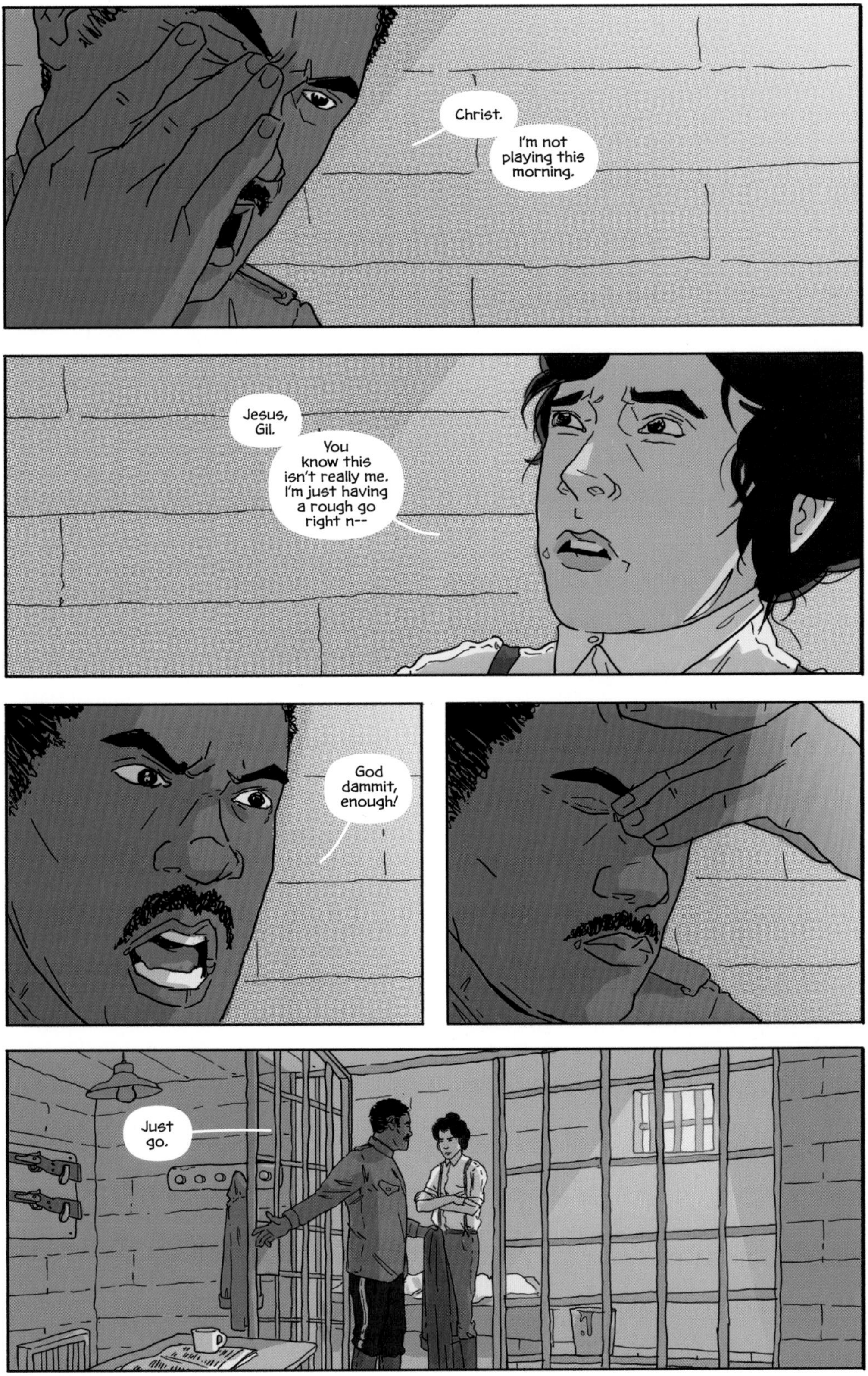
Christ.
I'm not playing this morning.
Jesus, Gil.
You know this isn't really me. I'm just having a rough go right n--
God dammit, enough!
Just go.

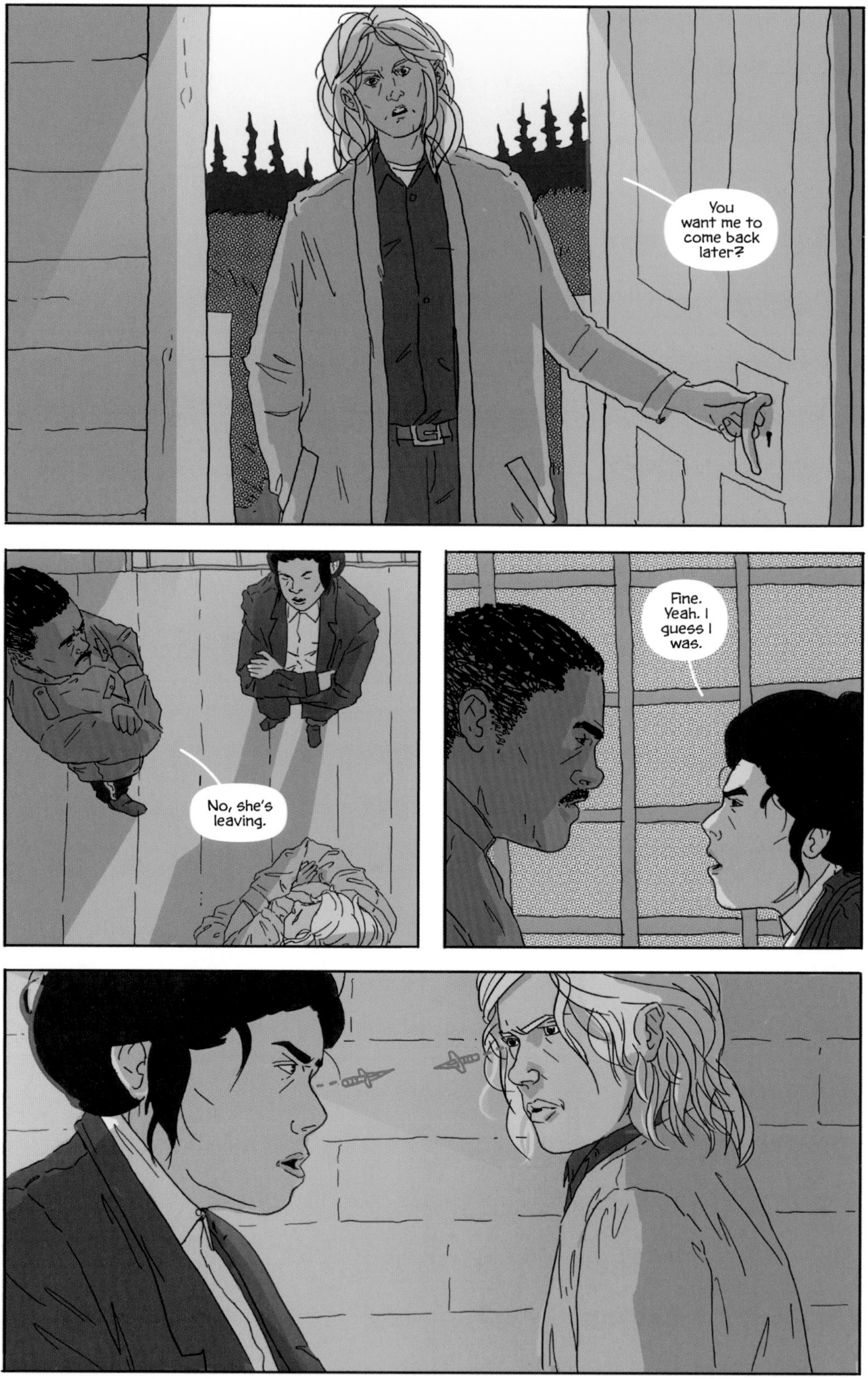
You want me to come back later?
No, she's leaving.
Fine. Yeah. I guess I was.

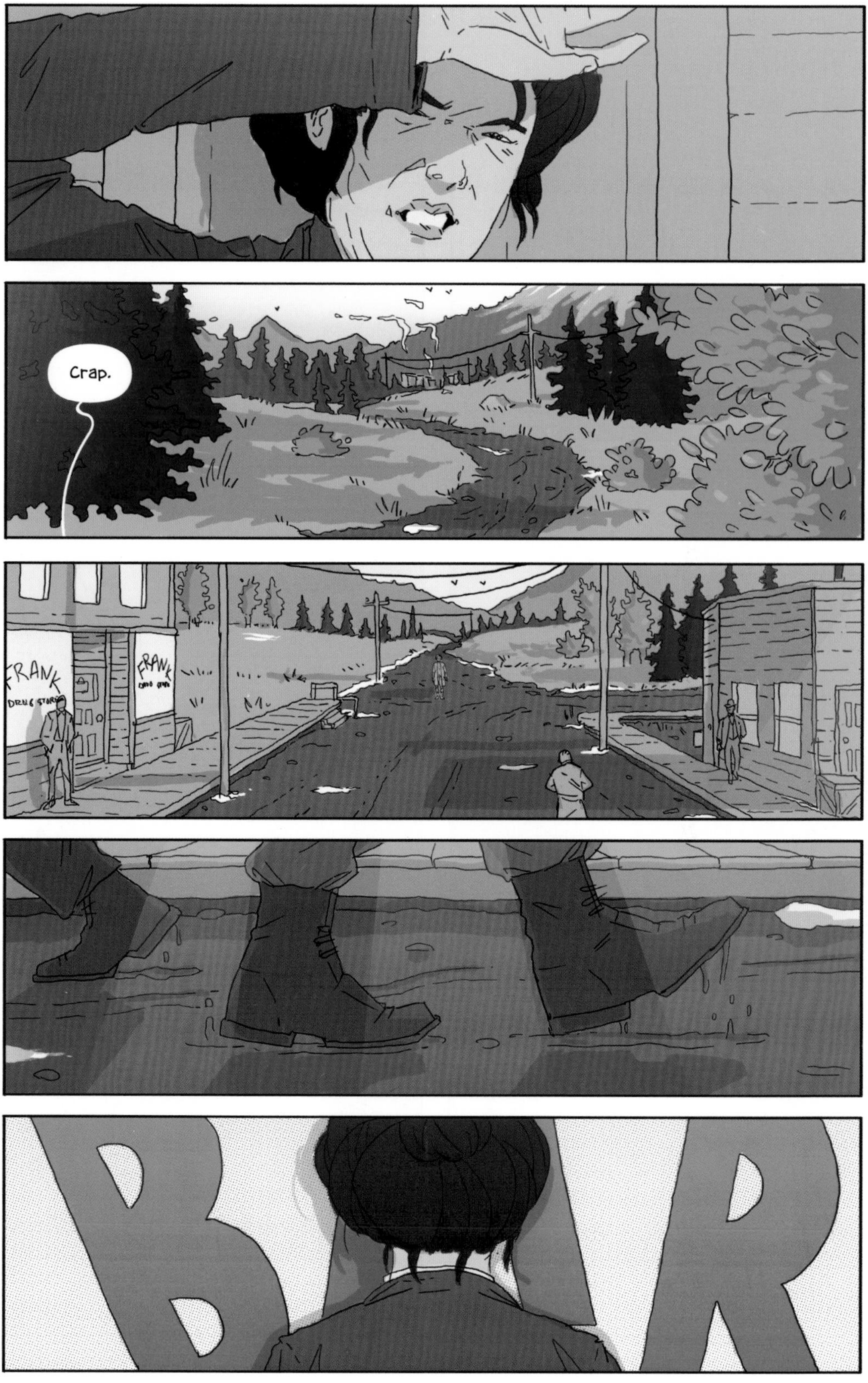
Crap.
FRANK
FRANK

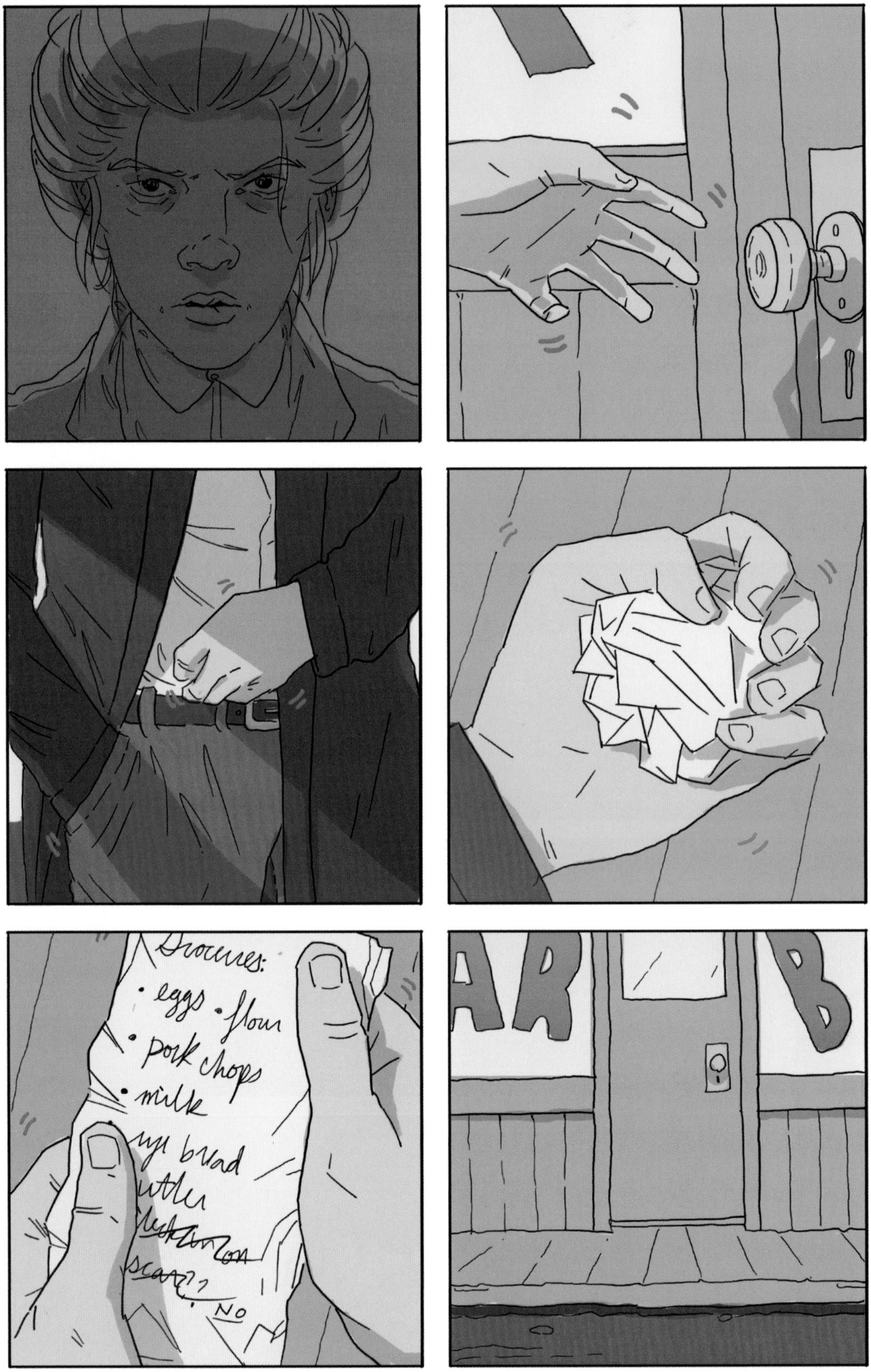

Groceries:
• eggs • flour
• pork chops
• milk
NO

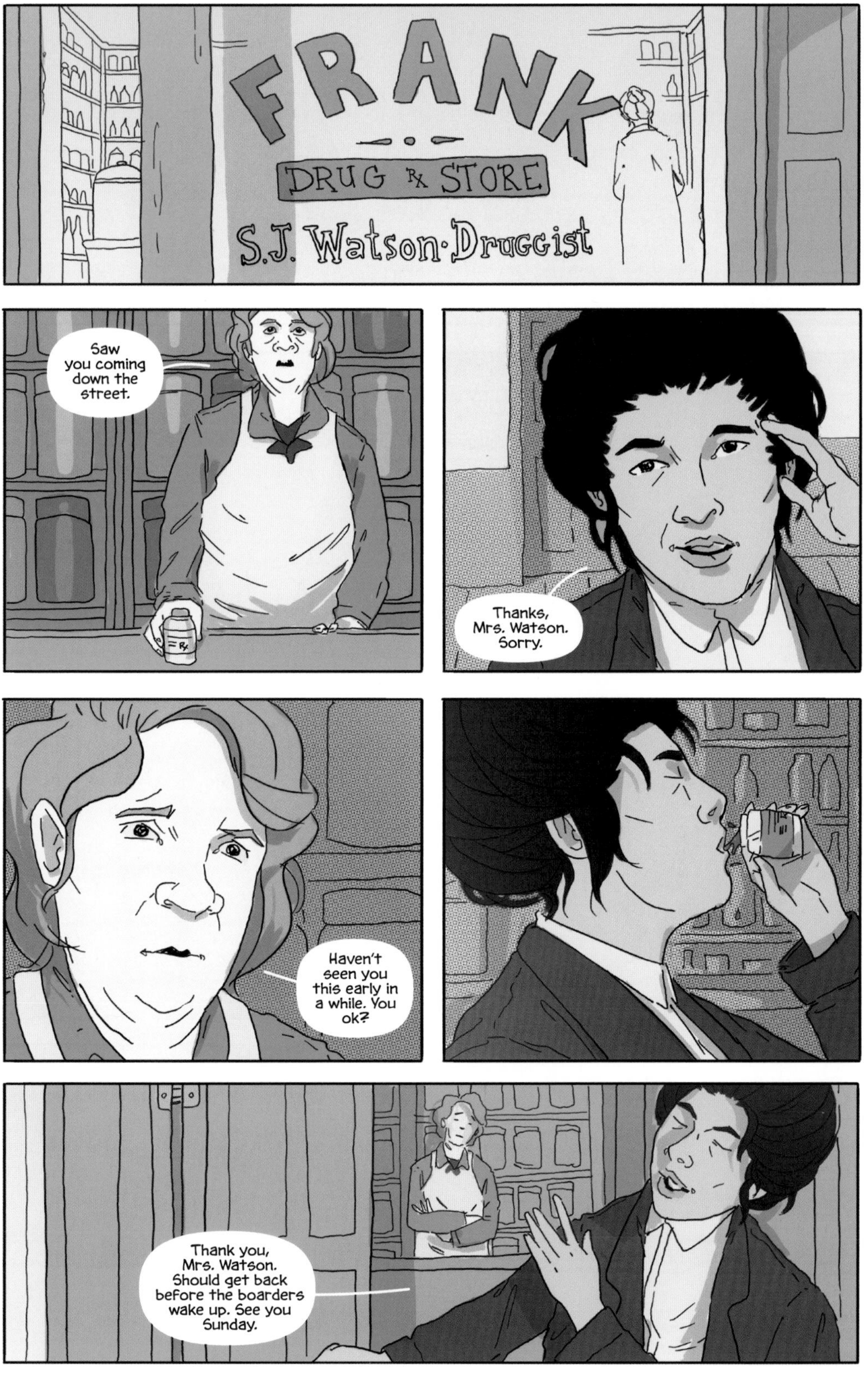
FRANK
DRUG Rx STORE
S.J. Watson·Druggist
Saw you coming down the street.
Thanks, Mrs. Watson. Sorry.
Haven't seen you this early in a while. You ok?
Thank you, Mrs. Watson. Should get back before the boarders wake up. See you Sunday.

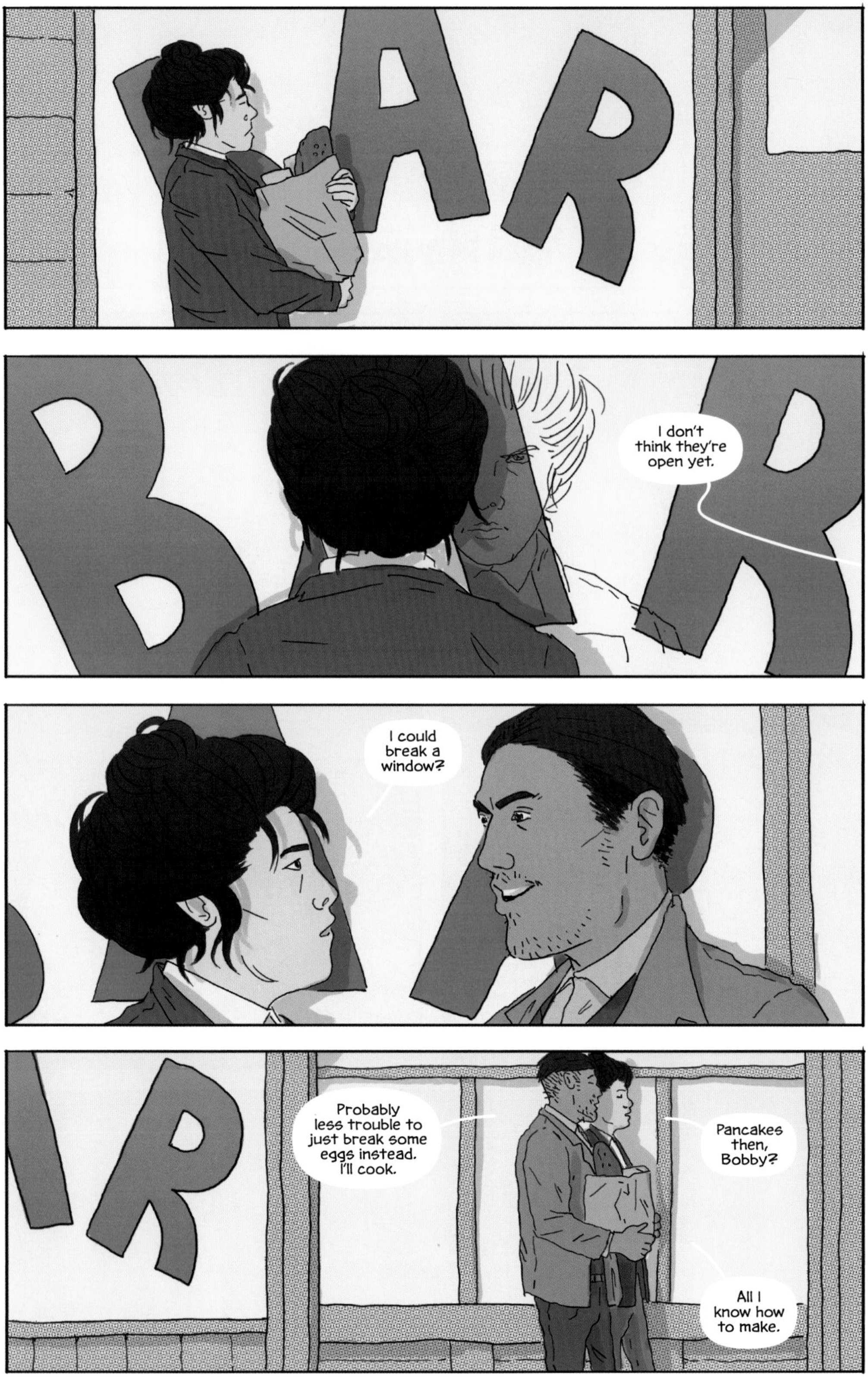

I don't think they're open yet.
I could break a window?
Probably less trouble to just break some eggs instead. I'll cook.
Pancakes then, Bobby?
All I know how to make.

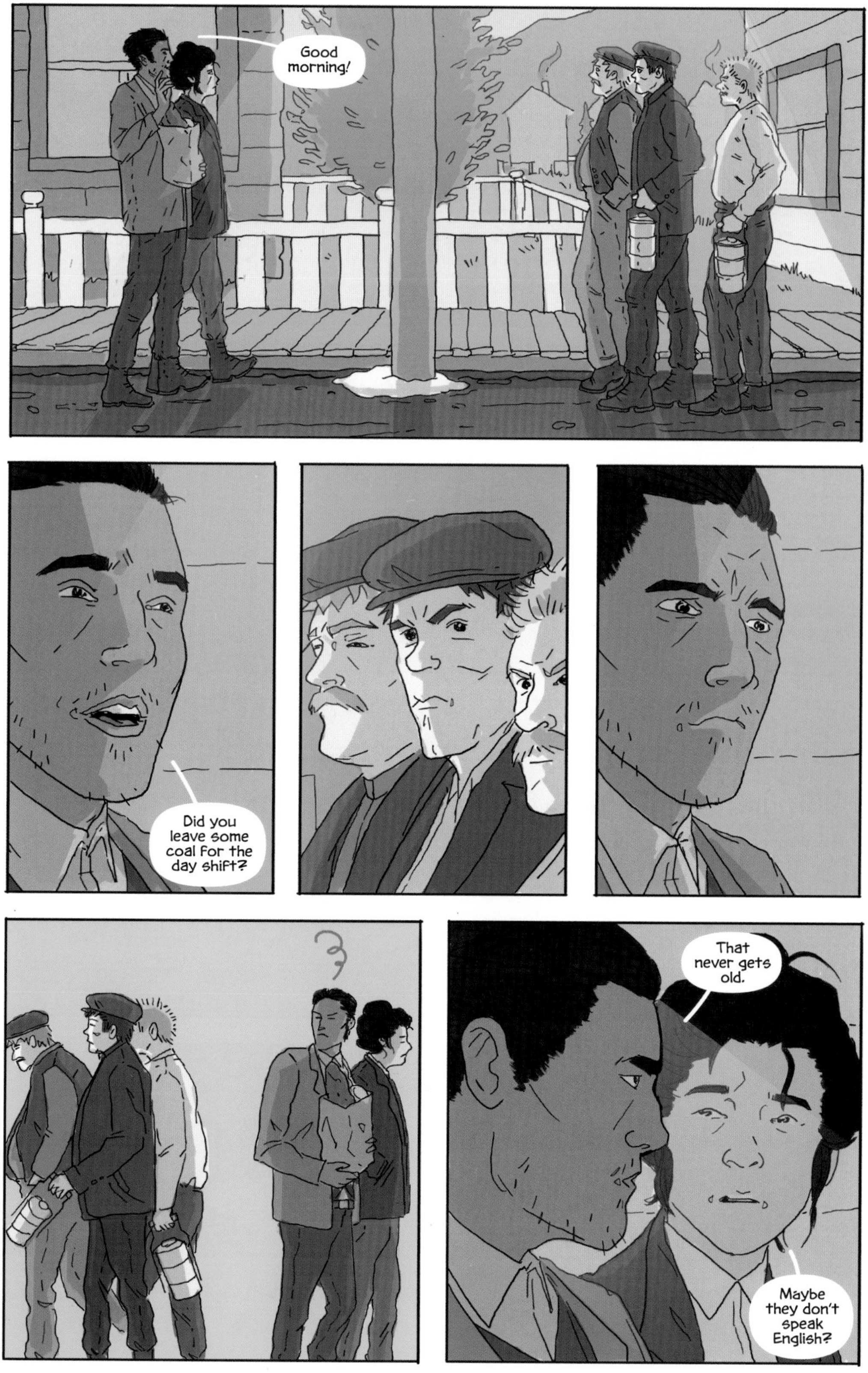
Good morning!
Did you leave some coal for the day shift?
That never gets old.
Maybe they don't speak English?

They wouldn't let us speak our language.

At the school they took us all to. They'd only talk to us in English. Expected a reply in the same, or else. I had never even heard English before.

Eventually I just forgot our language.

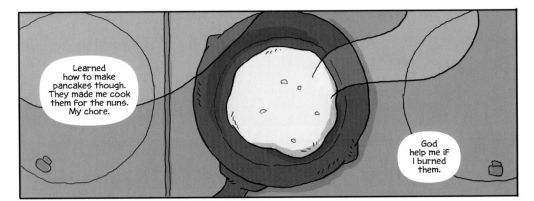

Learned how to make pancakes though. They made me cook them for the nuns. My chore.

God help me if I burned them.

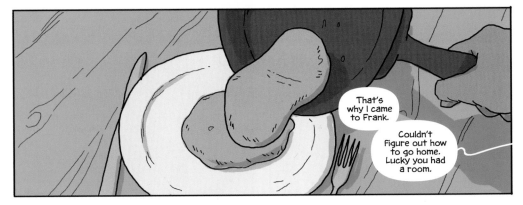

That's why I came to Frank.

Couldn't figure out how to go home. Lucky you had a room.

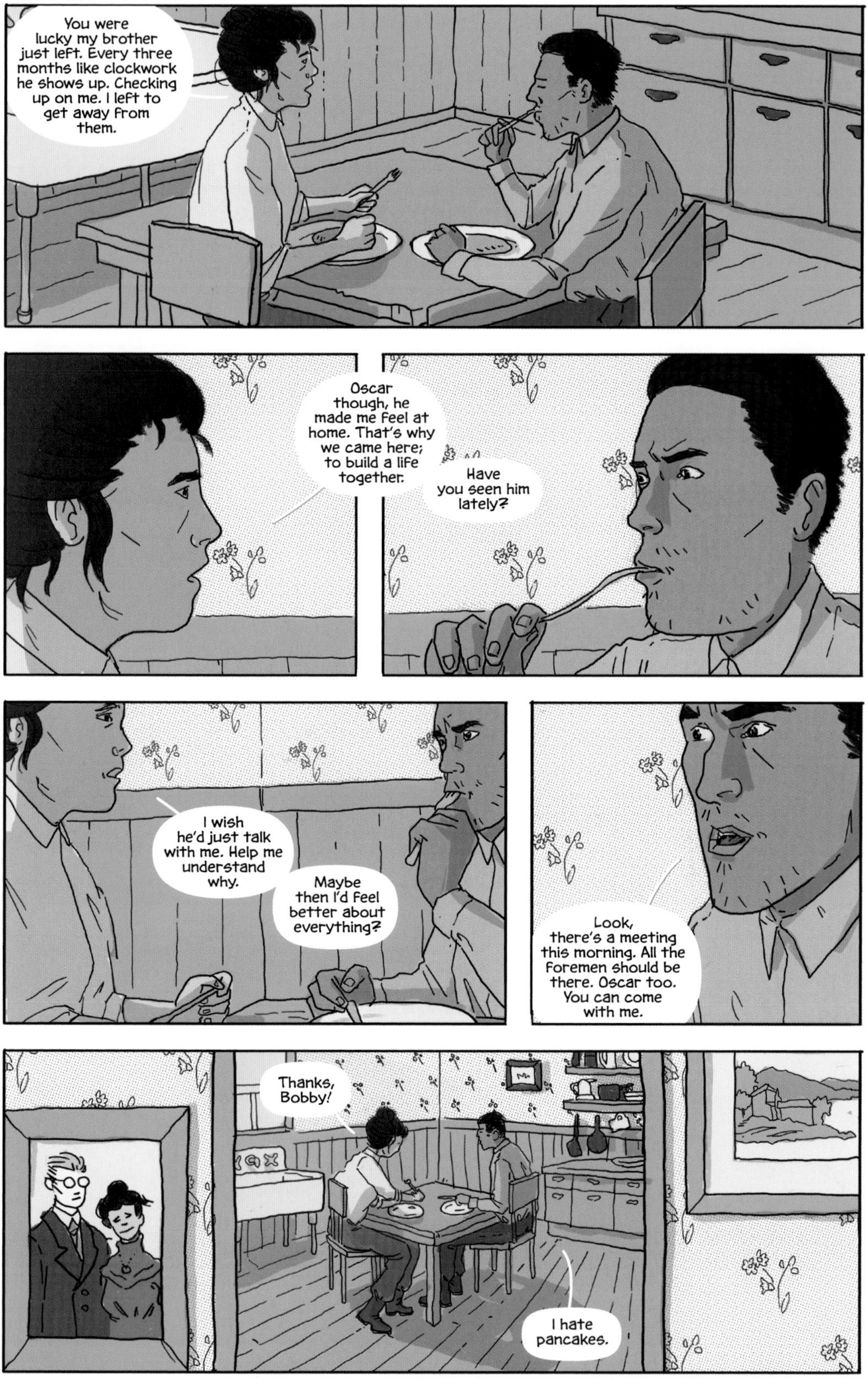
You were lucky my brother just left. Every three months like clockwork he shows up. Checking up on me. I left to get away from them.
Oscar though, he made me feel at home. That's why we came here; to build a life together.
Have you seen him lately?
I wish he'd just talk with me. Help me understand why.
Maybe then I'd feel better about everything?
Look, there's a meeting this morning. All the Foremen should be there. Oscar too. You can come with me.
Thanks, Bobby!
I hate pancakes.

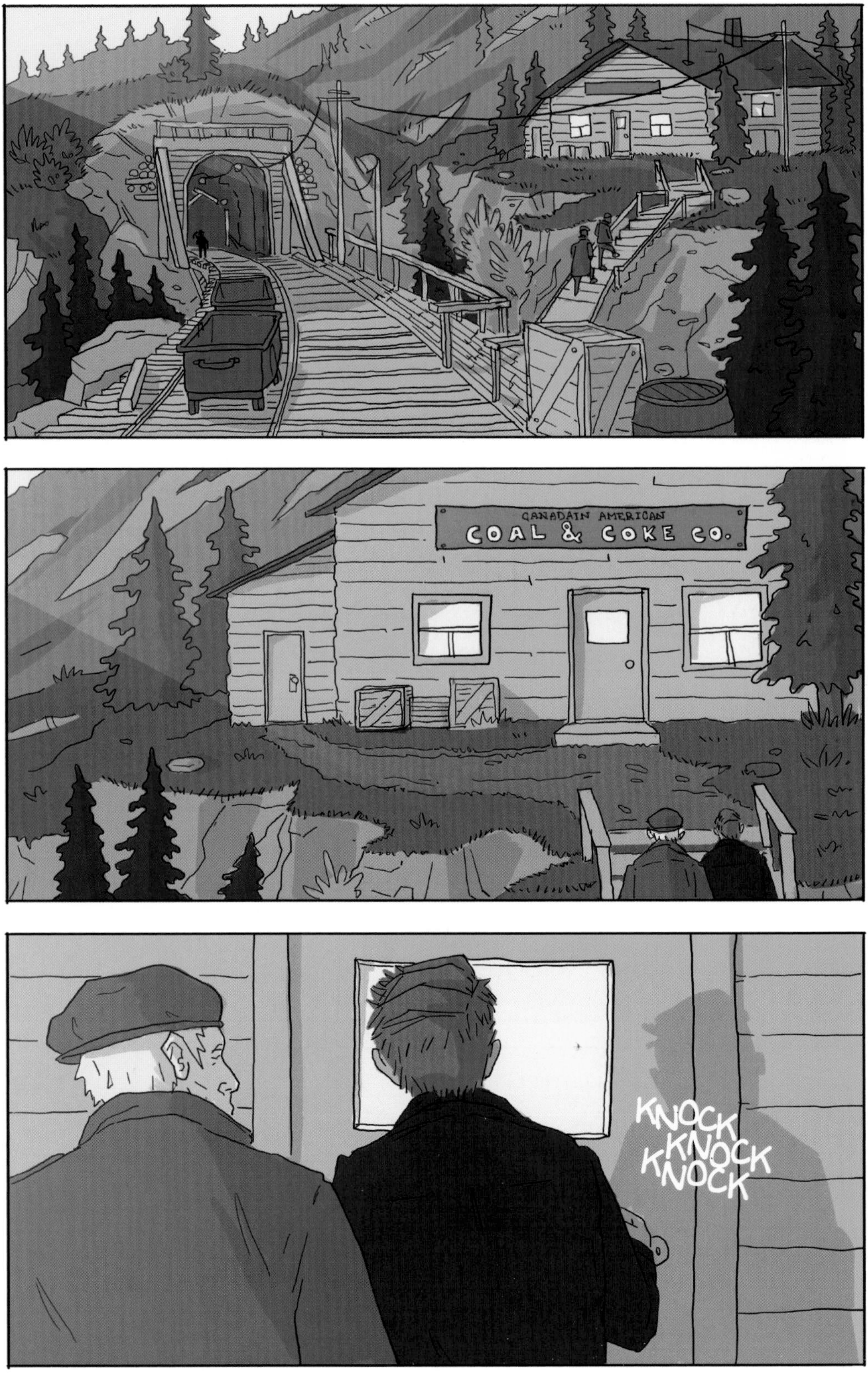
CANADAIN AMERICAN
COAL & COKE CO.
KNOCK
KNOCK
KNOCK

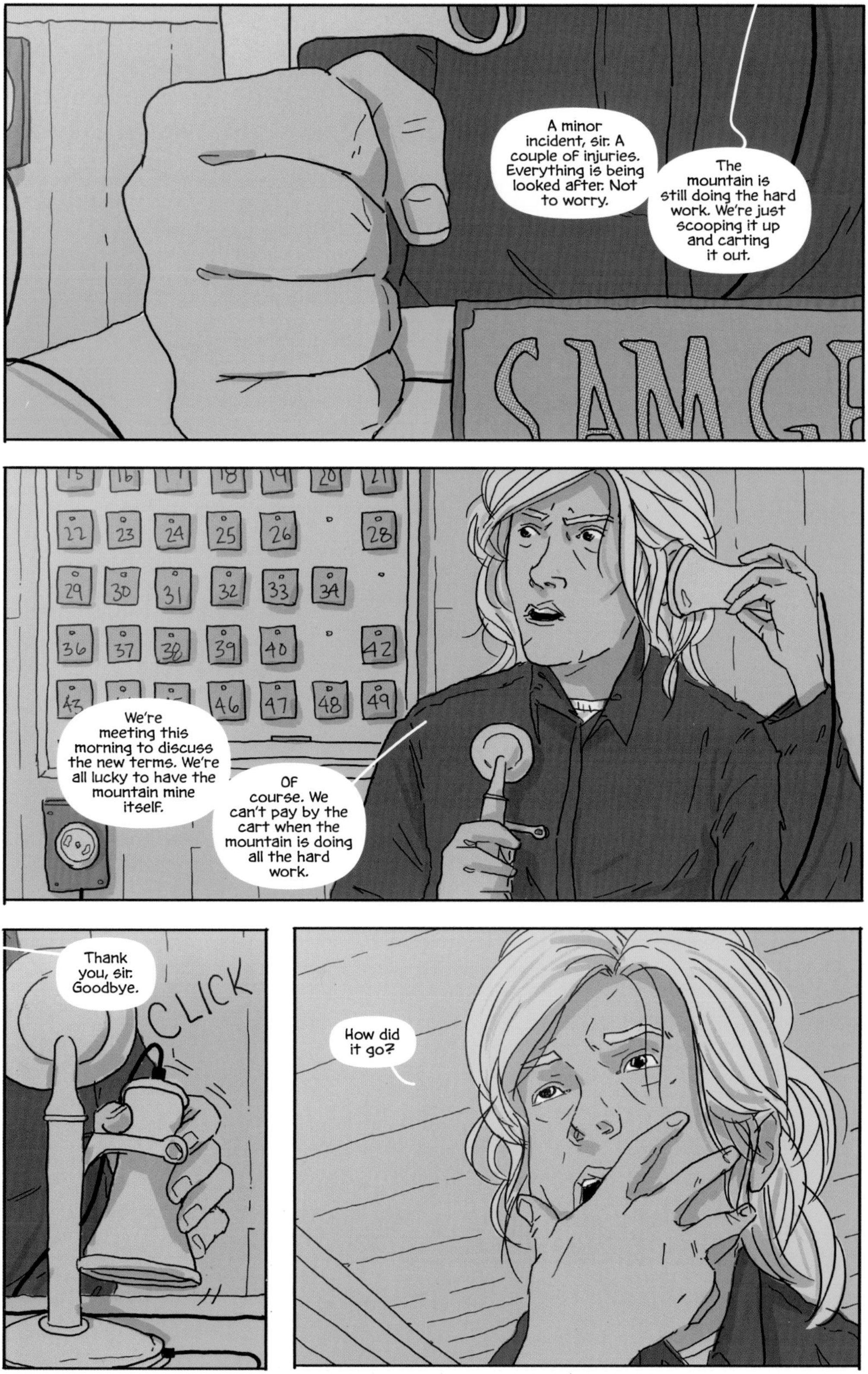
A minor incident, sir. A couple of injuries. Everything is being looked after. Not to worry.
The mountain is still doing the hard work. We're just scooping it up and carting it out.
SAMG
We're meeting this morning to discuss the new terms. We're all lucky to have the mountain mine itself.
Of course. We can't pay by the cart when the mountain is doing all the hard work.
Thank you, sir. Goodbye.
CLICK
How did it go?

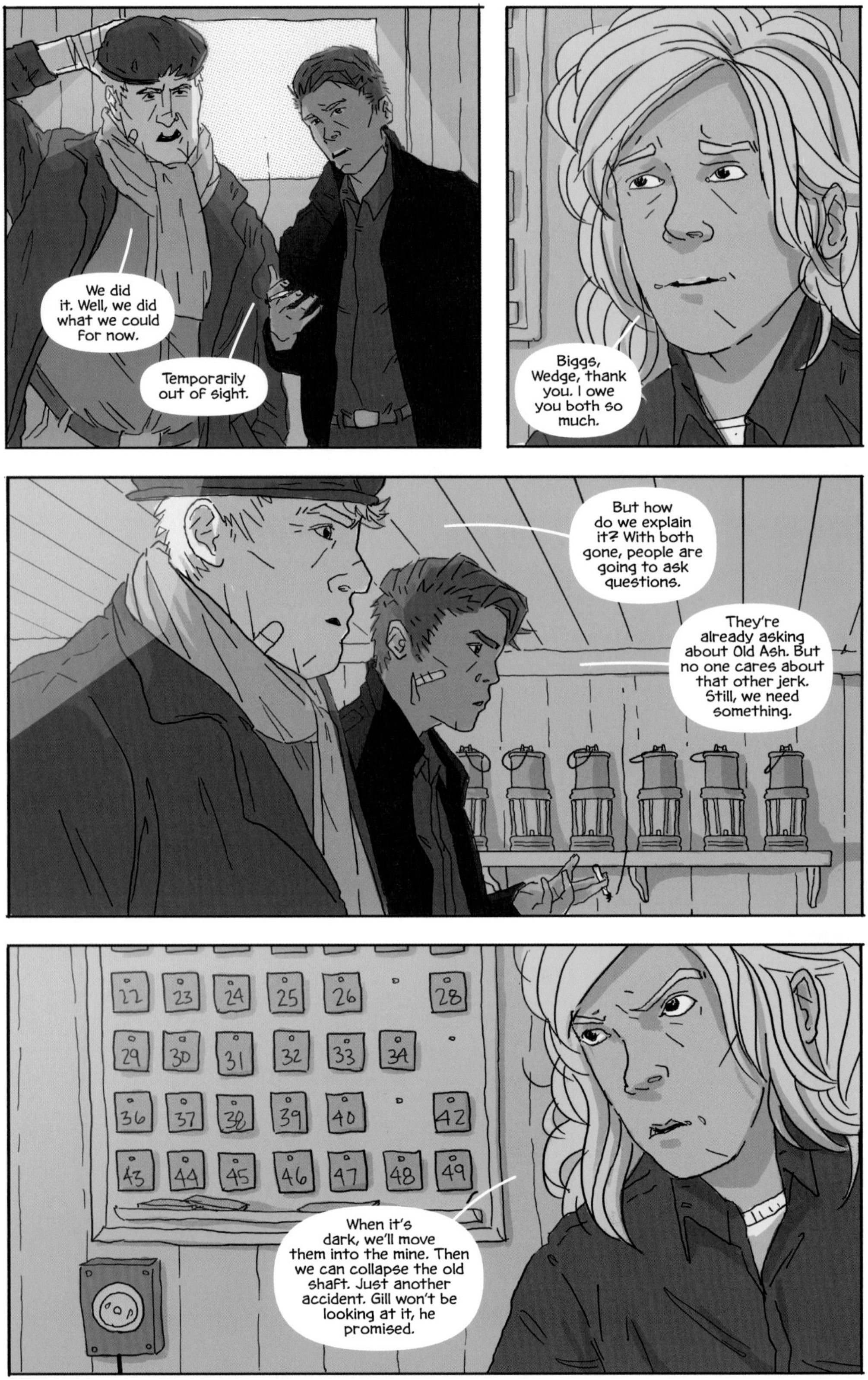
We did it. Well, we did what we could for now.
Temporarily out of sight.
Biggs, Wedge, thank you. I owe you both so much.
But how do we explain it? With both gone, people are going to ask questions.
They're already asking about Old Ash. But no one cares about that other jerk. Still, we need something.
22 23 24 25 26 28
29 30 31 32 33 34
36 37 38 39 40 42
43 44 45 46 47 48 49
When it's dark, we'll move them into the mine. Then we can collapse the old shaft. Just another accident. Gill won't be looking at it, he promised.

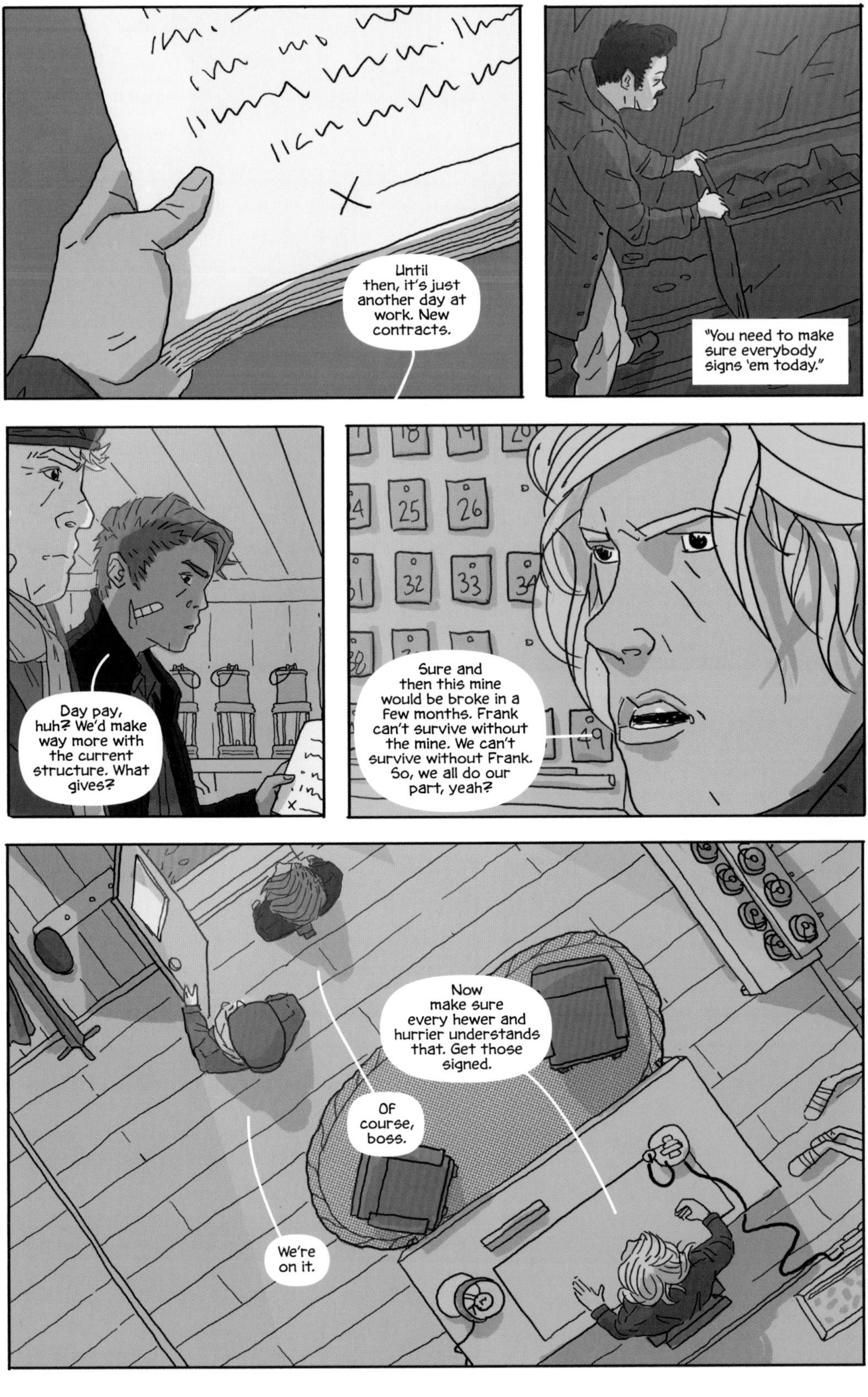
Until then, it's just another day at work. New contracts.
"You need to make sure everybody signs 'em today."
Day pay, huh? We'd make way more with the current structure. What gives?
Sure and then this mine would be broke in a few months. Frank can't survive without the mine. We can't survive without Frank. So, we all do our part, yeah?
Now make sure every hewer and hurrier understands that. Get those signed.
Of course, boss.
We're on it.

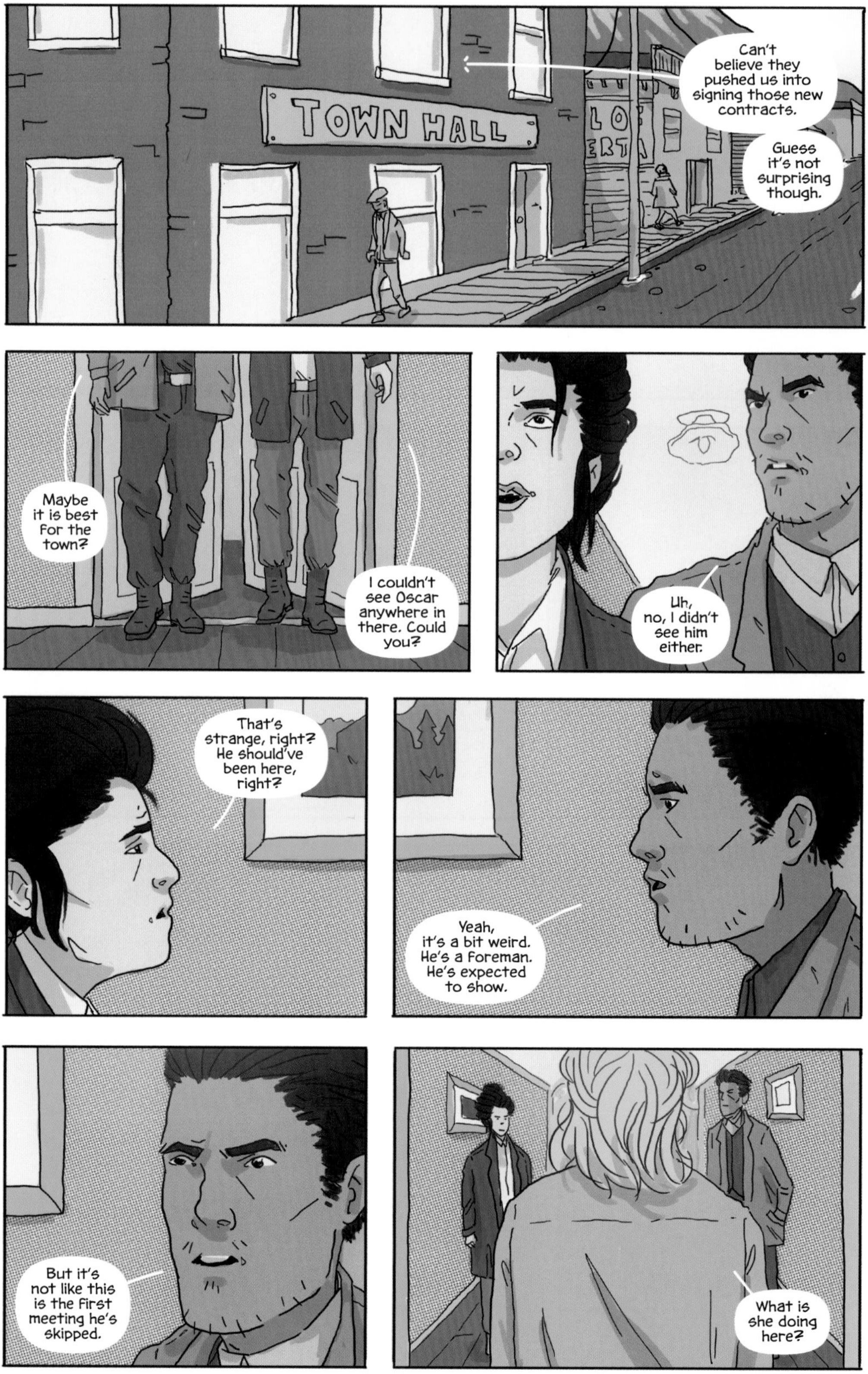
TOWN HALL
Can't believe they pushed us into signing those new contracts.
Guess it's not surprising though.
Maybe it is best for the town?
I couldn't see Oscar anywhere in there. Could you?
Uh, no, I didn't see him either.
That's strange, right? He should've been here, right?
Yeah, it's a bit weird. He's a foreman. He's expected to show.
But it's not like this is the first meeting he's skipped.
What is she doing here?

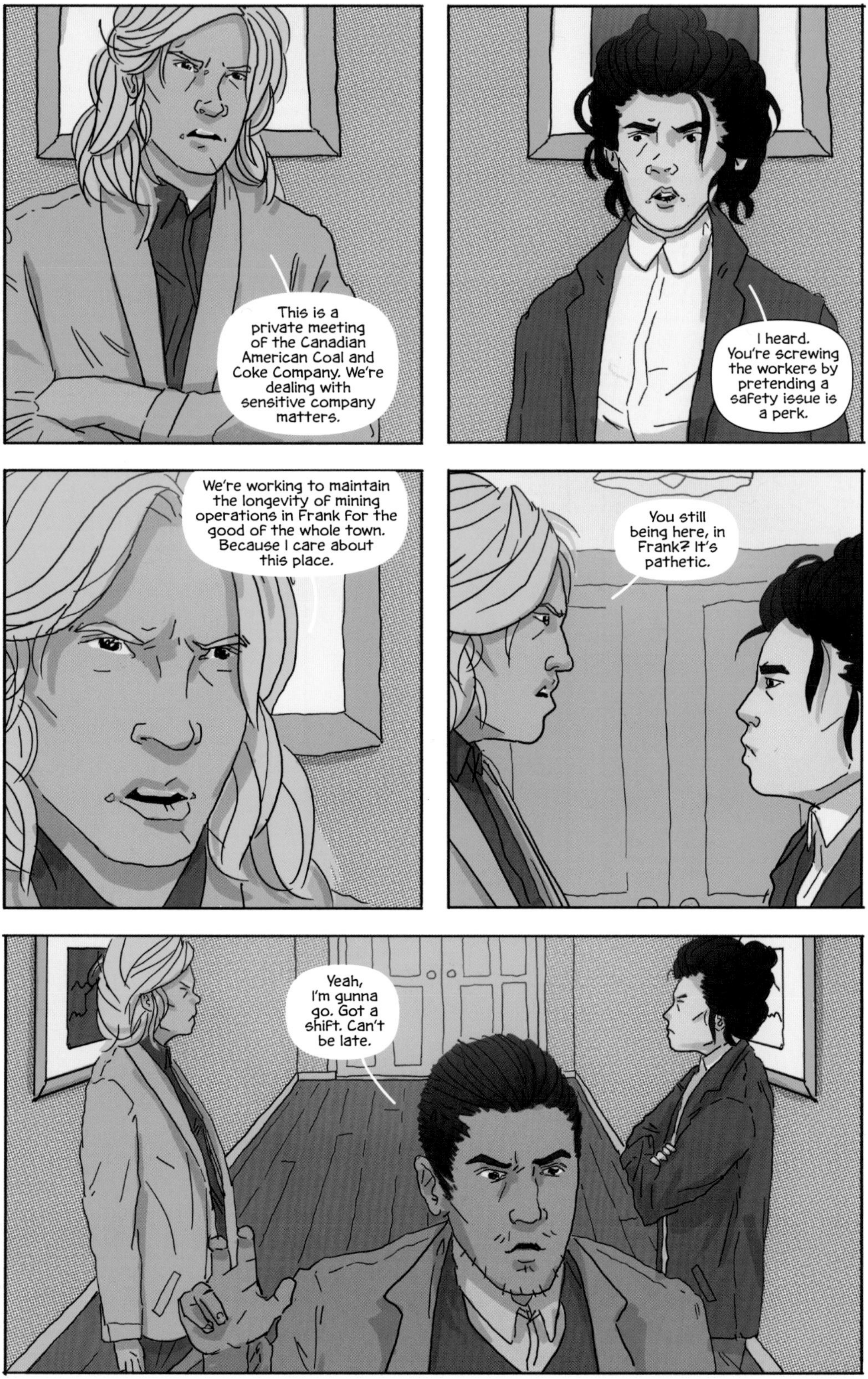
This is a private meeting of the Canadian American Coal and Coke Company. We're dealing with sensitive company matters.
I heard. You're screwing the workers by pretending a safety issue is a perk.
We're working to maintain the longevity of mining operations in Frank for the good of the whole town. Because I care about this place.
You still being here, in Frank? It's pathetic.
Yeah, I'm gunna go. Got a shift. Can't be late.

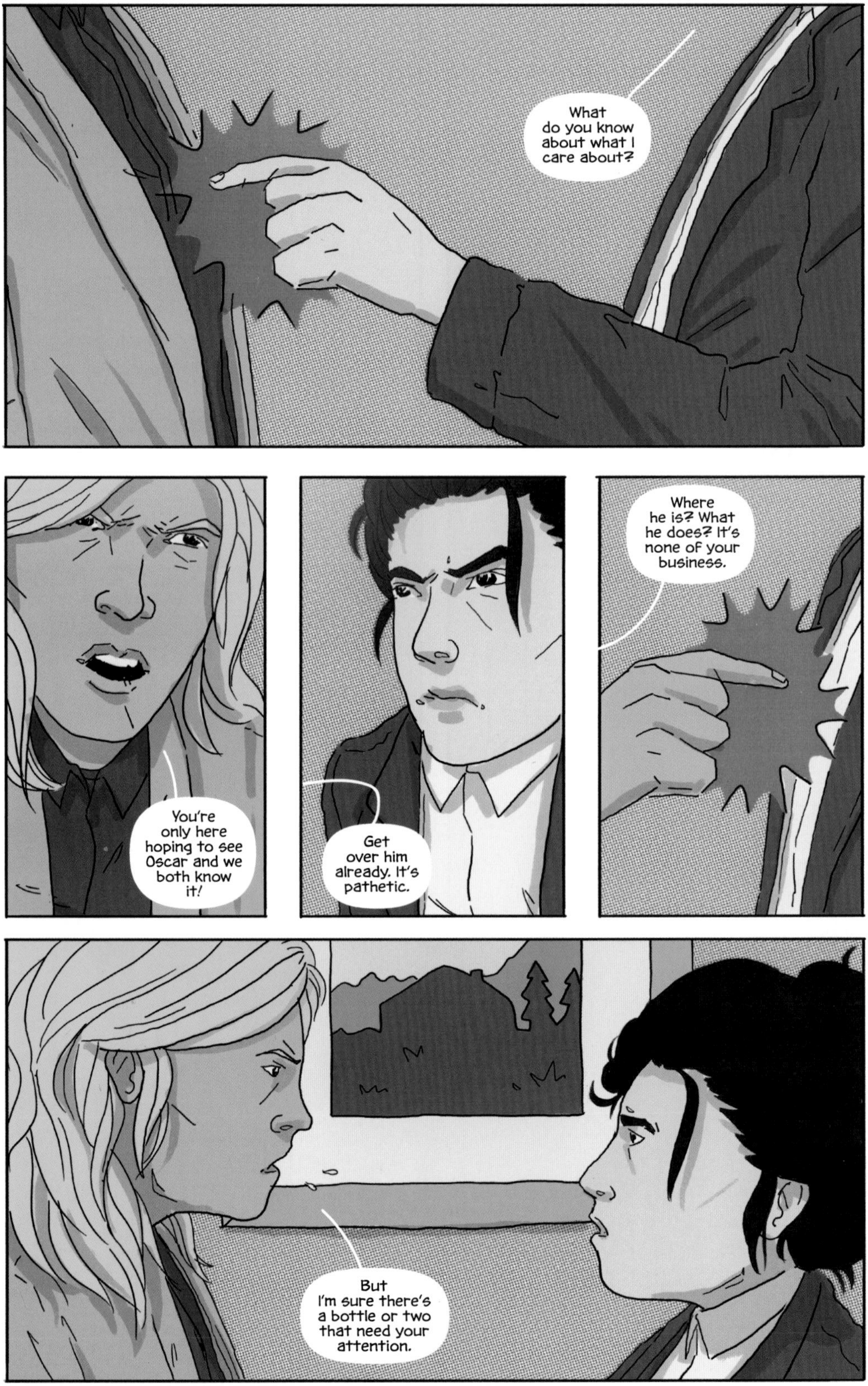
What do you know about what I care about?
You're only here hoping to see Oscar and we both know it!
Get over him already. It's pathetic.
Where he is? What he does? It's none of your business.
But I'm sure there's a bottle or two that need your attention.

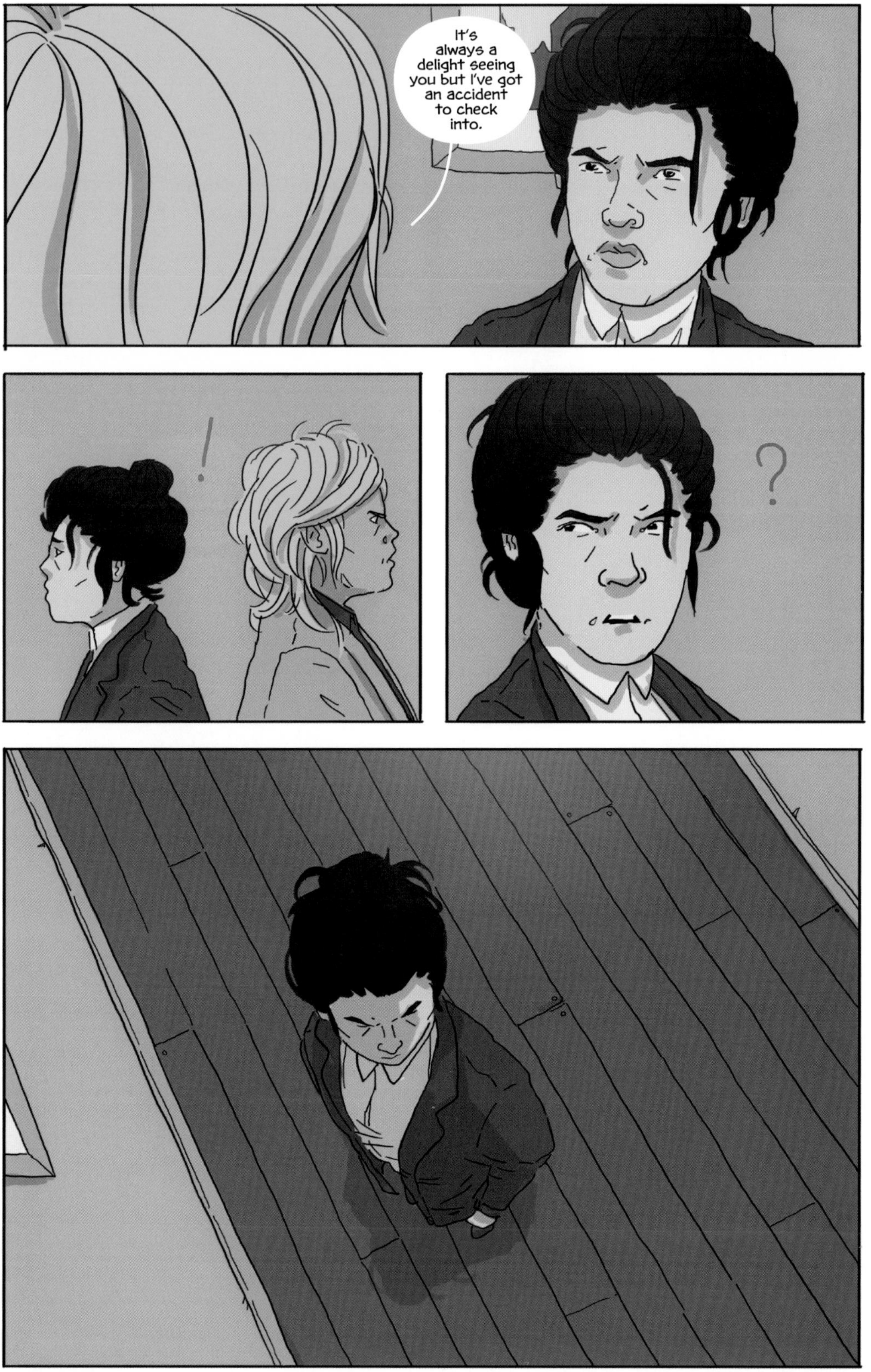
It's always a delight seeing you but I've got an accident to check into.
!
?

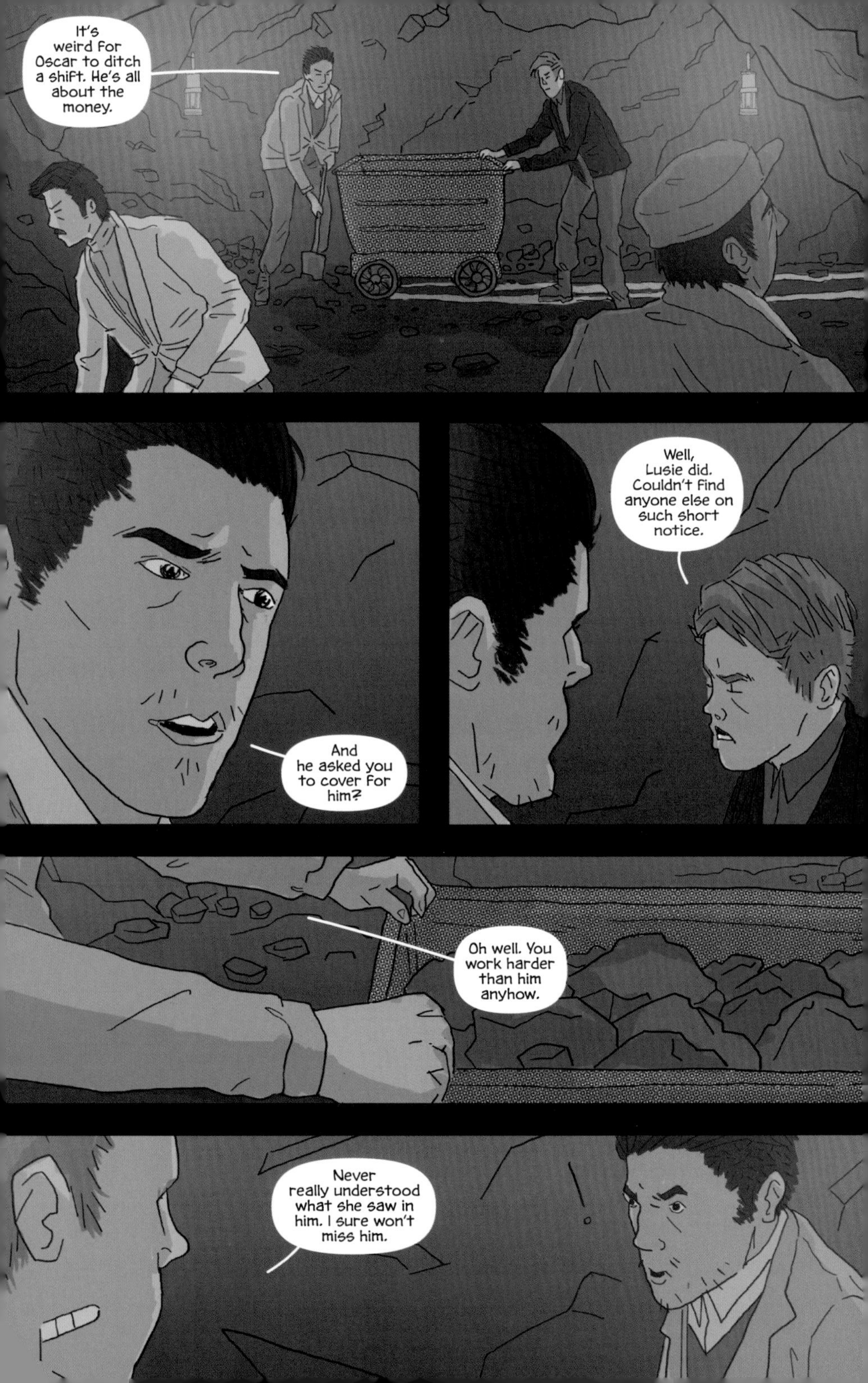
It's weird for Oscar to ditch a shift. He's all about the money.
And he asked you to cover for him?
Well, Lusie did. Couldn't find anyone else on such short notice.
Oh well. You work harder than him anyhow.
Never really understood what she saw in him. I sure won't miss him.

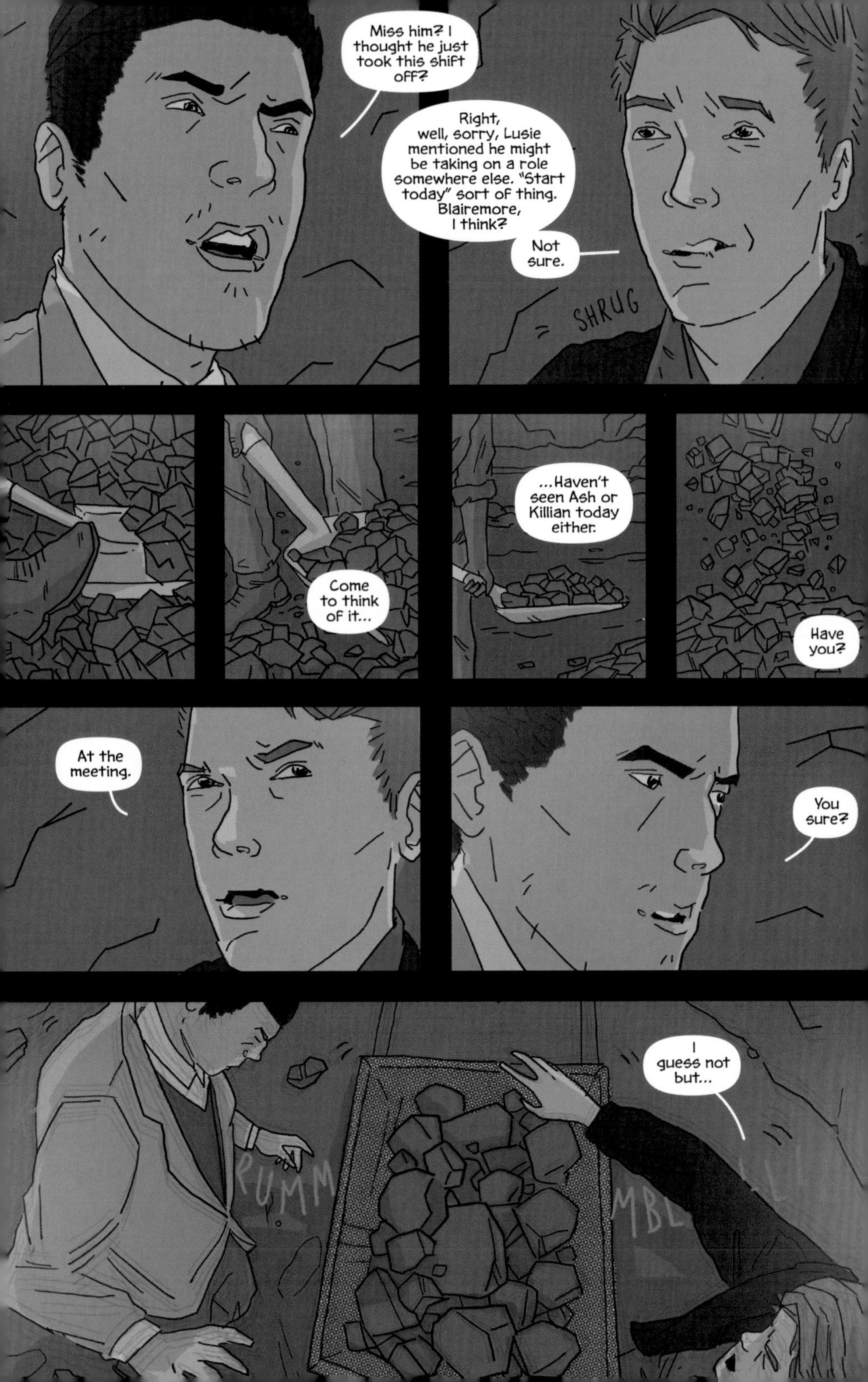
Miss him? I thought he just took this shift off?
Right, well, sorry, Lusie mentioned he might be taking on a role somewhere else. "Start today" sort of thing. Blairemore, I think?
Not sure.
SHRUG
Come to think of it...
...Haven't seen Ash or Killian today either.
Have you?
At the meeting.
You sure?
I guess not but...
RUMM
MBL

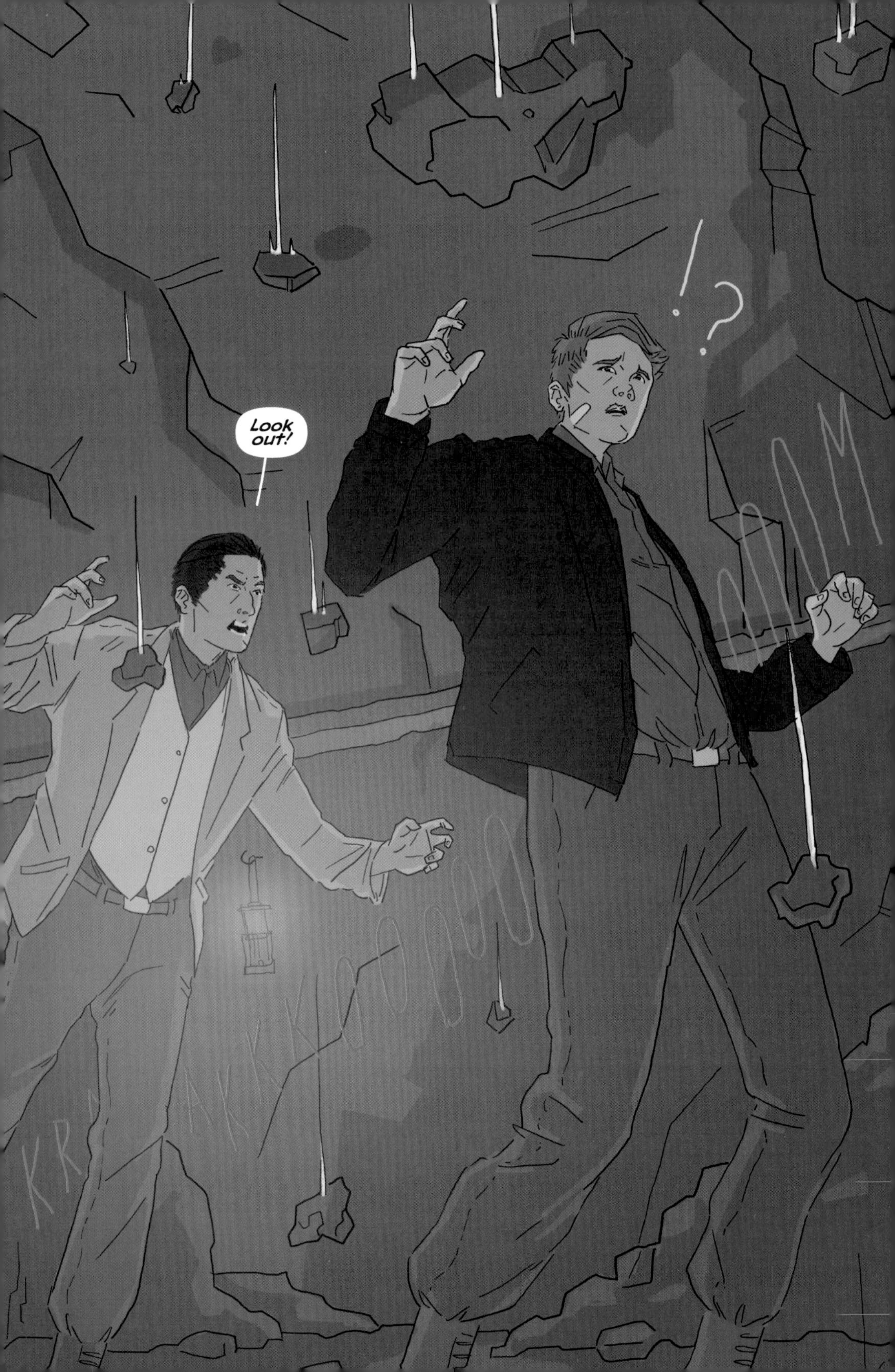
Look out!
!?

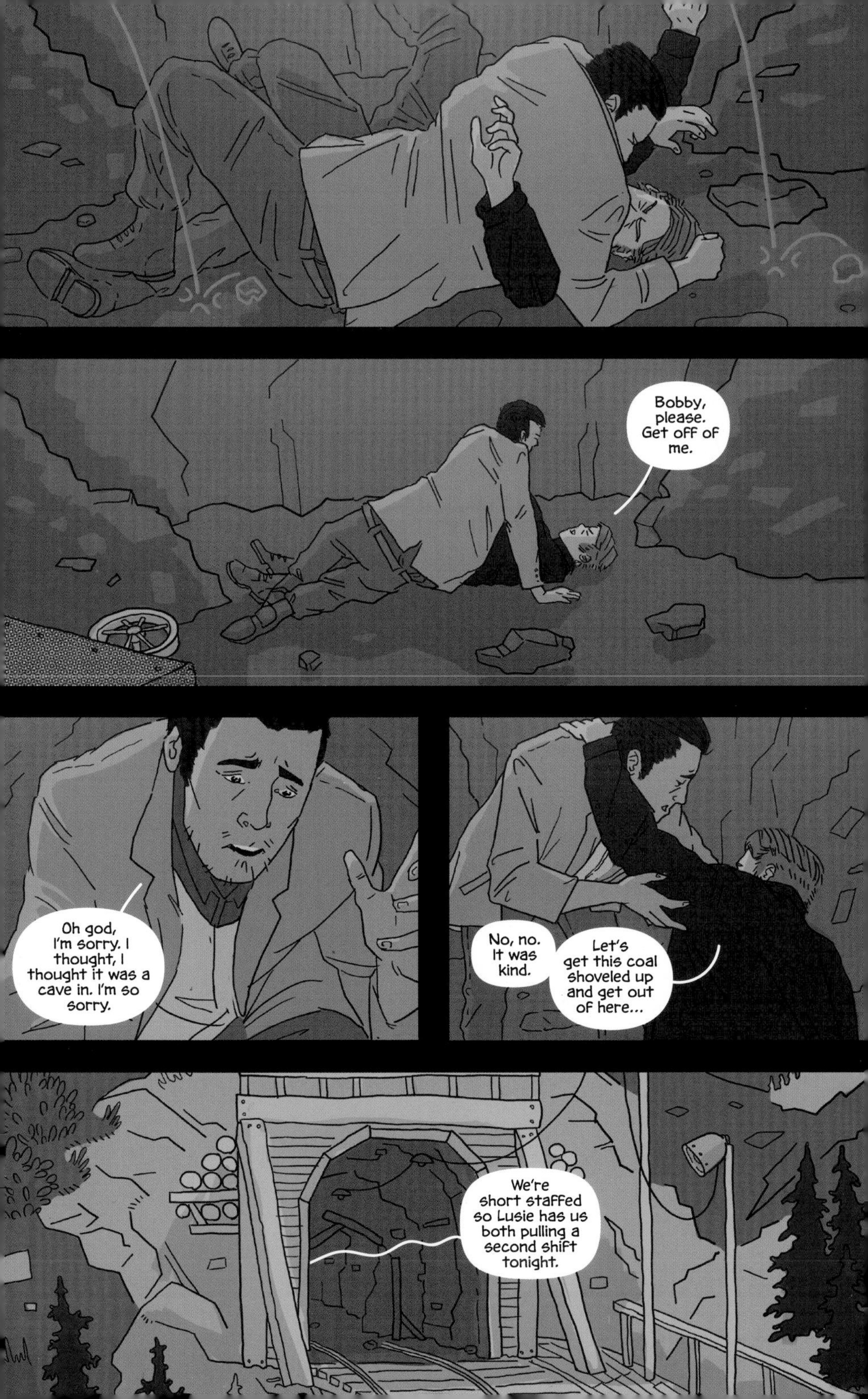
Bobby, please. Get off of me.
Oh god, I'm sorry. I thought, I thought it was a cave in. I'm so sorry.
No, no. It was kind.
Let's get this coal shoveled up and get out of here...
We're short staffed so Lusie has us both pulling a second shift tonight.

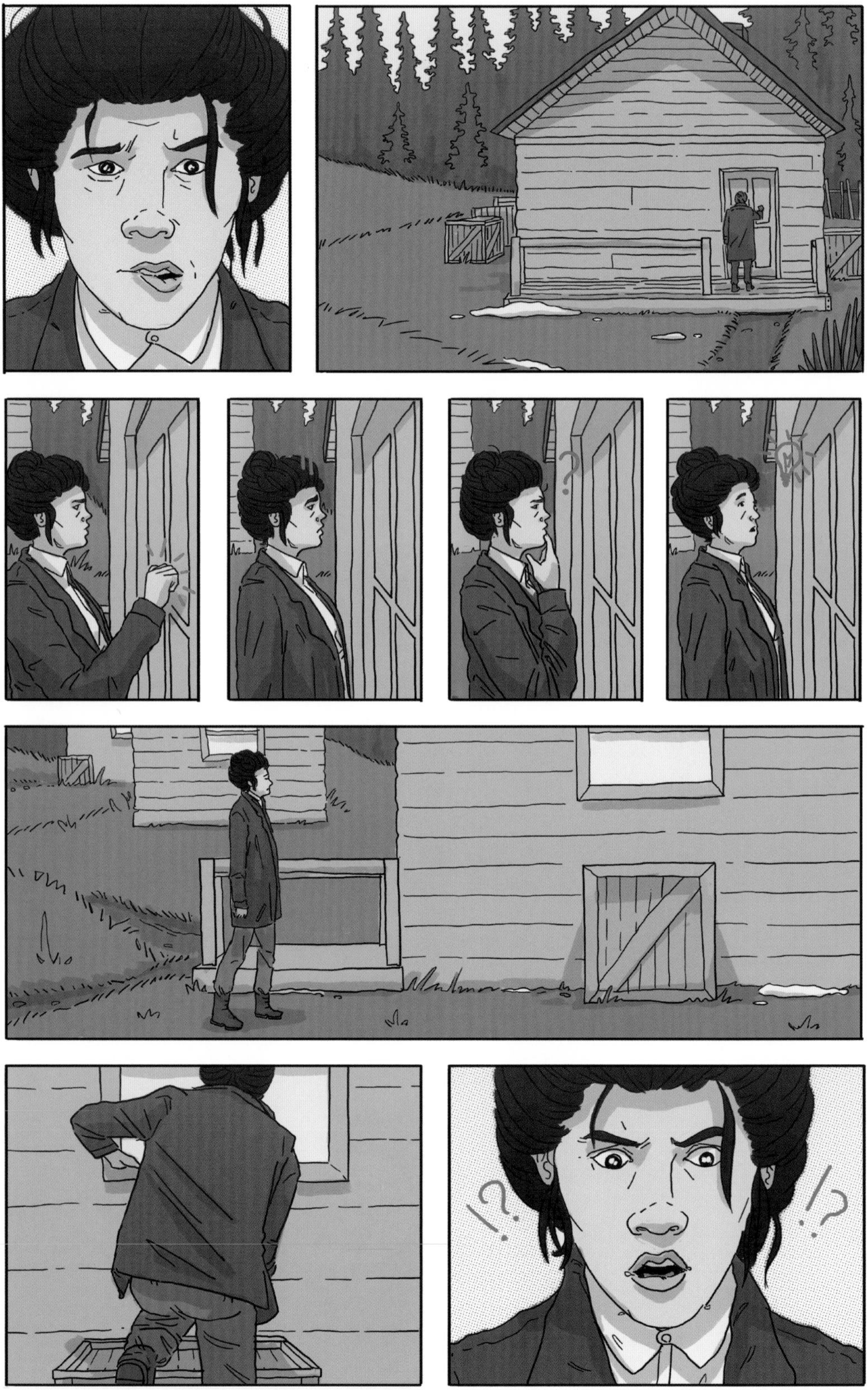
?
!?
!?

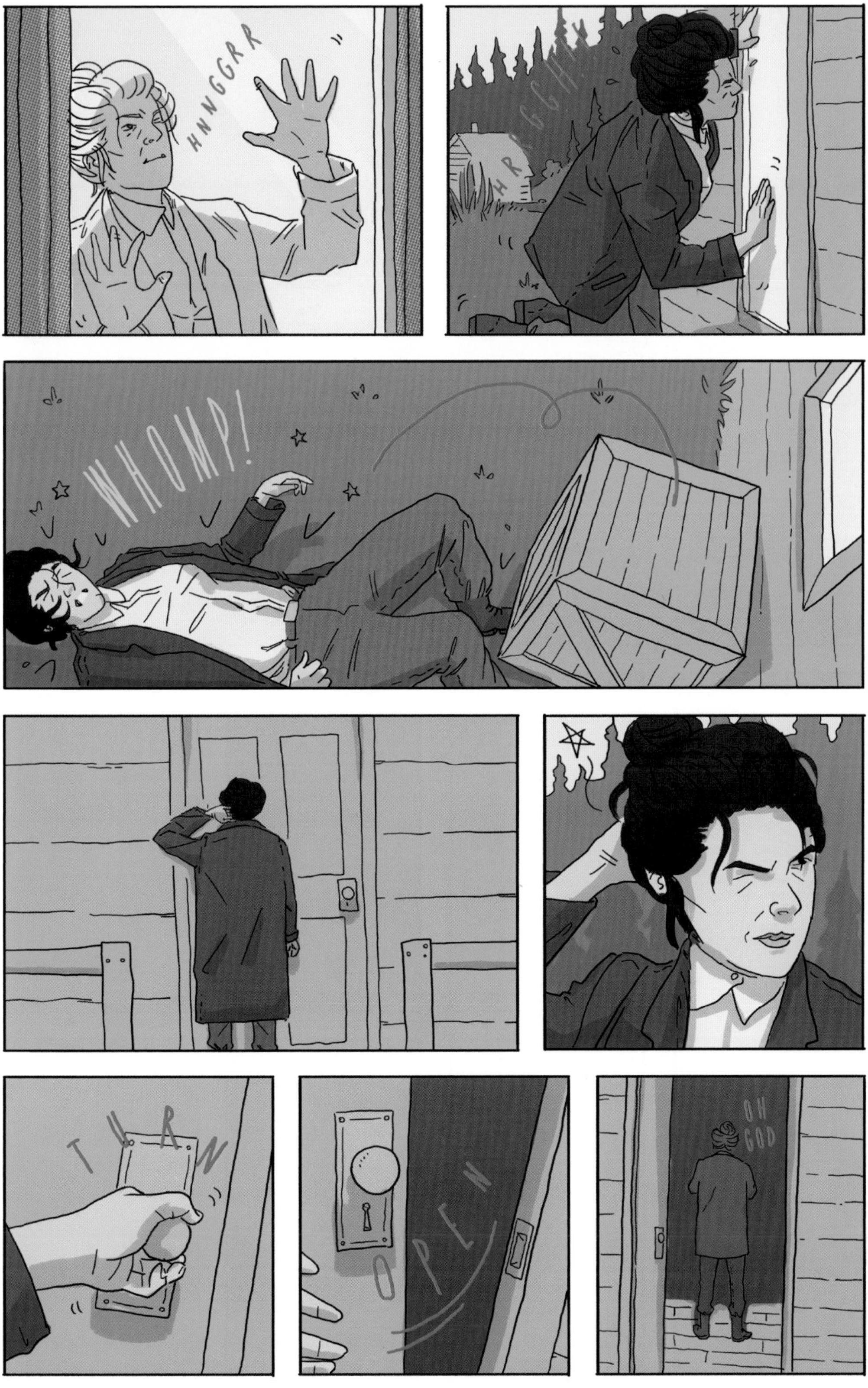
HNNGGRR
HRRGGHH
WHOMP!
TURN
OPEN
OH GOD

SAFETY REPORT

COAL MIN
IS NOW

UNSTA
DANGE

RECOMM
CLOSUR

SHAFT IN
CAN'T BE MAINT...

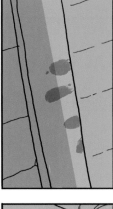

THE HOUND
OF THE
BASKERVILLES
CONAN DOYLE

Oh god, oh no!

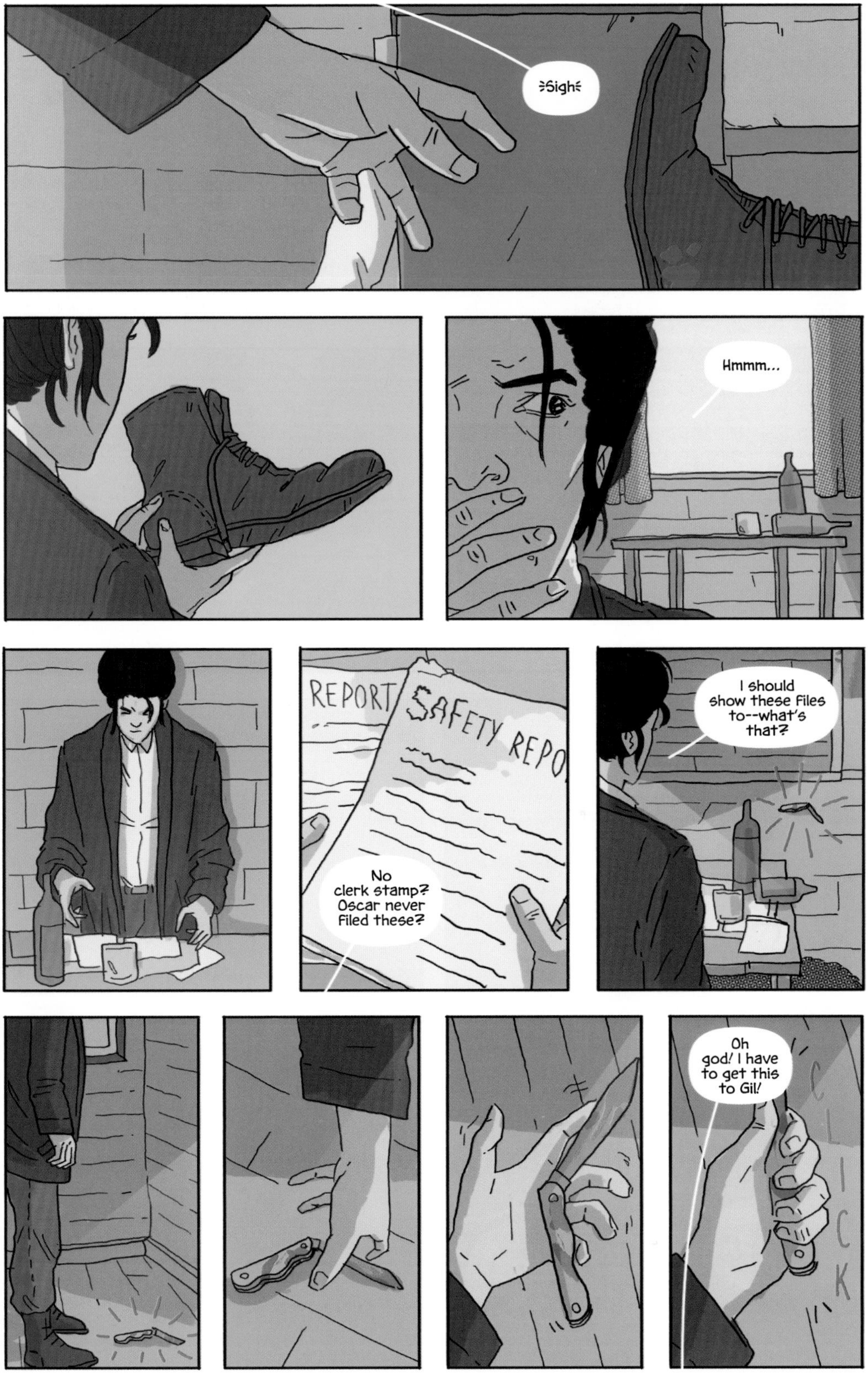

Sigh
Hmmm...
REPORT
SAFETY REPO
No clerk stamp? Oscar never filed these?
I should show these files to--what's that?
Oh god! I have to get this to Gil!
CLICK

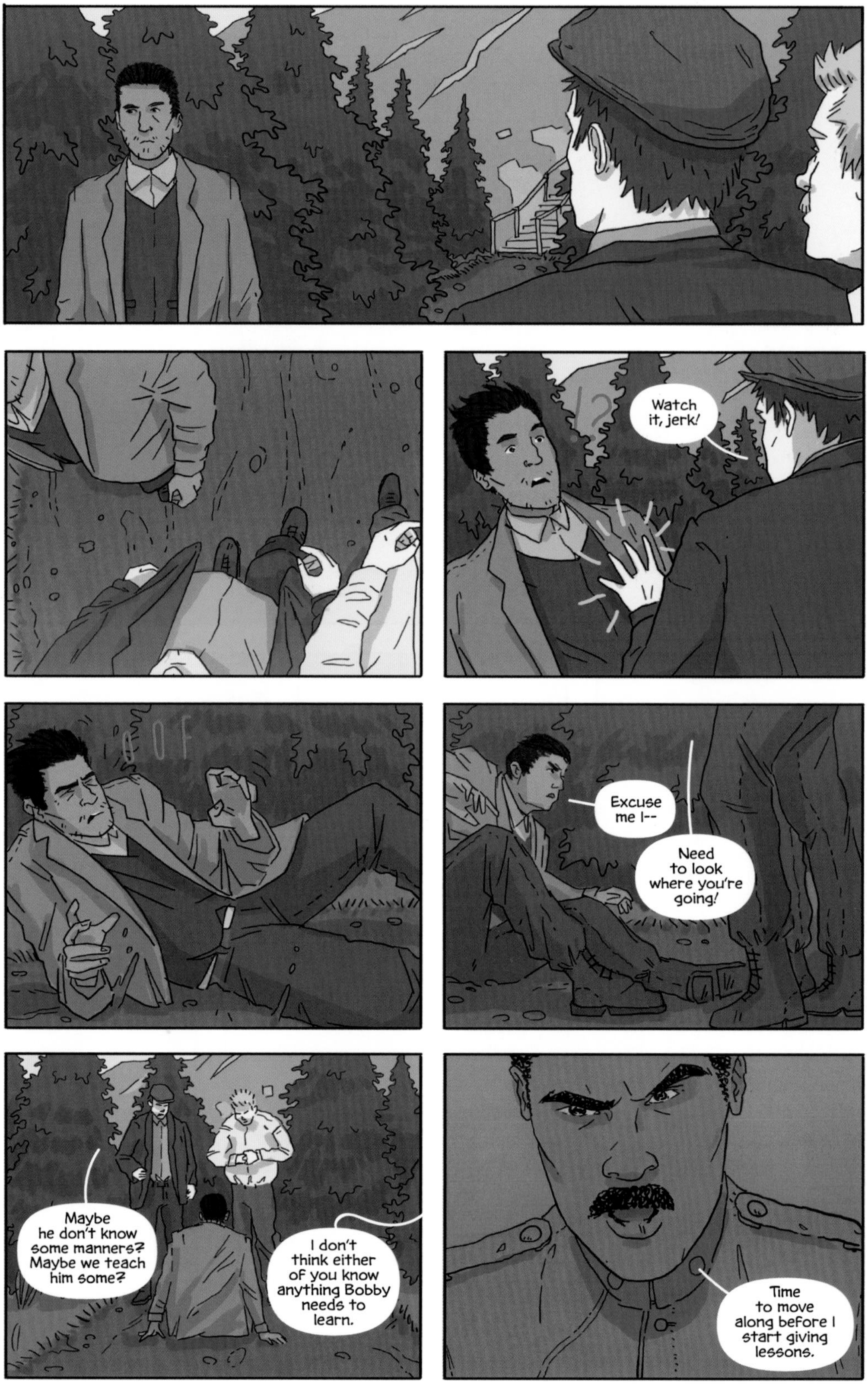
!?
Watch it, jerk!
OOF
Excuse me I--
Need to look where you're going!
Maybe he don't know some manners? Maybe we teach him some?
I don't think either of you know anything Bobby needs to learn.
Time to move along before I start giving lessons.

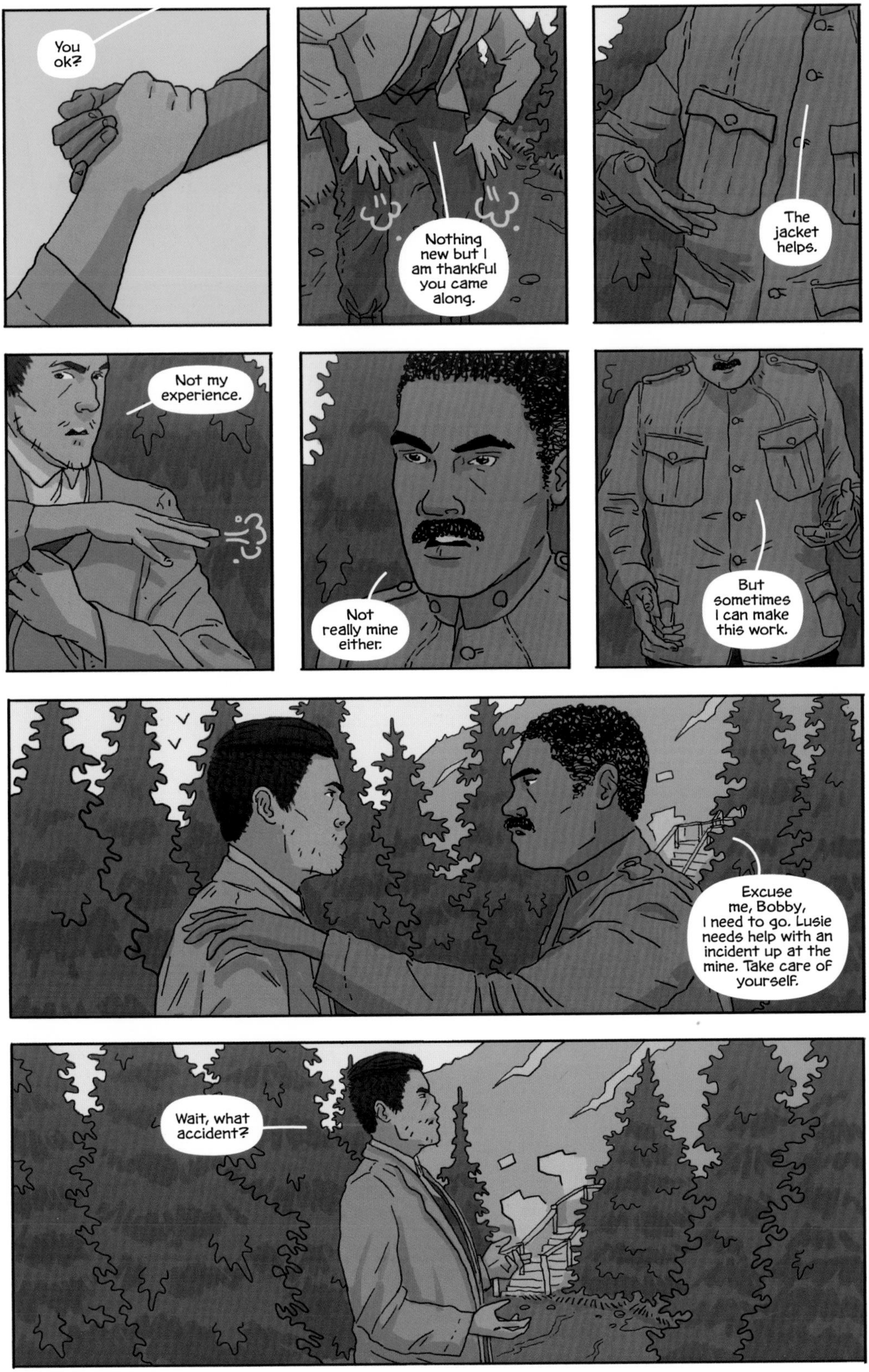
You ok?
Nothing new but I am thankful you came along.
The jacket helps.
Not my experience.
Not really mine either.
But sometimes I can make this work.
Excuse me, Bobby, I need to go. Lusie needs help with an incident up at the mine. Take care of yourself.
Wait, what accident?

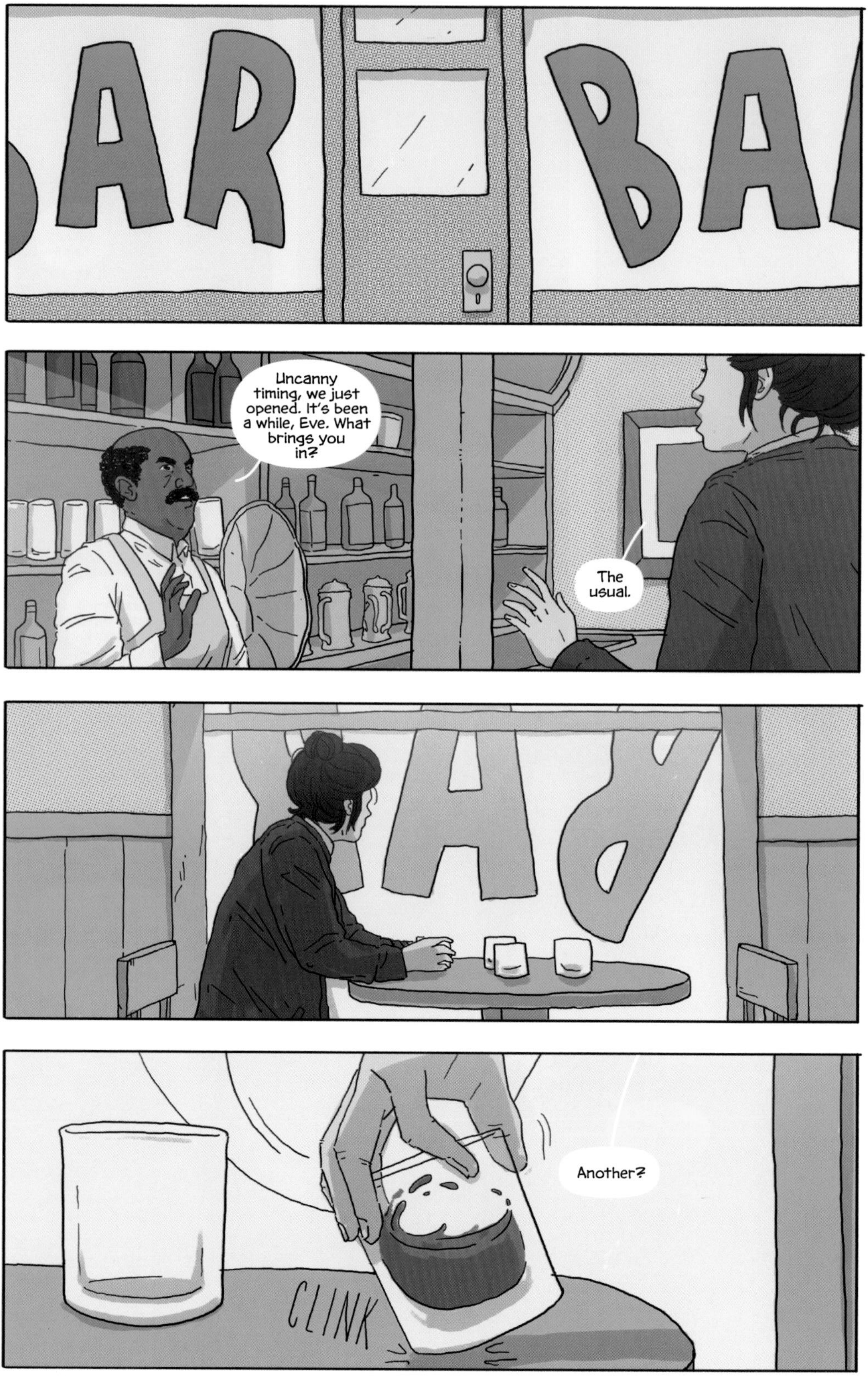
Uncanny timing, we just opened. It's been a while, Eve. What brings you in?
The usual.
CLINK
Another?

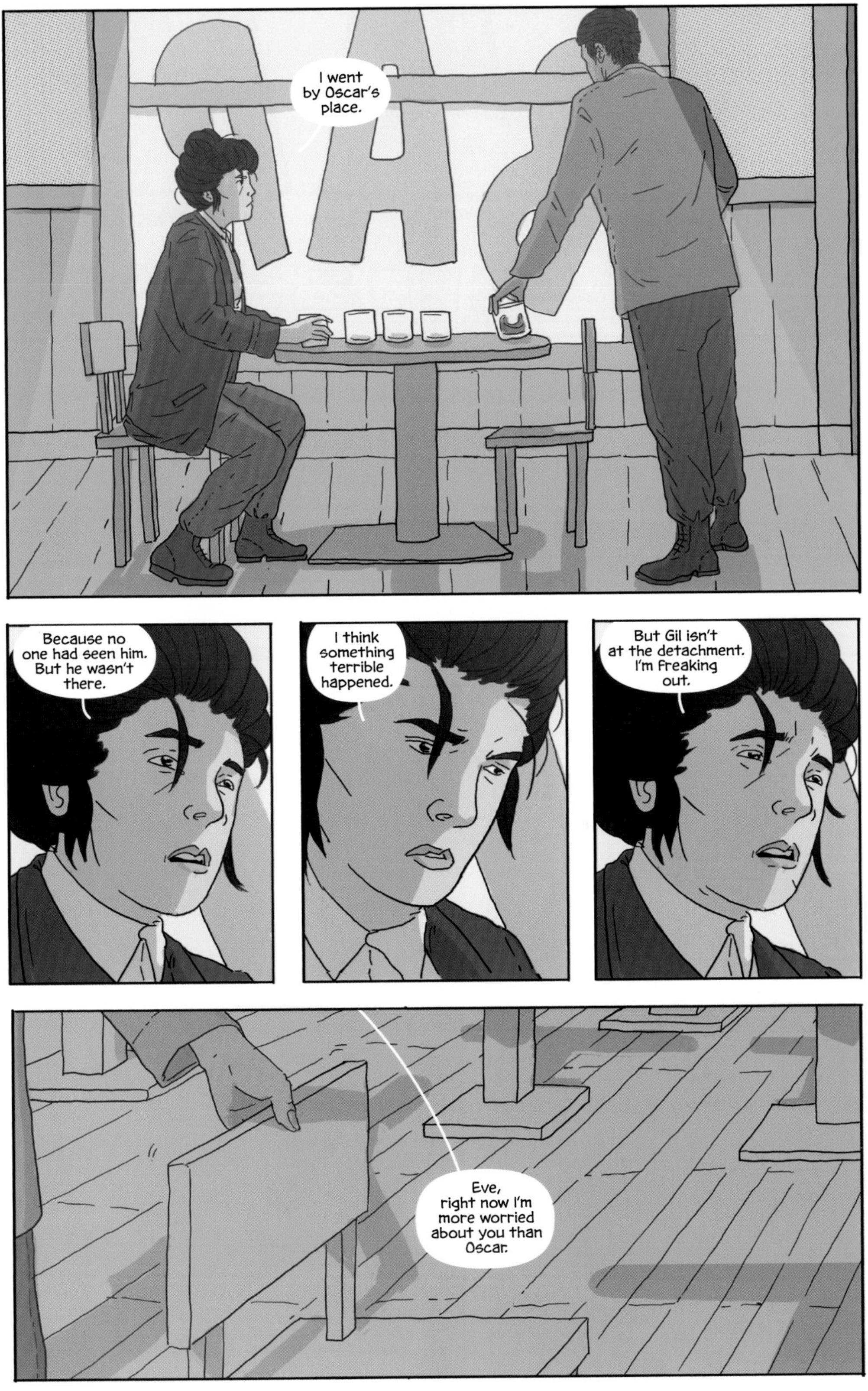
I went by Oscar's place.
Because no one had seen him. But he wasn't there.
I think something terrible happened.
But Gil isn't at the detachment. I'm freaking out.
Eve, right now I'm more worried about you than Oscar.

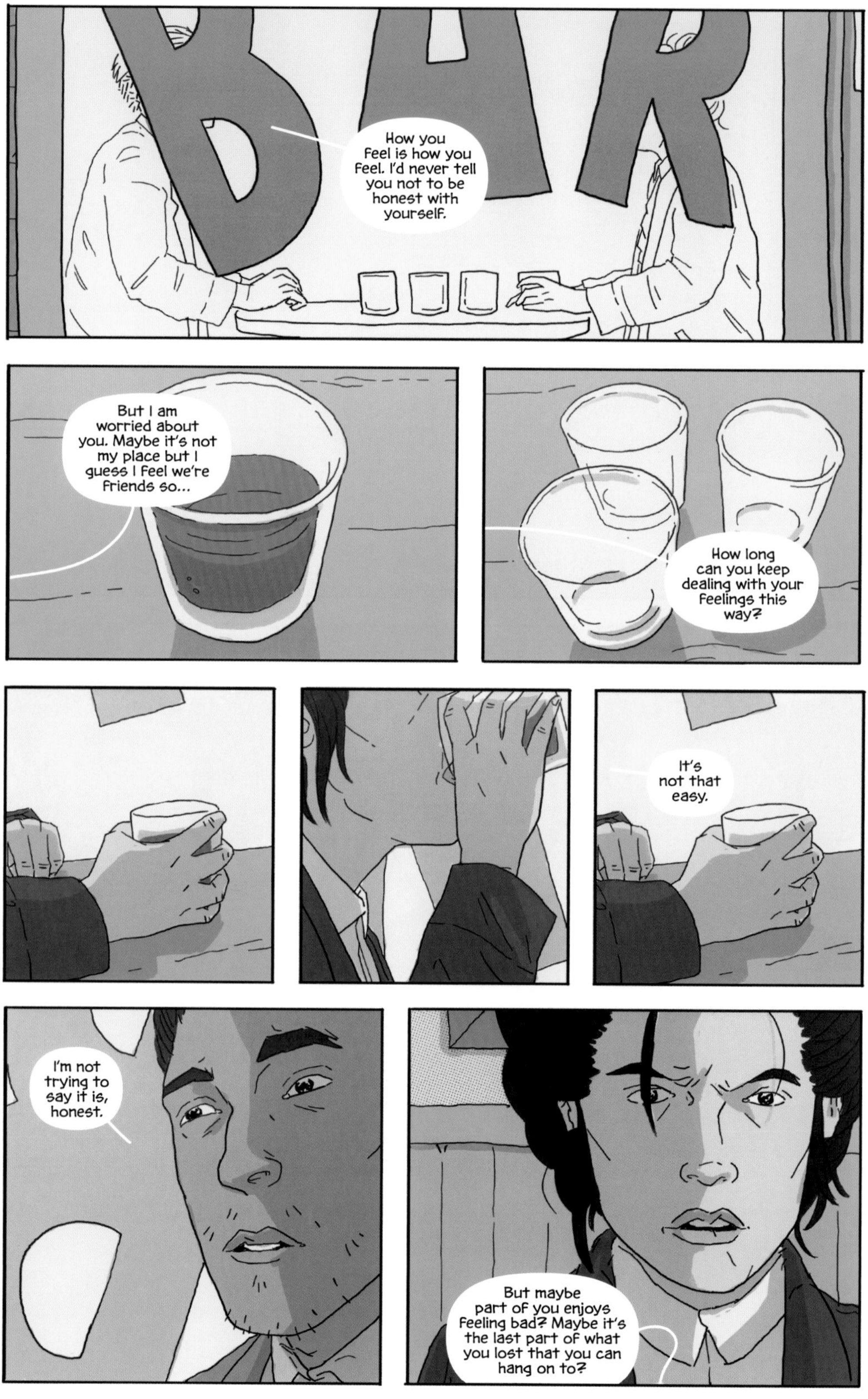
BAR
How you feel is how you feel. I'd never tell you not to be honest with yourself.
But I am worried about you. Maybe it's not my place but I guess I feel we're friends so...
How long can you keep dealing with your feelings this way?
It's not that easy.
I'm not trying to say it is, honest.
But maybe part of you enjoys feeling bad? Maybe it's the last part of what you lost that you can hang on to?

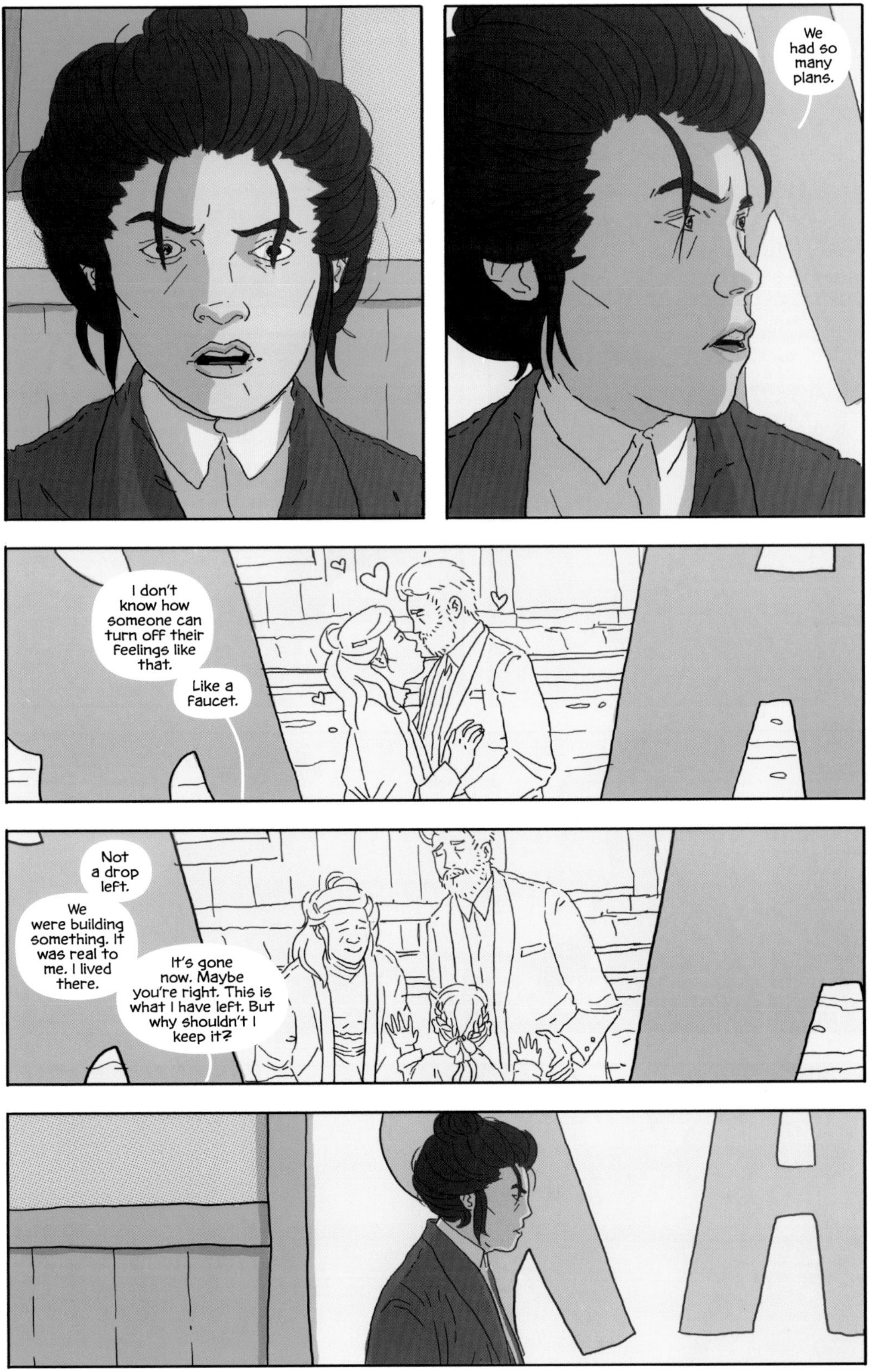
We had so many plans.
I don't know how someone can turn off their feelings like that.
Like a faucet.
Not a drop left.
We were building something. It was real to me. I lived there.
It's gone now. Maybe you're right. This is what I have left. But why shouldn't I keep it?

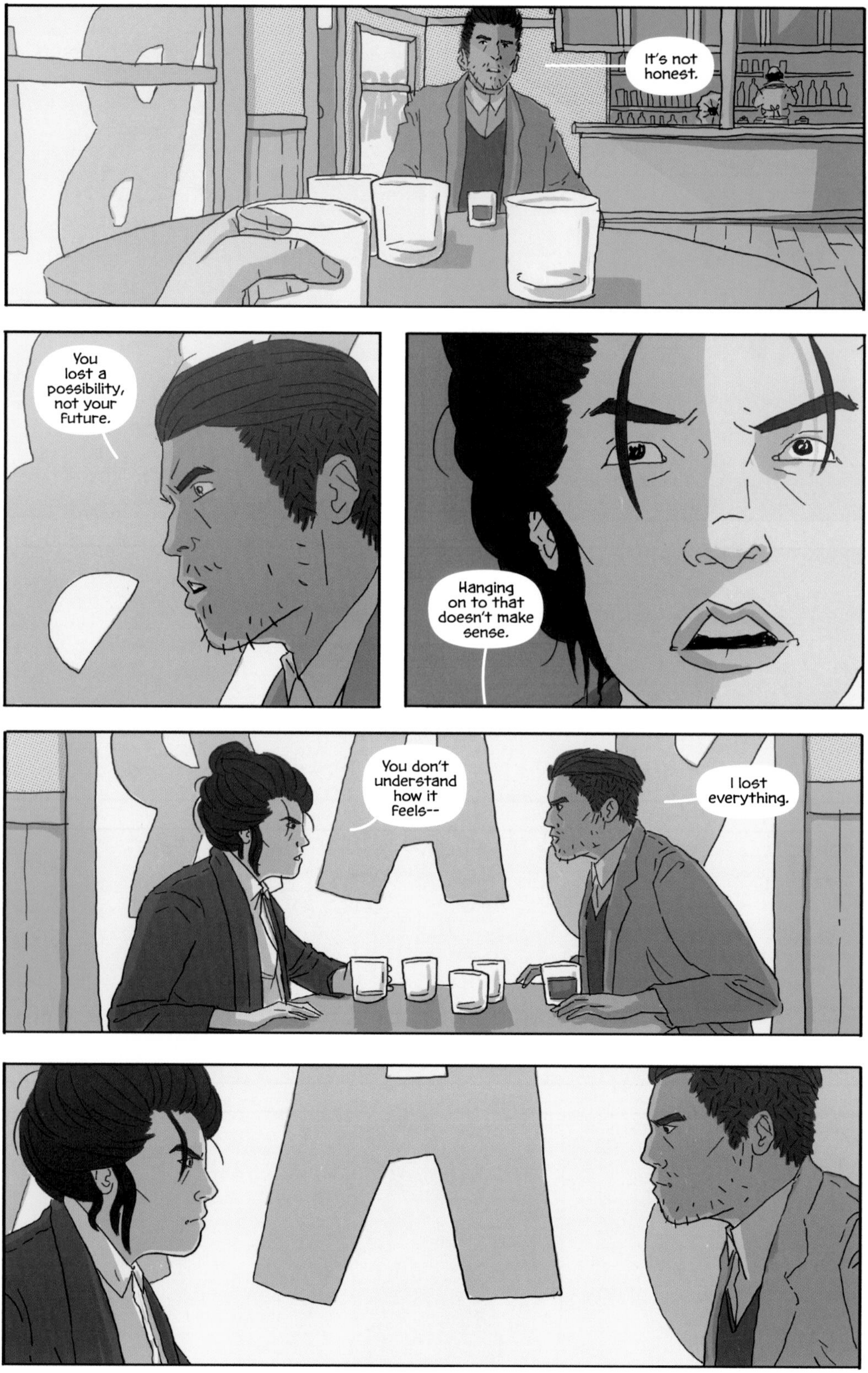
It's not honest.
You lost a possibility, not your future.
Hanging on to that doesn't make sense.
You don't understand how it feels--
I lost everything.

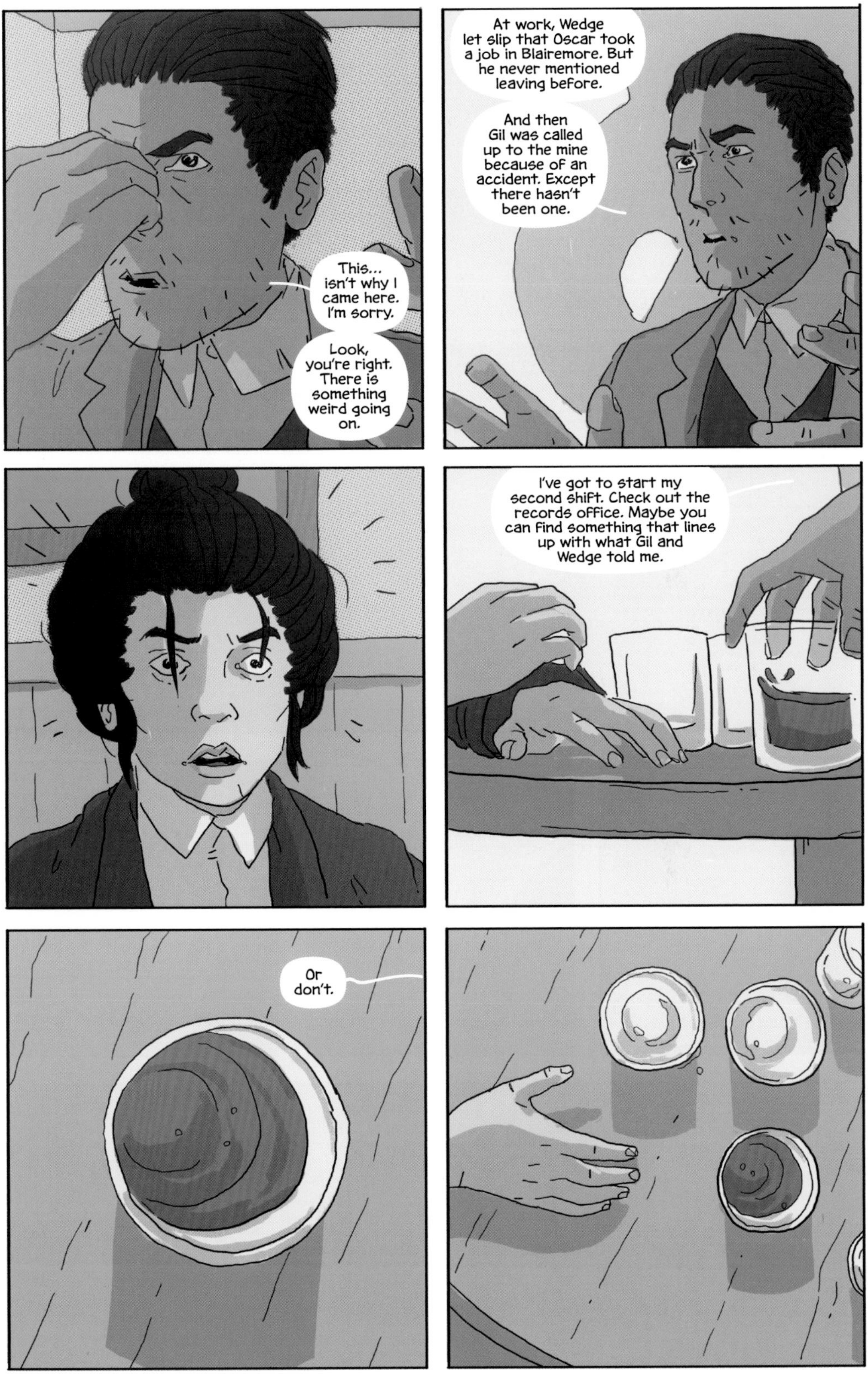
This... isn't why I came here. I'm sorry.
Look, you're right. There is something weird going on.
At work, Wedge let slip that Oscar took a job in Blairemore. But he never mentioned leaving before.
And then Gil was called up to the mine because of an accident. Except there hasn't been one.
I've got to start my second shift. Check out the records office. Maybe you can find something that lines up with what Gil and Wedge told me.
Or don't.

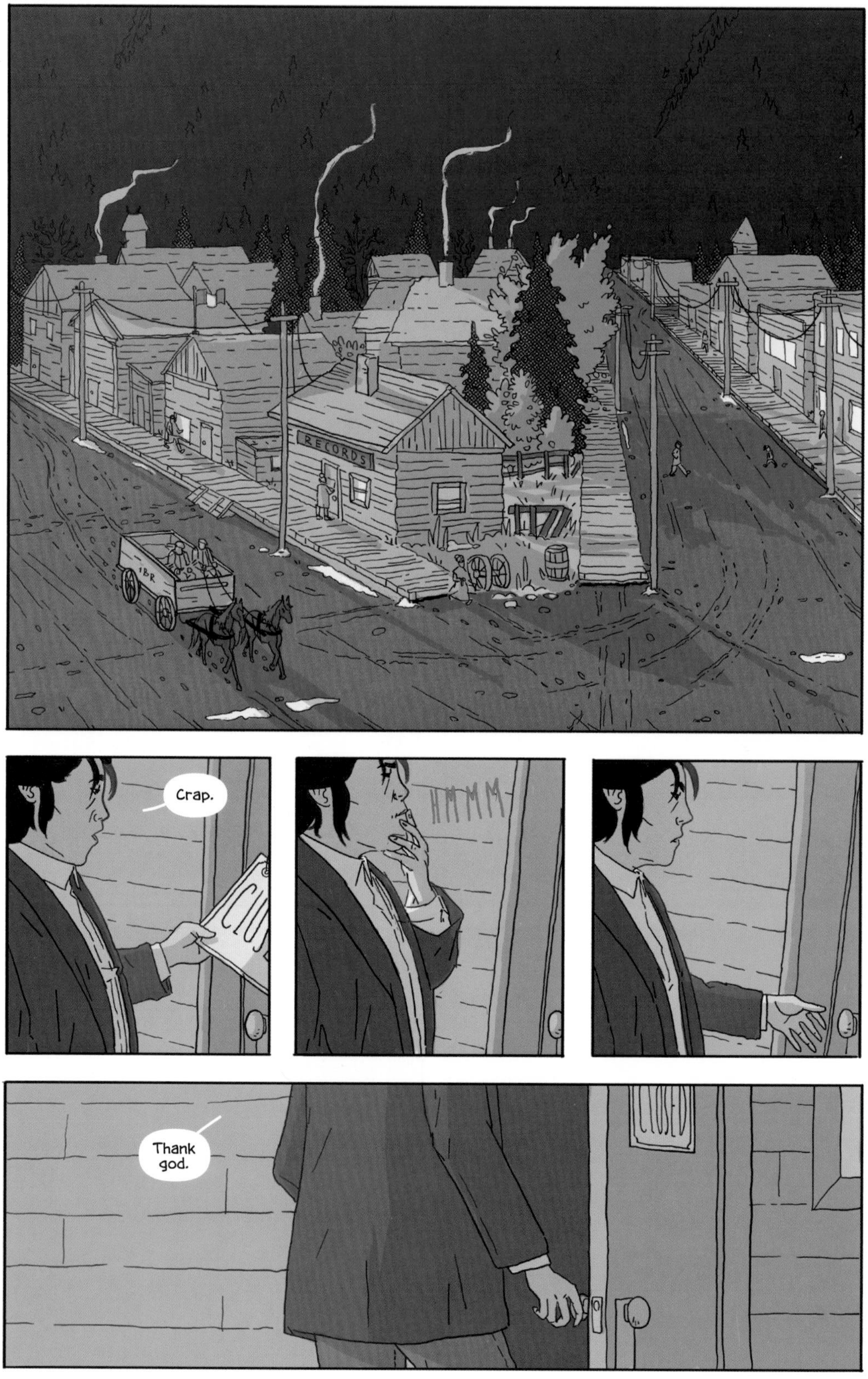
RECORDS
IBR
Crap.
HMMM
Thank god.
CLOSED

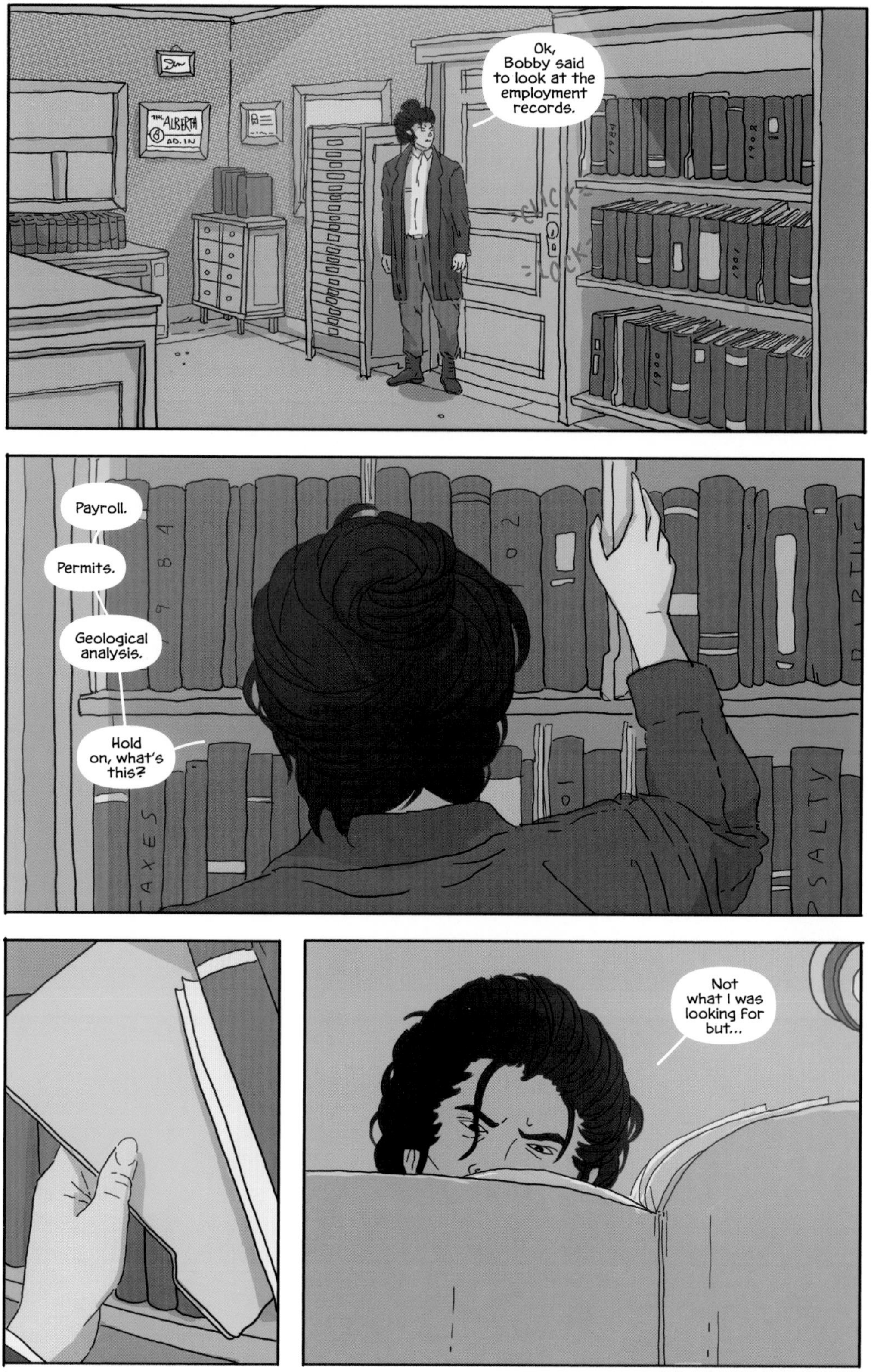

Ok, Bobby said to look at the employment records.
CLICK
LOCK
Payroll.
Permits.
Geological analysis.
Hold on, what's this?
Not what I was looking for but...

What's this? April 29, but that's tomorrow. Two dead? This doesn't make any sense.
TOSS
Some jerk put the wrong date on this?
CAC&Co
WORKER TERMINATIONS

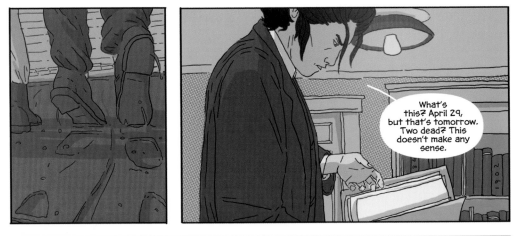

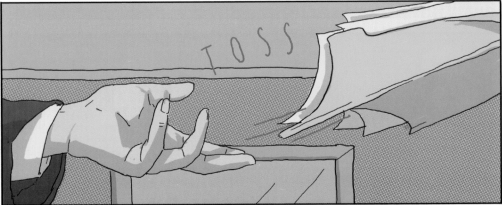

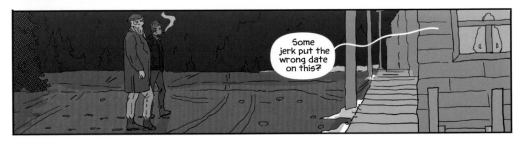

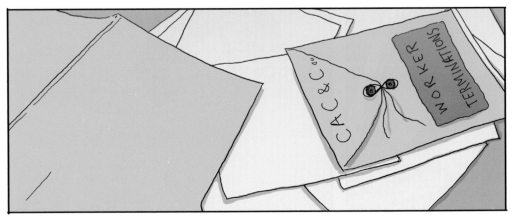

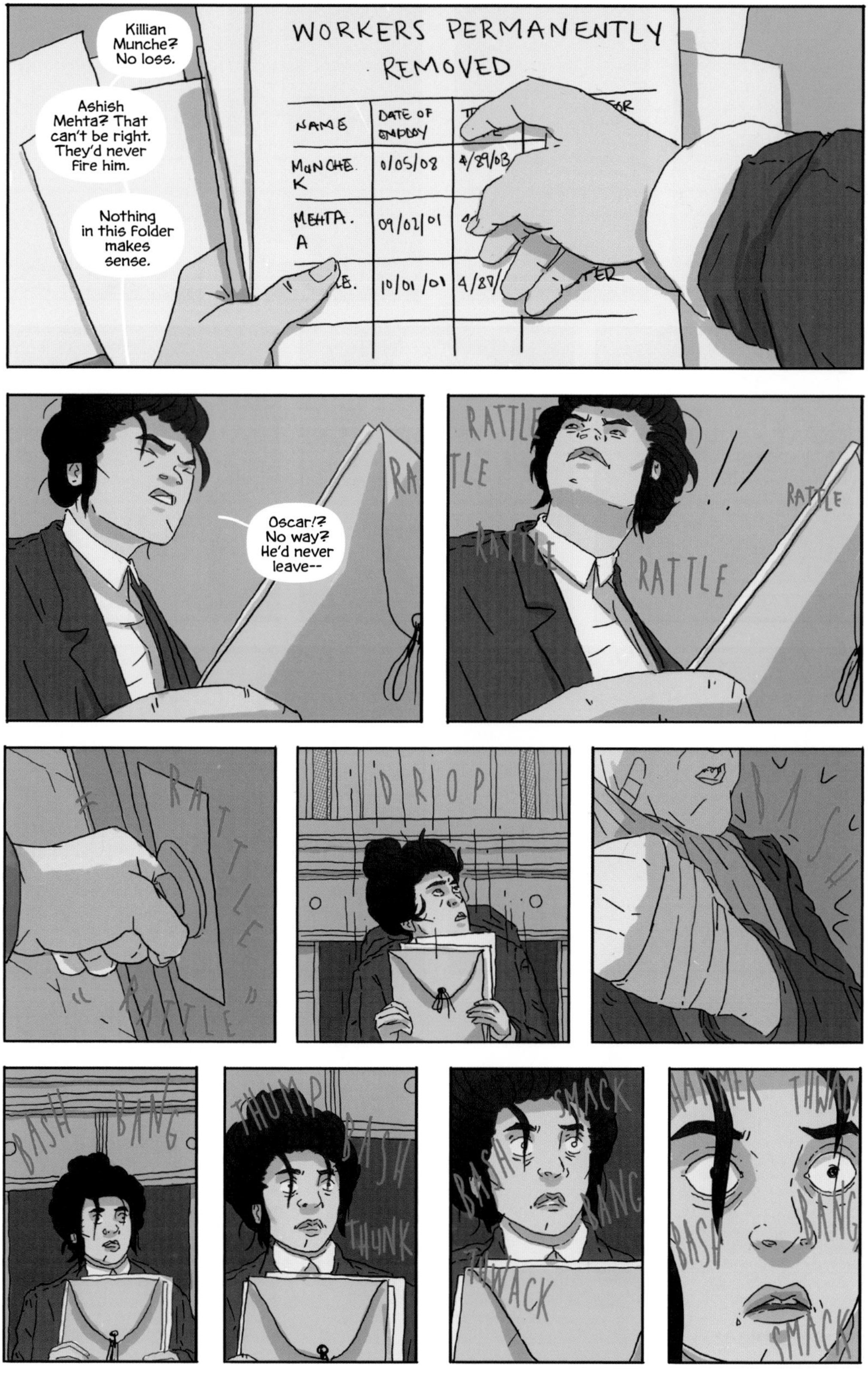
WORKERS PERMANENTLY REMOVED
NAME
DATE OF EMPLOY
MUNCHE. K
0/05/08
MEHTA. A
09/02/01
10/01/01
Killian Munche? No loss.
Ashish Mehta? That can't be right. They'd never fire him.
Nothing in this folder makes sense.
RATTLE
Oscar!? No way? He'd never leave--
RATTLE
RATTLE
RATTLE
RATTLE
RATTLE
RATTLE
DROP
BASH
BASH
BANG
THUMP
BASH
THUNK
SMACK
BASH
BANG
THWACK
HAMMER
THWACK
BASH
BANG
SMACK

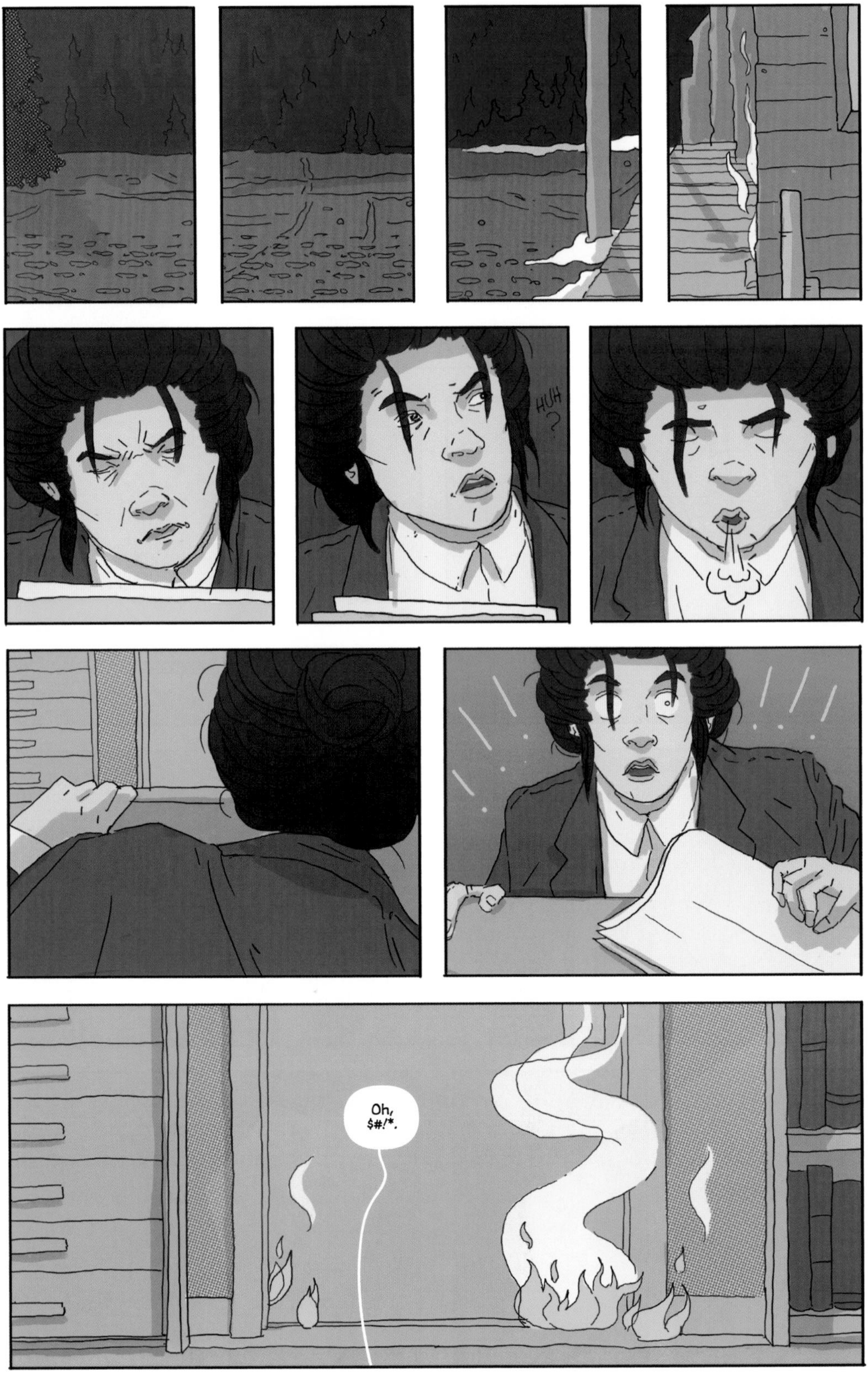
HUH
?
Oh,
$#!*.

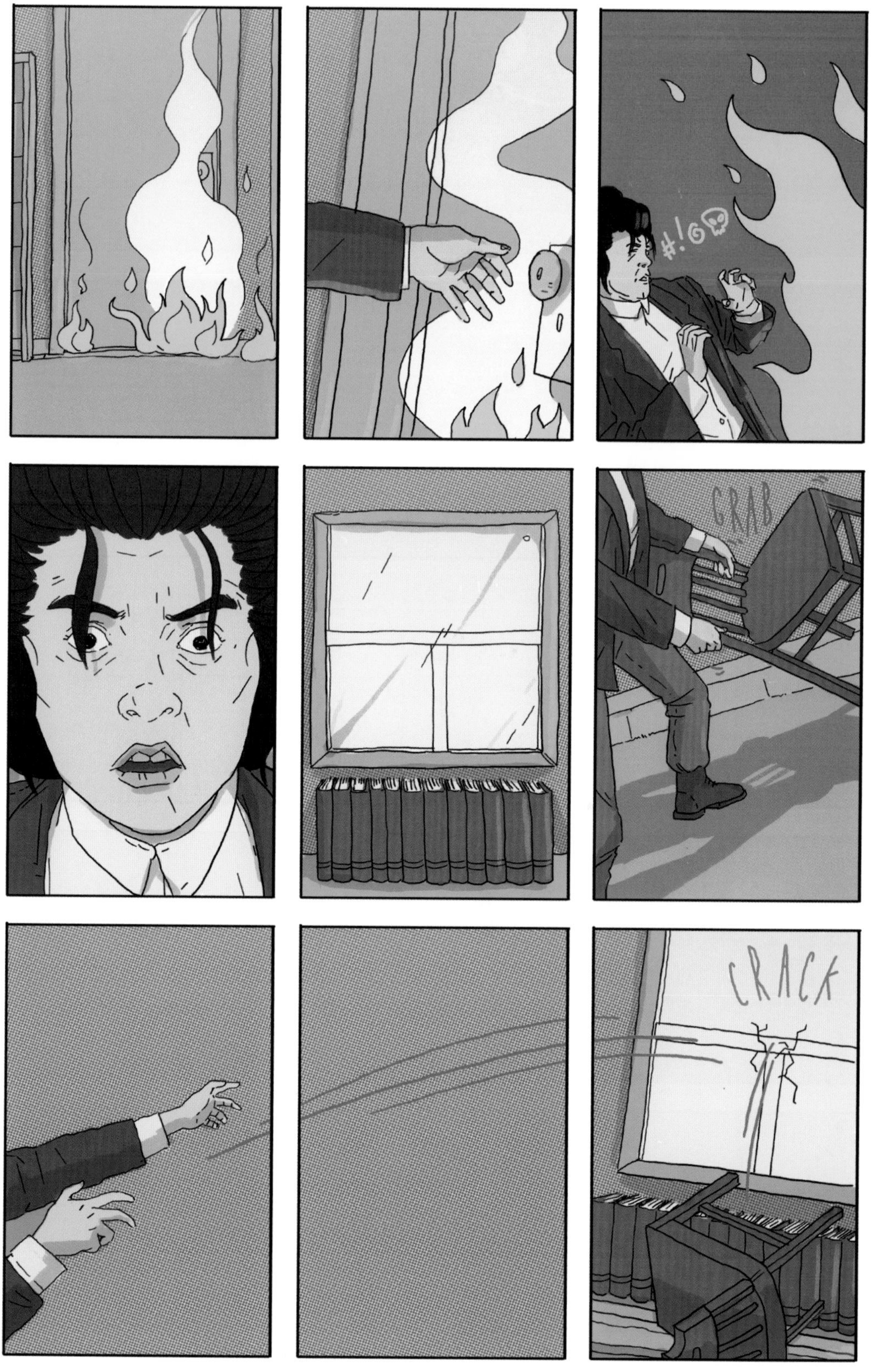
#!@
GRAB
CRACK

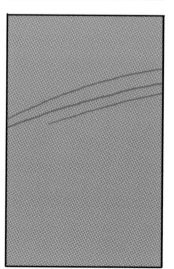

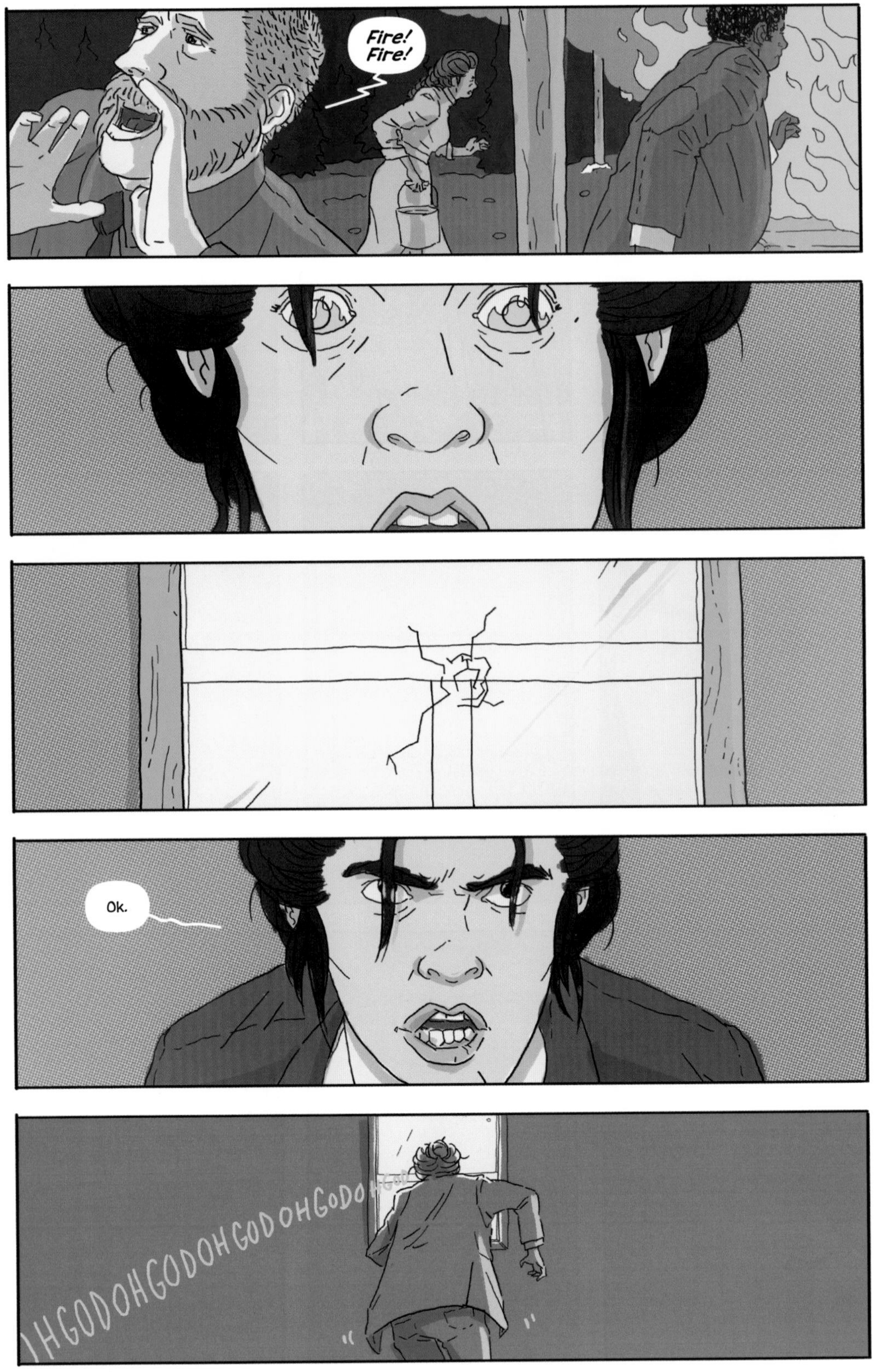
Fire! Fire!
Ok.
HGODOHGODOHGODOHGODOHGOD

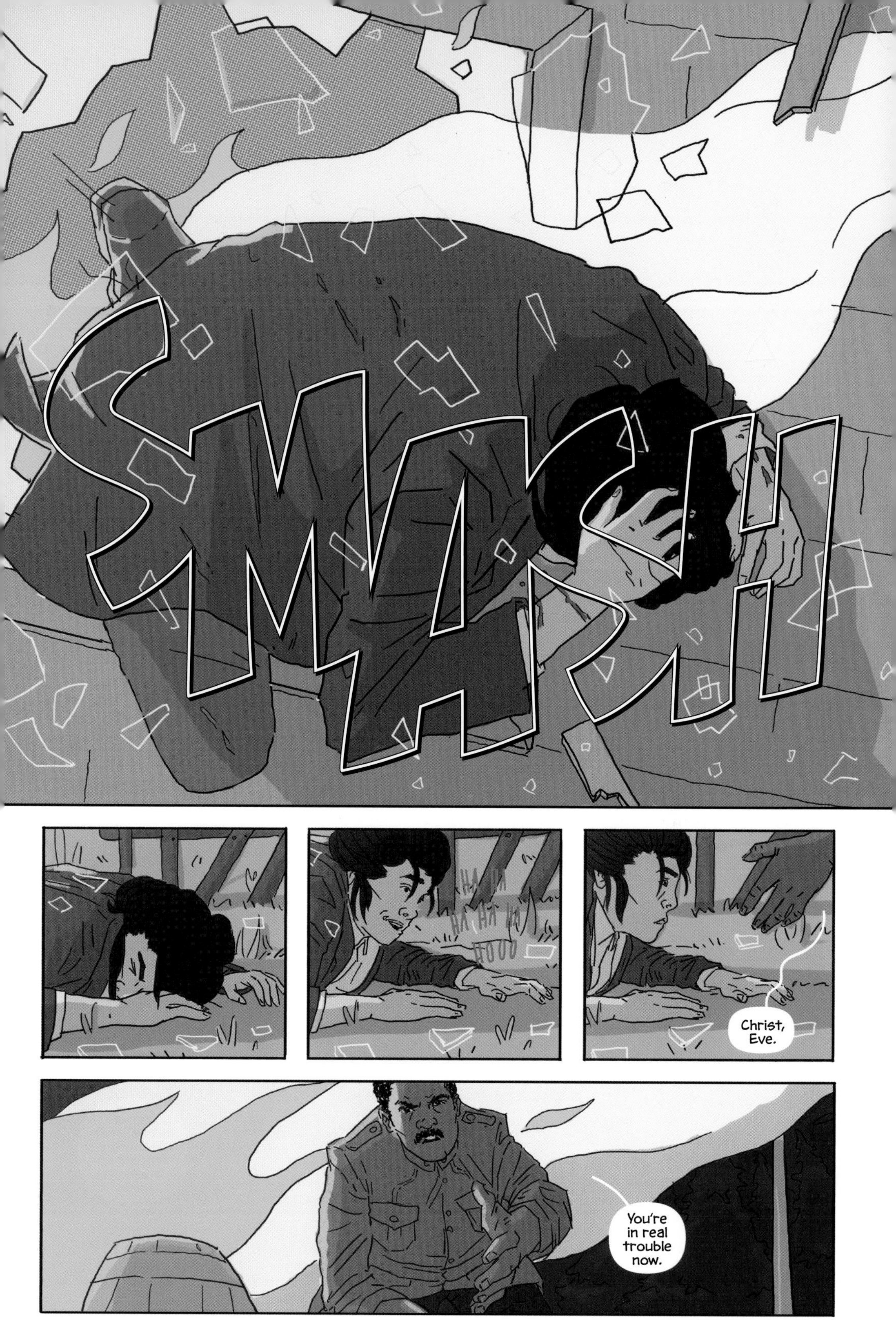
SMASH
Christ, Eve.
You're in real trouble now.

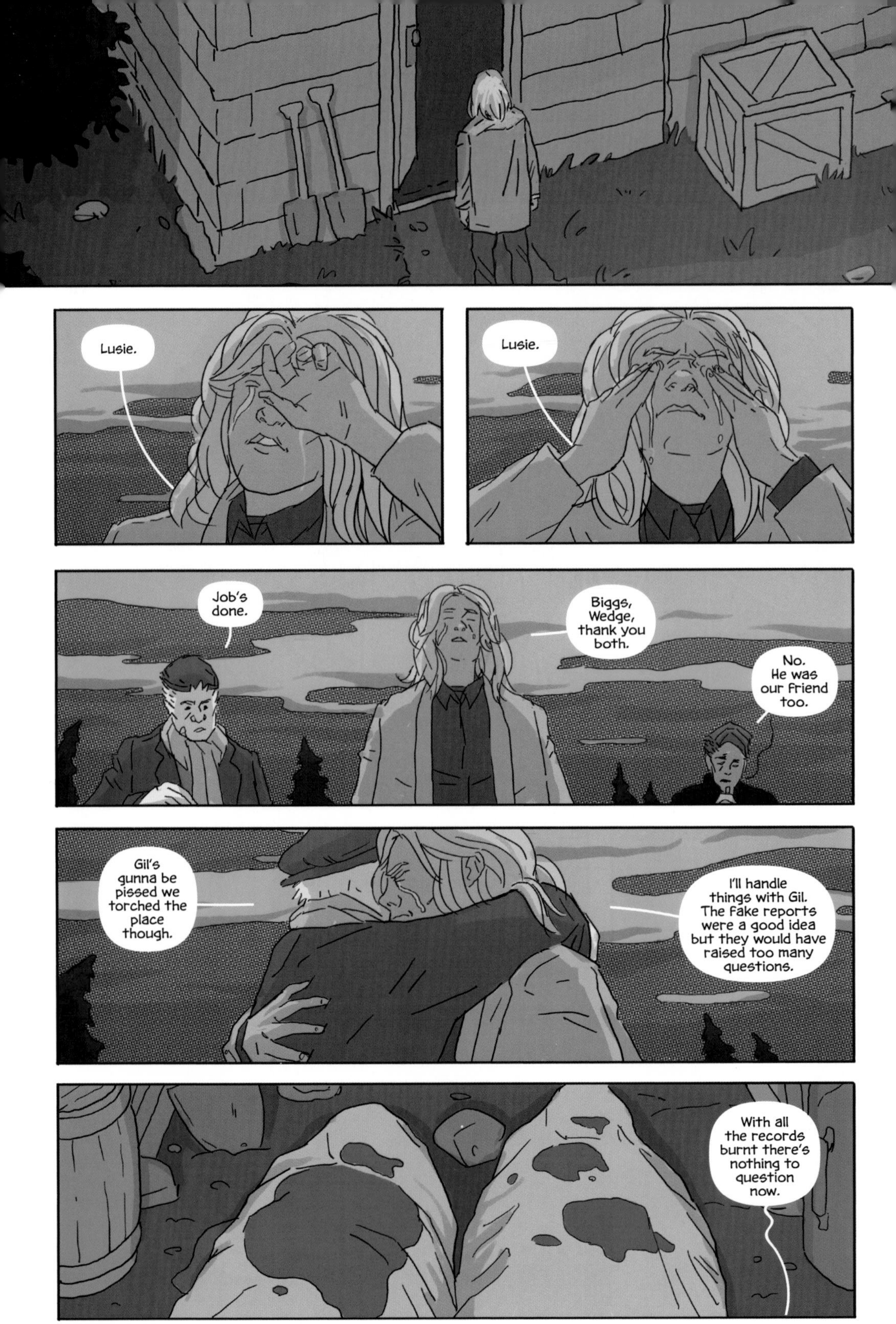
Lusie.
Lusie.
Job's done.
Biggs, Wedge, thank you both.
No. He was our friend too.
Gil's gunna be pissed we torched the place though.
I'll handle things with Gil. The fake reports were a good idea but they would have raised too many questions.
With all the records burnt there's nothing to question now.

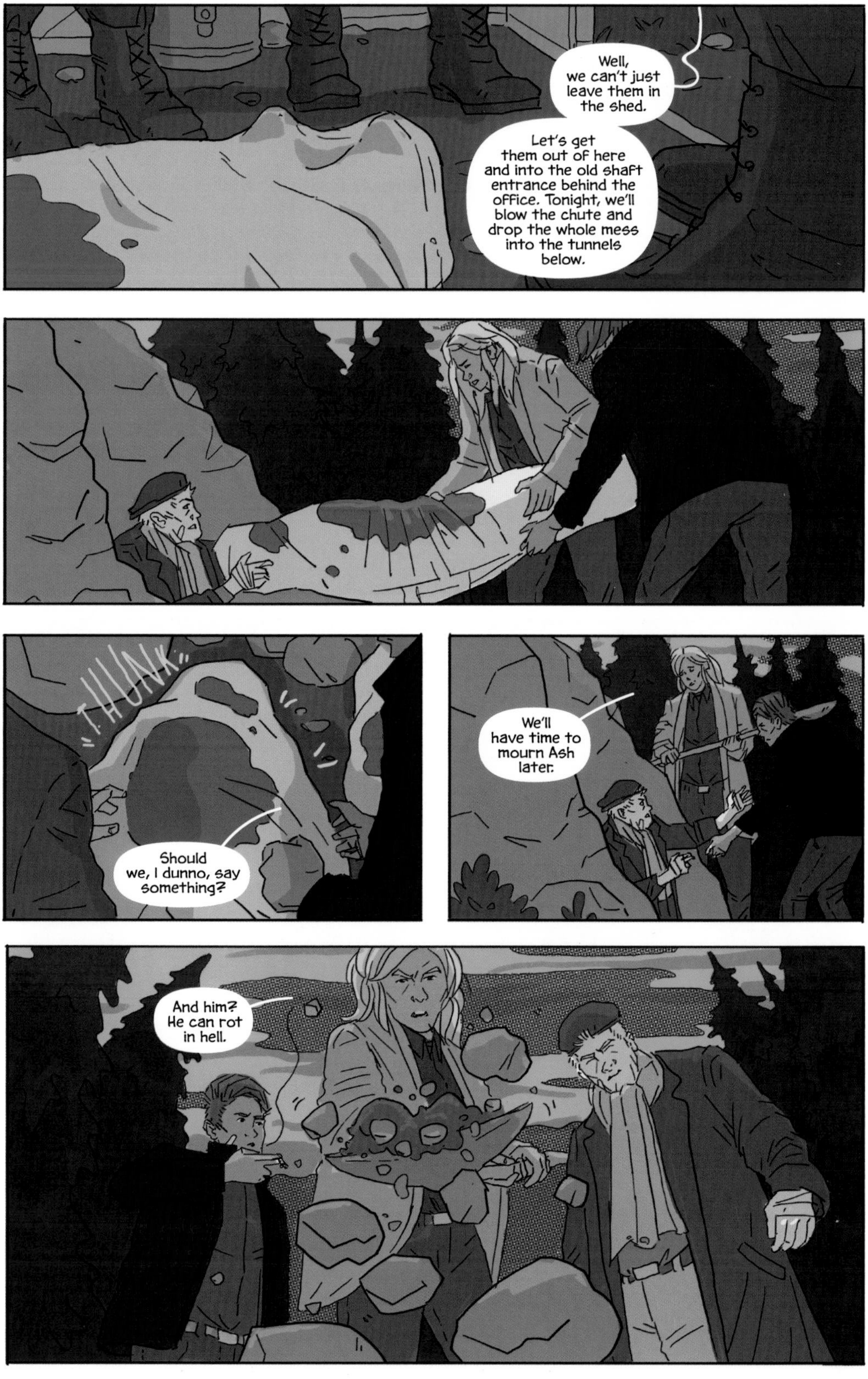
Well, we can't just leave them in the shed.
Let's get them out of here and into the old shaft entrance behind the office. Tonight, we'll blow the chute and drop the whole mess into the tunnels below.
THUNK
Should we, I dunno, say something?
We'll have time to mourn Ash later.
And him? He can rot in hell.

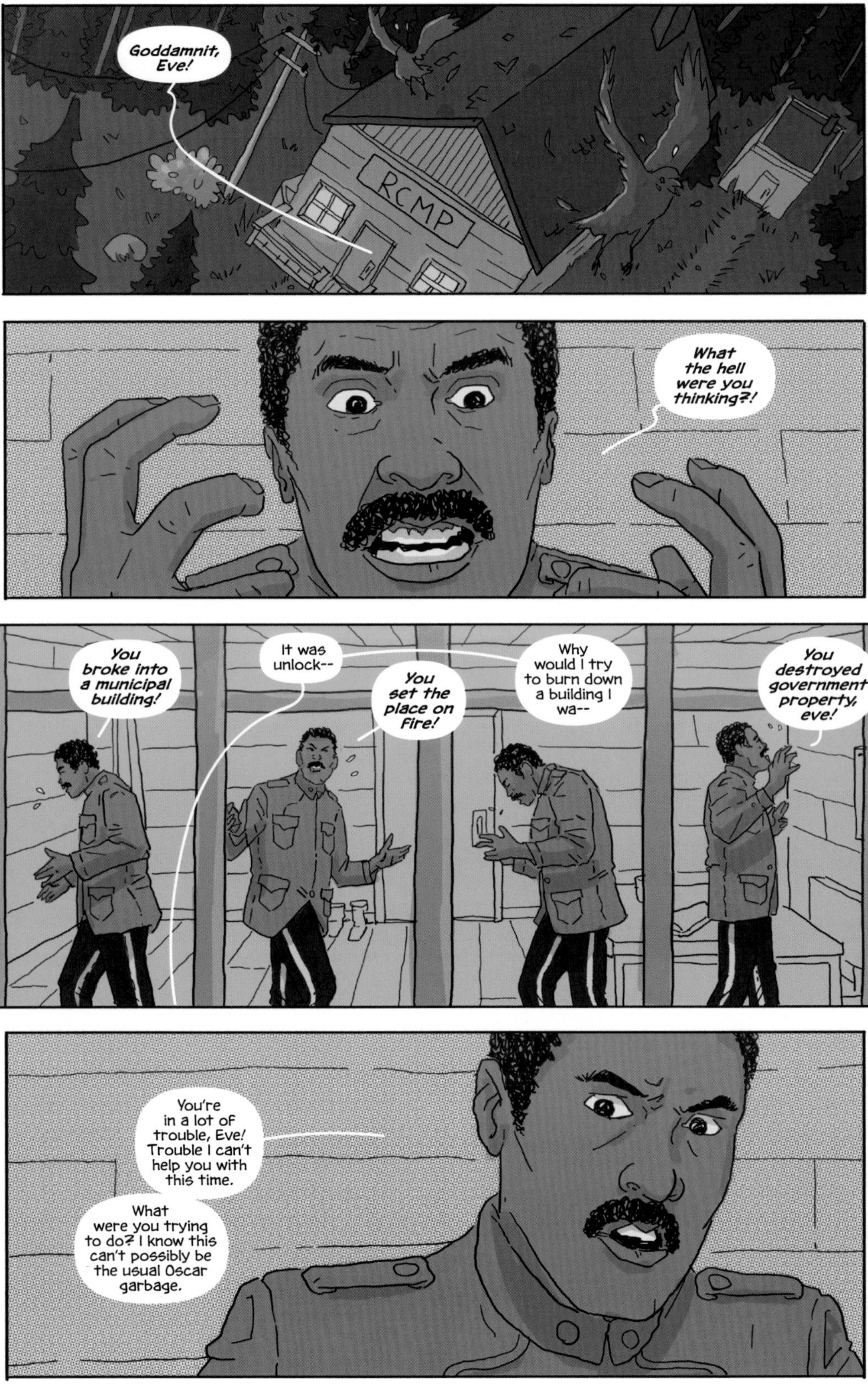
Goddamnit, Eve!
RCMP
What the hell were you thinking?!
You broke into a municipal building!
It was unlock--
You set the place on Fire!
Why would I try to burn down a building I wa--
You destroyed government property, eve!
You're in a lot of trouble, Eve! Trouble I can't help you with this time.
What were you trying to do? I know this can't possibly be the usual Oscar garbage.

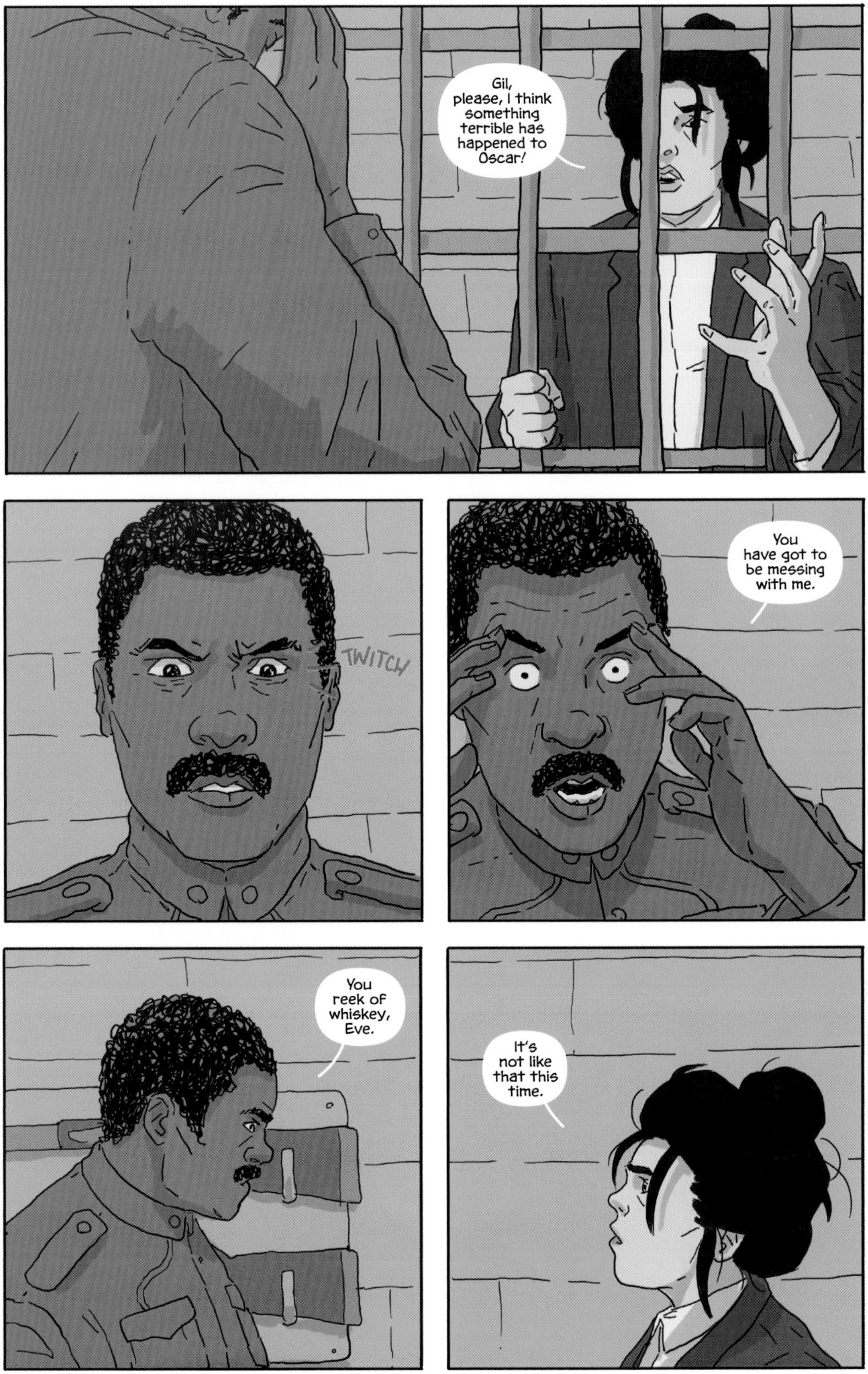
Gil, please, I think something terrible has happened to Oscar!
TWITCH
You have got to be messing with me.
You reek of whiskey, Eve.
It's not like that this time.

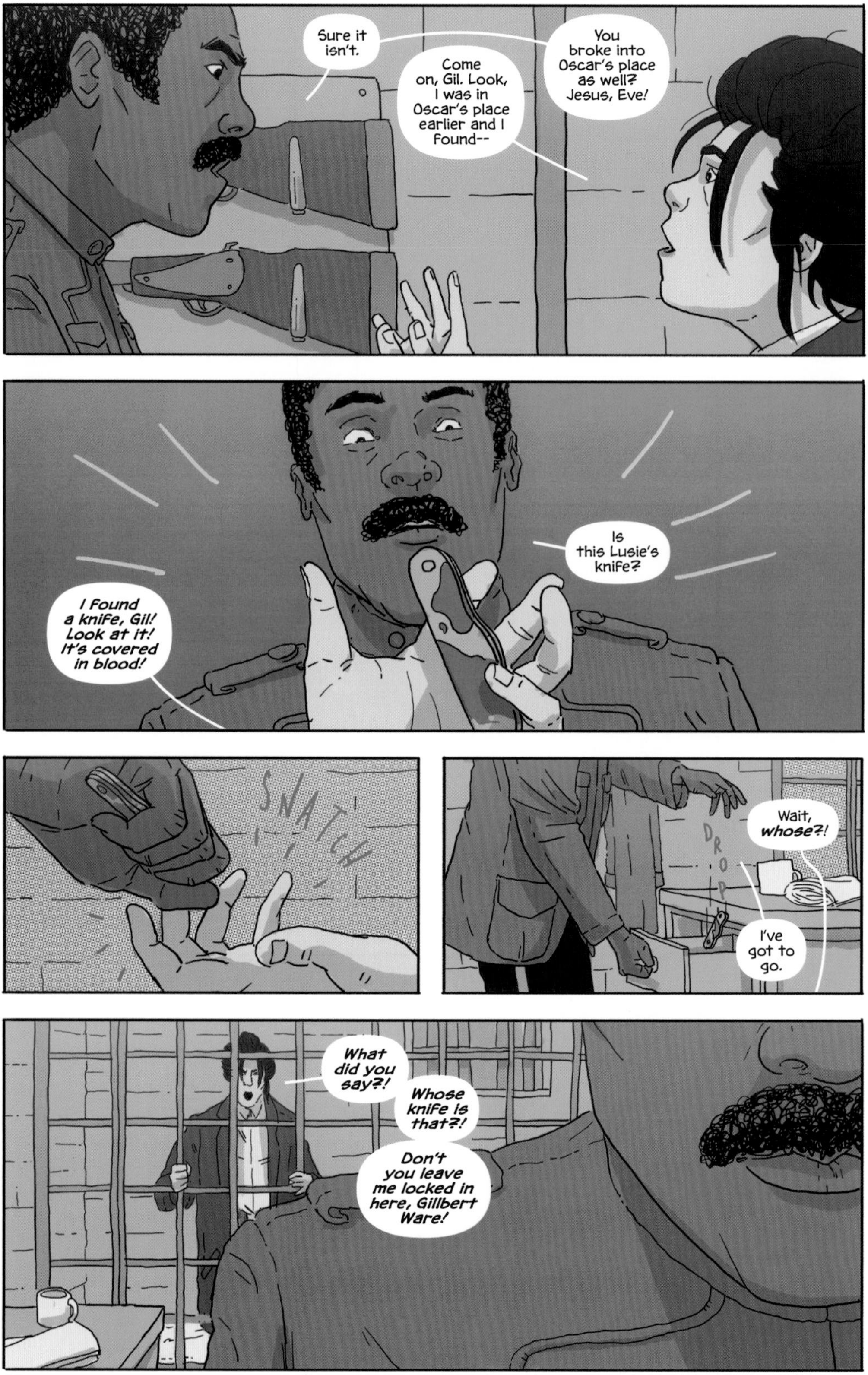
Sure it isn't.
Come on, Gil. Look, I was in Oscar's place earlier and I found--
You broke into Oscar's place as well? Jesus, Eve!
I found a knife, Gil! Look at it! It's covered in blood!
Is this Lusie's knife?
SNATCH
DROP
Wait, whose?!
I've got to go.
What did you say?!
Whose knife is that?!
Don't you leave me locked in here, Gillbert Ware!

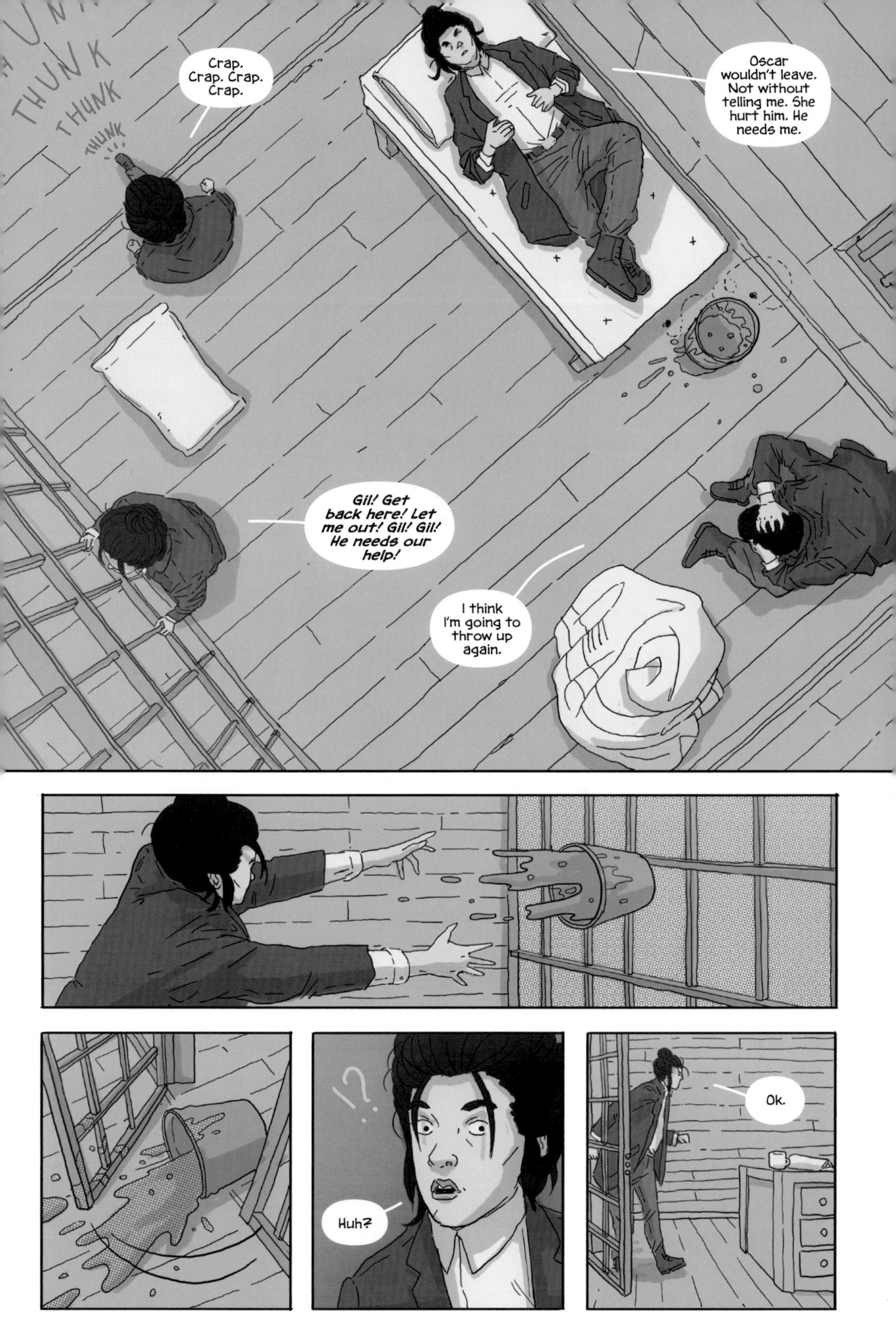
THUNK
THUNK
THUNK
Crap. Crap. Crap. Crap.
Oscar wouldn't leave. Not without telling me. She hurt him. He needs me.
Gil! Get back here! Let me out! Gil! Gil! He needs our help!
I think I'm going to throw up again.
Huh?
Ok.

Locked.
God dang it!
THUNK
Canadian
Whisky
FLICK

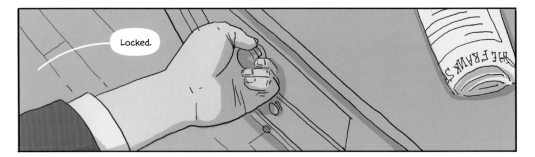

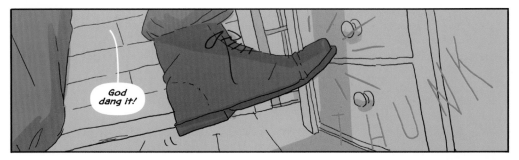

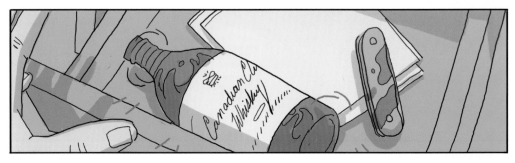

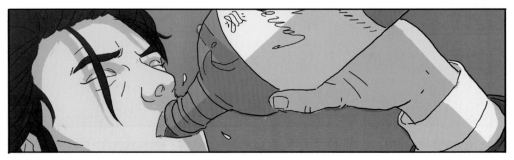

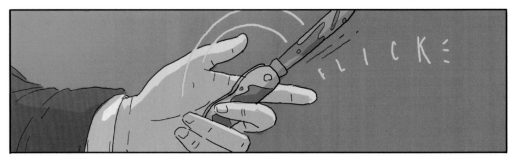

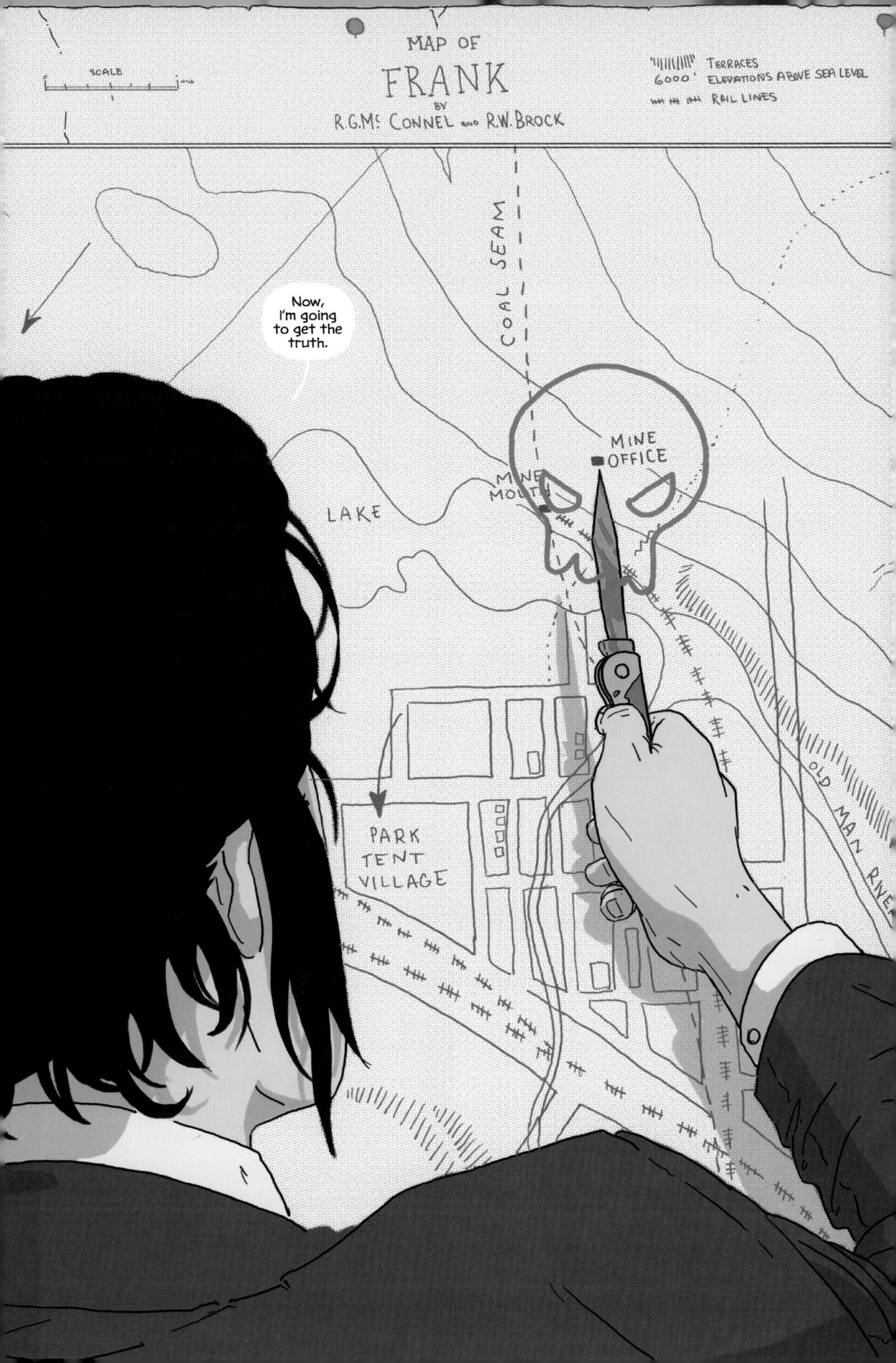
MAP OF
FRANK
BY
R.G.Mc CONNEL AND R.W. BROCK
SCALE
TERRACES
6000' ELEVATIONS ABOVE SEA LEVEL
RAIL LINES
COAL SEAM
Now, I'm going to get the truth.
MINE OFFICE
MINE MOUTH
LAKE
PARK TENT VILLAGE
OLD MAN RIVER

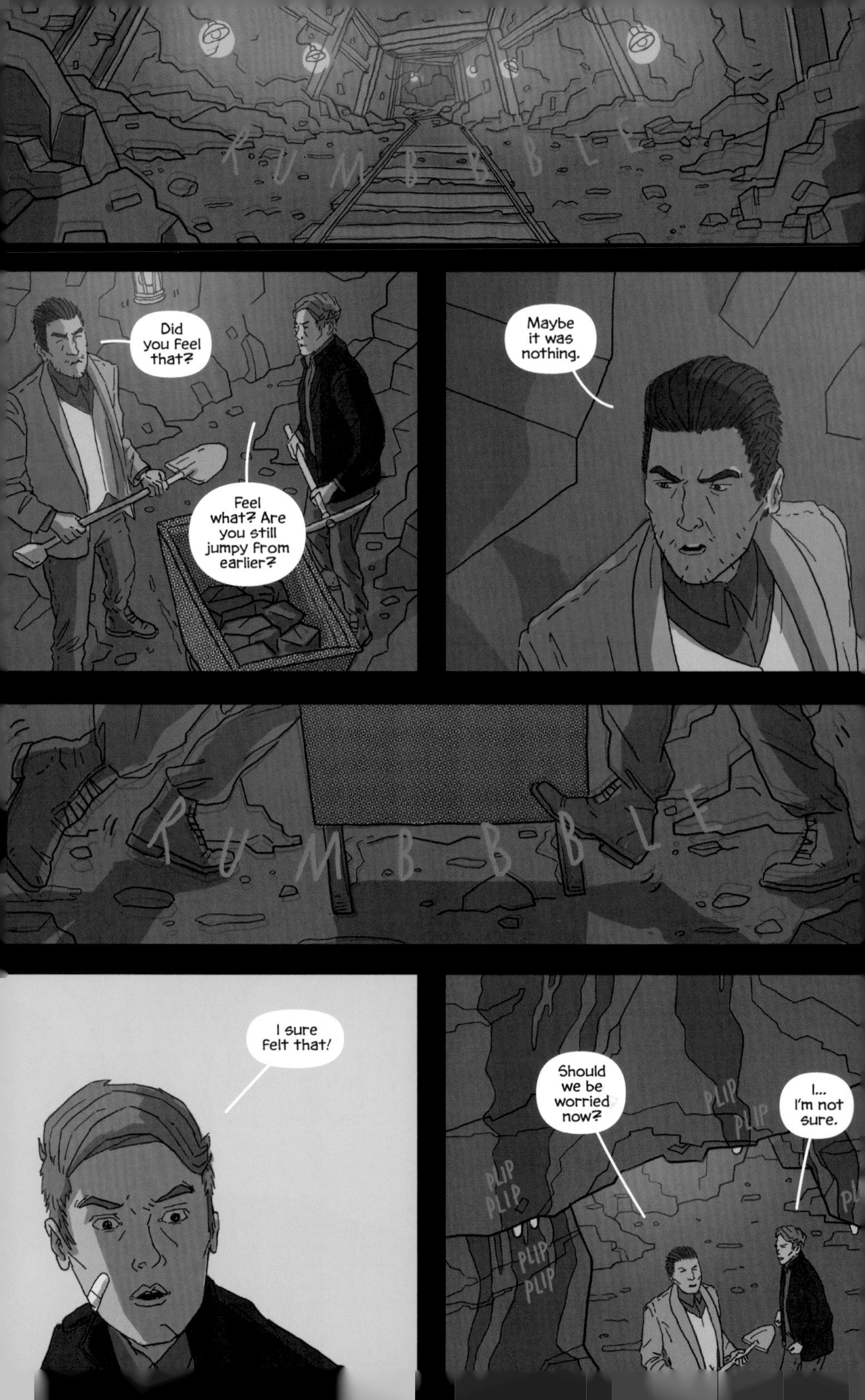
RUMBBBLE
Did you feel that?
Feel what? Are you still jumpy from earlier?
Maybe it was nothing.
RUMBBBLE
I sure felt that!
Should we be worried now?
PLIP PLIP
PLIP PLIP
PLIP PLIP
I... I'm not sure.

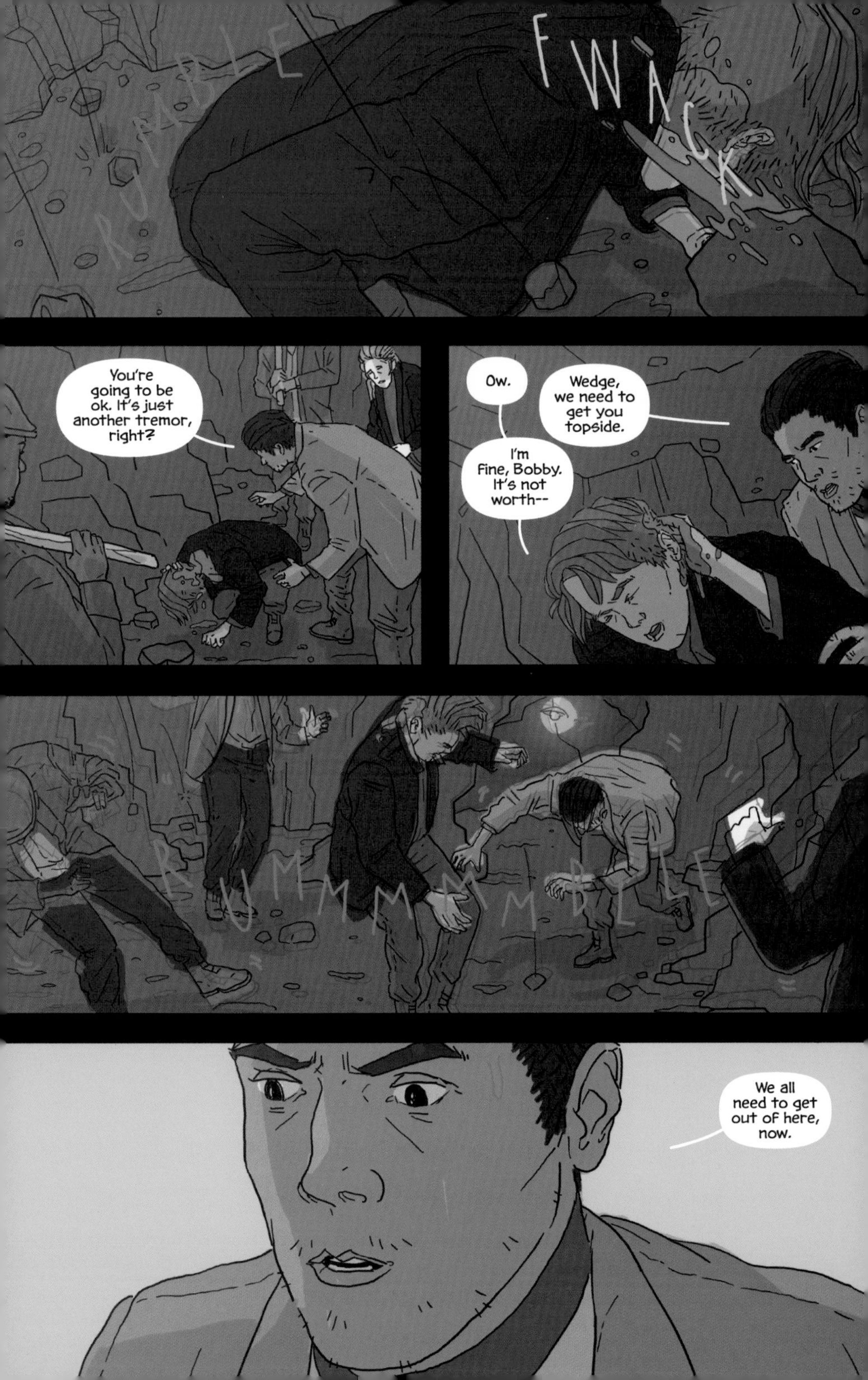
RUMBLE
FWACK
You're going to be ok. It's just another tremor, right?
Ow.
Wedge, we need to get you topside.
I'm Fine, Bobby. It's not worth--
RUMMMMMBLE
We all need to get out of here, now.

BRRRRR

BEA[

[ST]ING CAPS

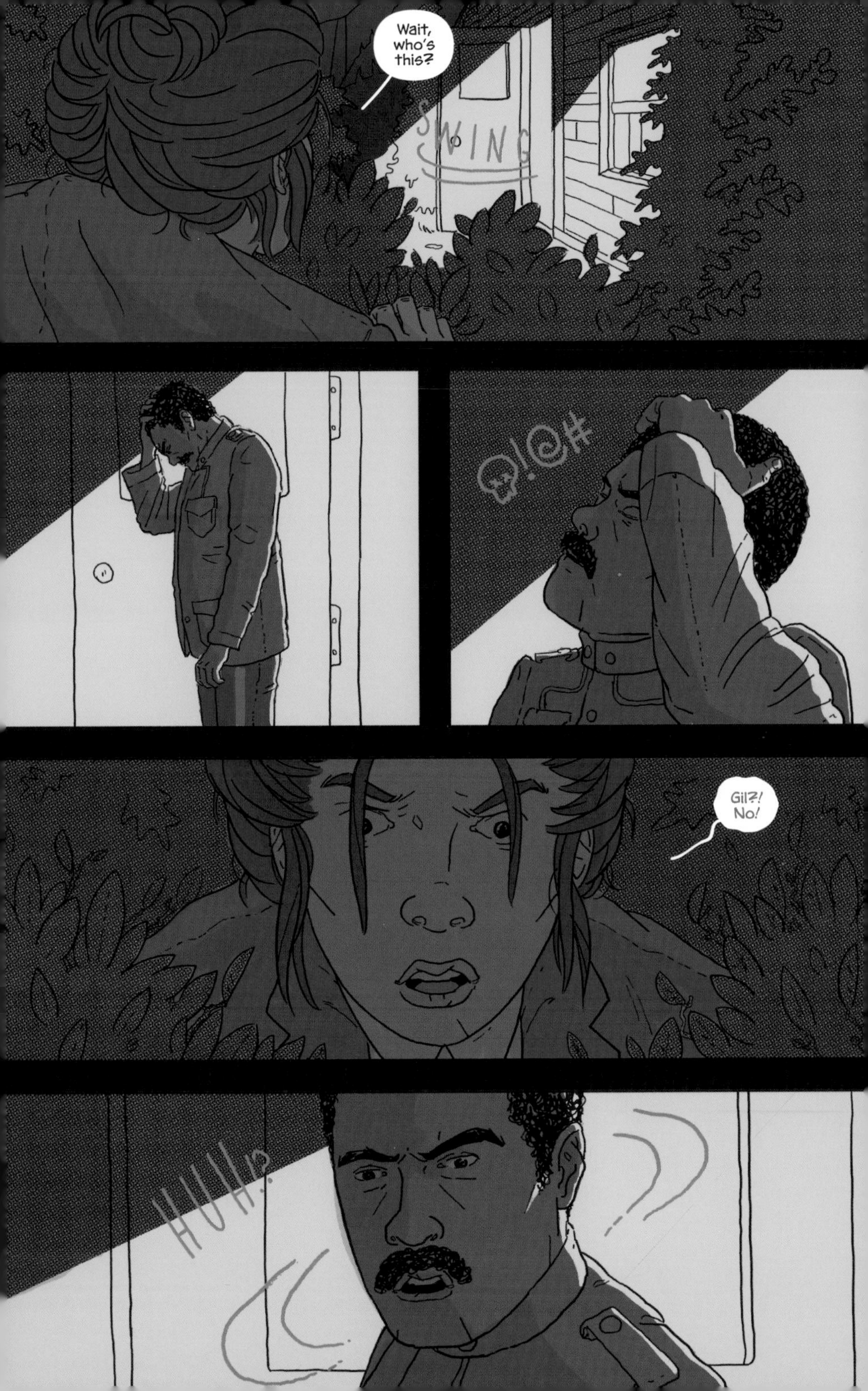
Wait, who's this?
SWING
Gil?! No!
HUH!?

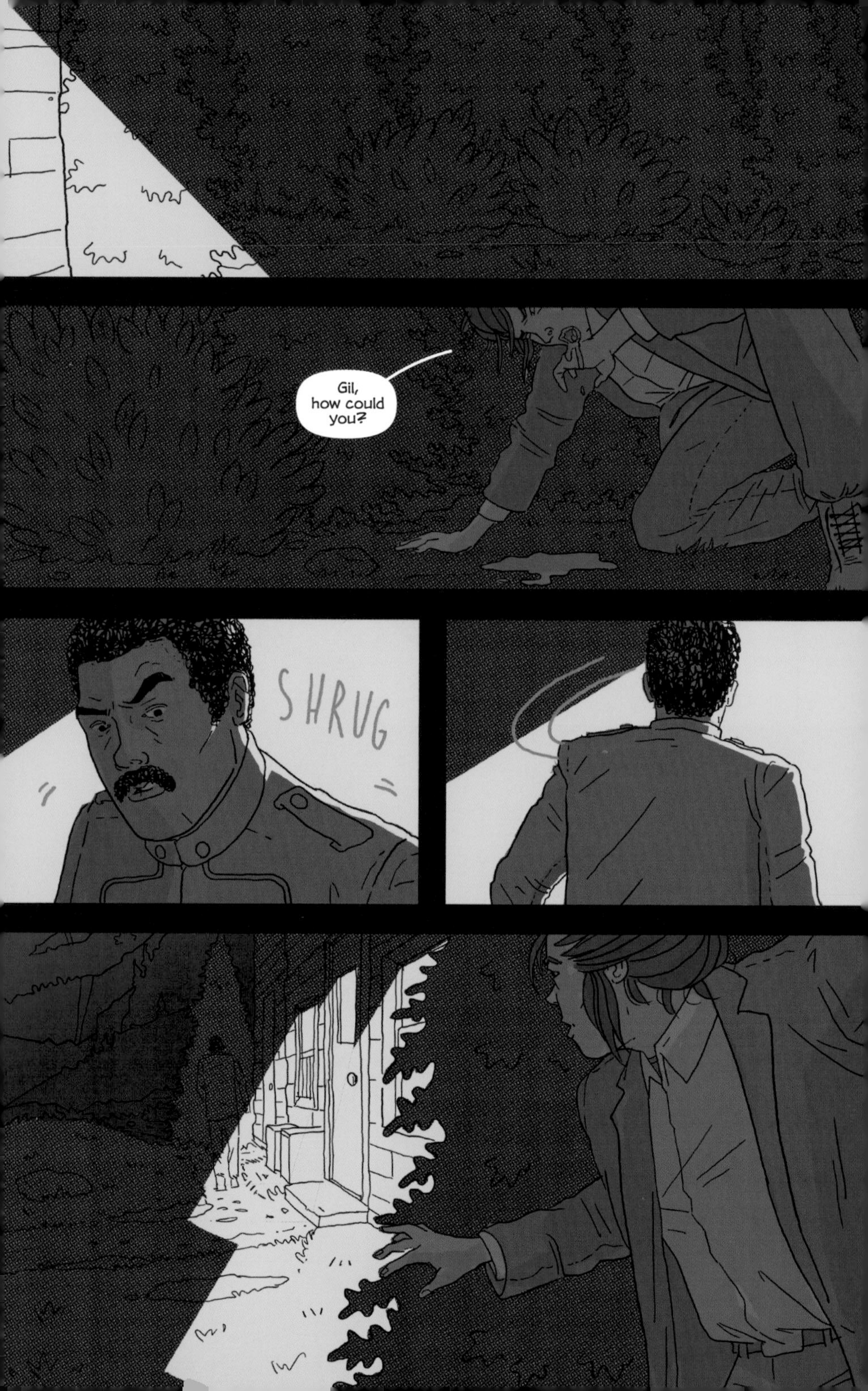
Gil, how could you?
SHRUG

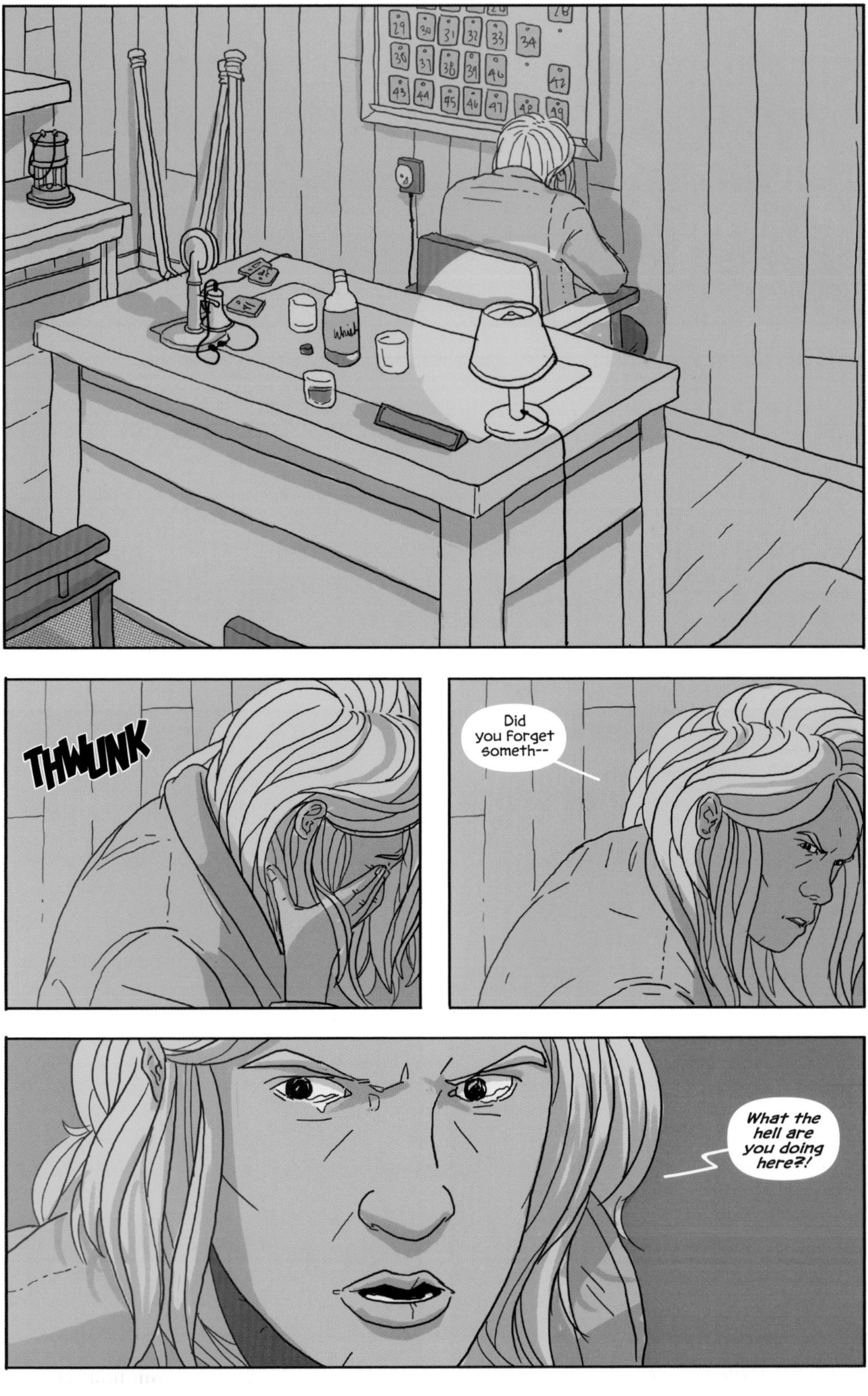
THWUNK
Did you forget someth--
What the hell are you doing here?!

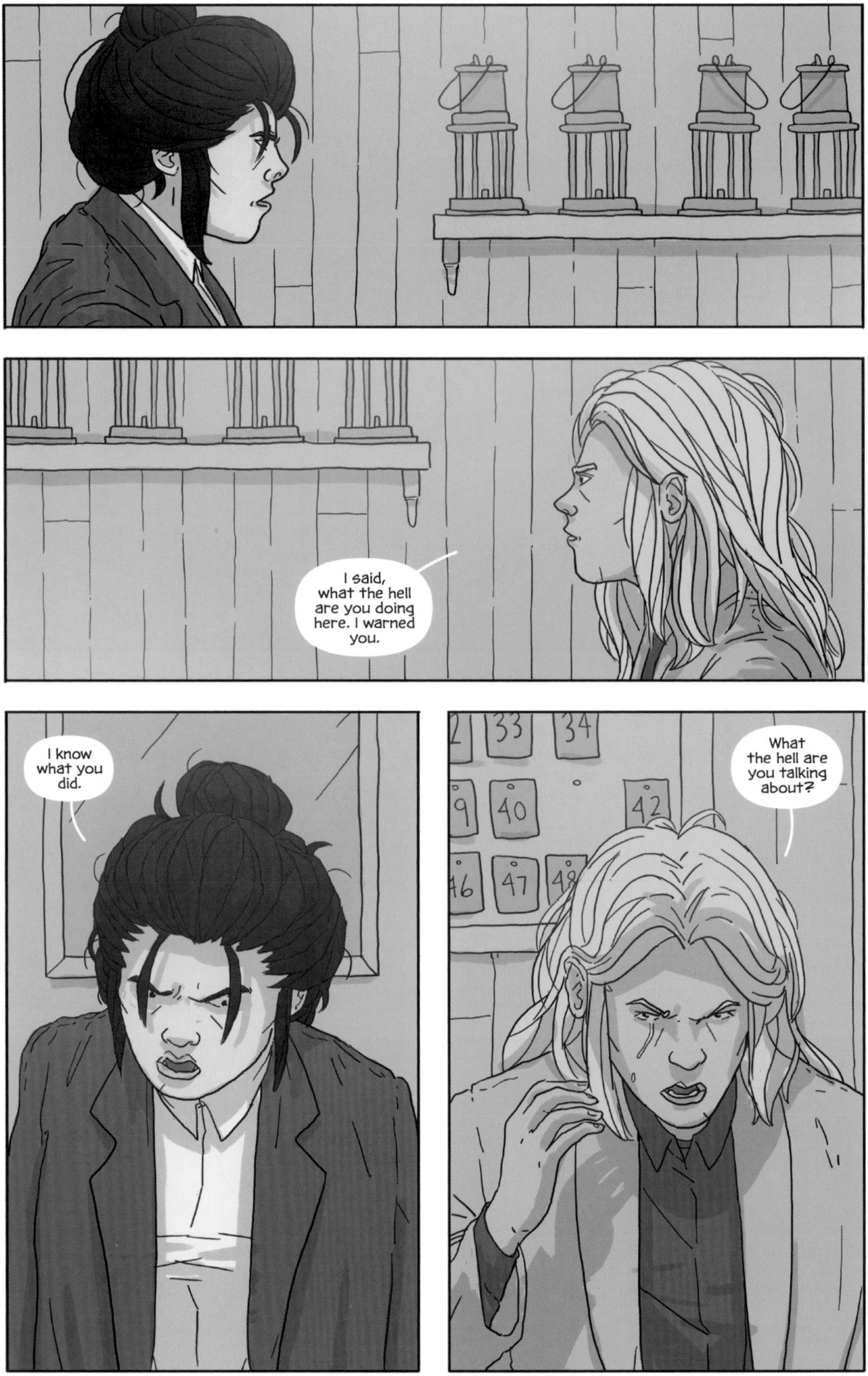
I said, what the hell are you doing here. I warned you.
I know what you did.
What the hell are you talking about?

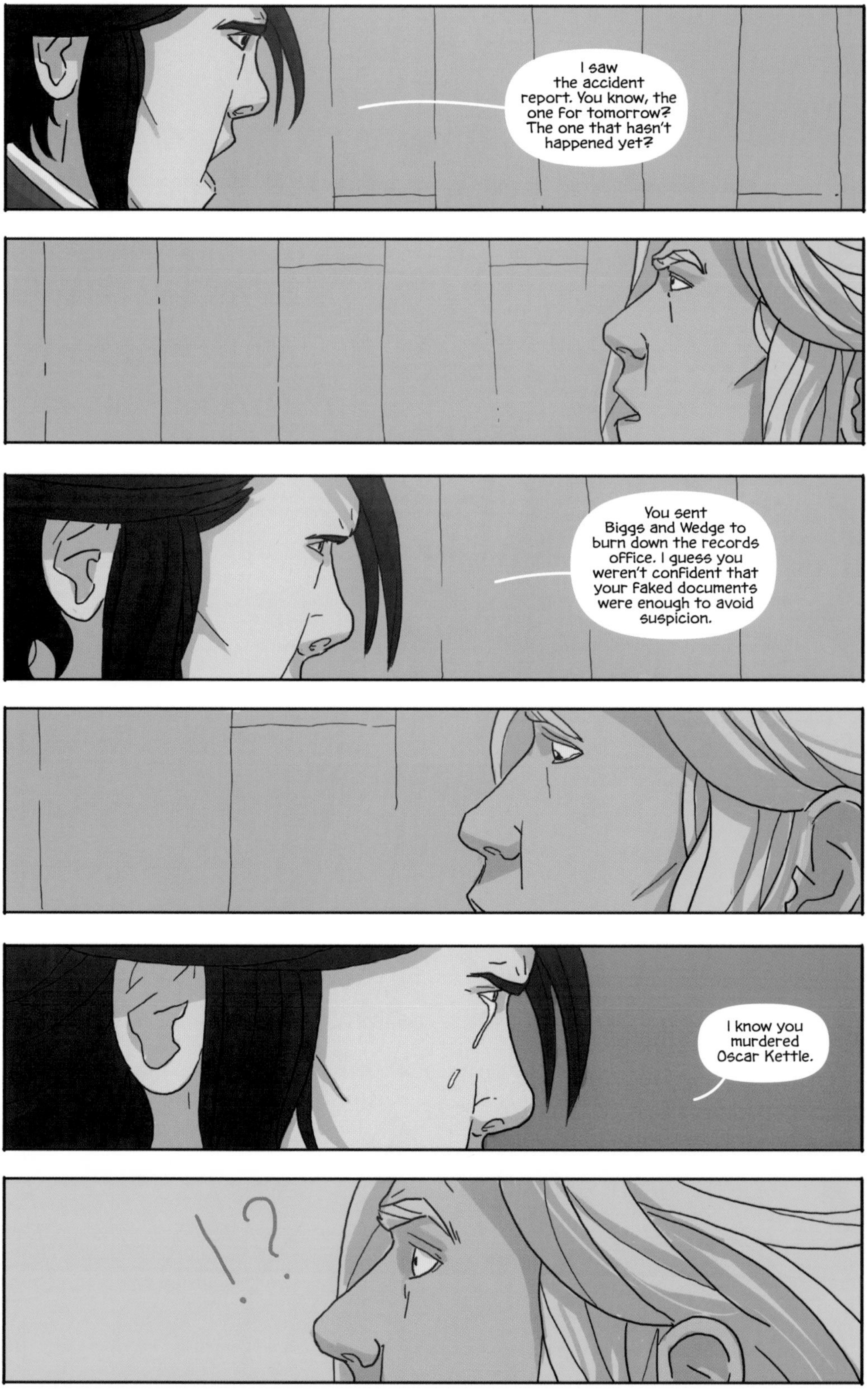
I saw the accident report. You know, the one for tomorrow? The one that hasn't happened yet?
You sent Biggs and Wedge to burn down the records office. I guess you weren't confident that your faked documents were enough to avoid suspicion.
I know you murdered Oscar Kettle.
!?

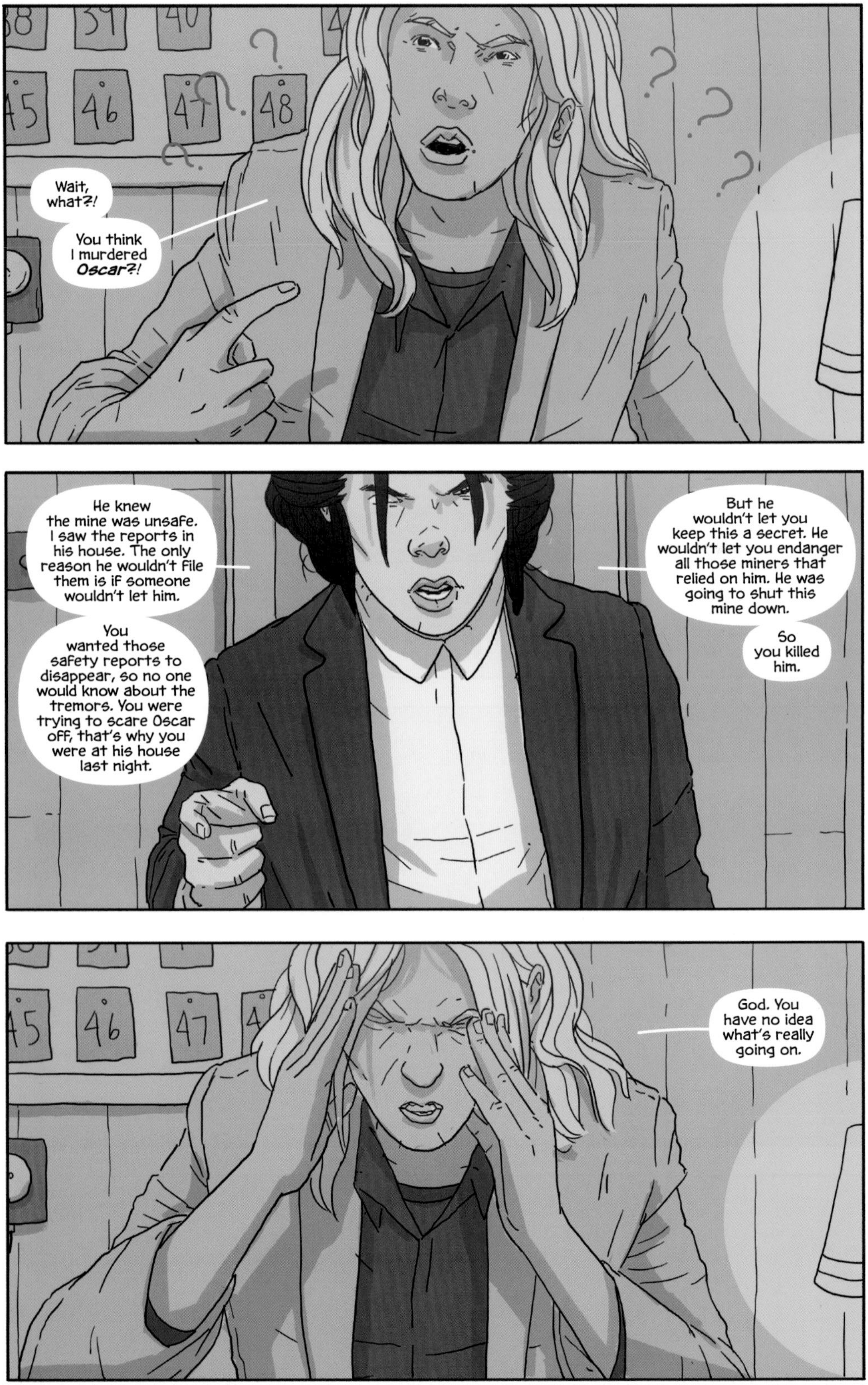

Wait, what?!
You think I murdered Oscar?!
He knew the mine was unsafe. I saw the reports in his house. The only reason he wouldn't file them is if someone wouldn't let him.
You wanted those safety reports to disappear, so no one would know about the tremors. You were trying to scare Oscar off, that's why you were at his house last night.
But he wouldn't let you keep this a secret. He wouldn't let you endanger all those miners that relied on him. He was going to shut this mine down.
So you killed him.
God. You have no idea what's really going on.

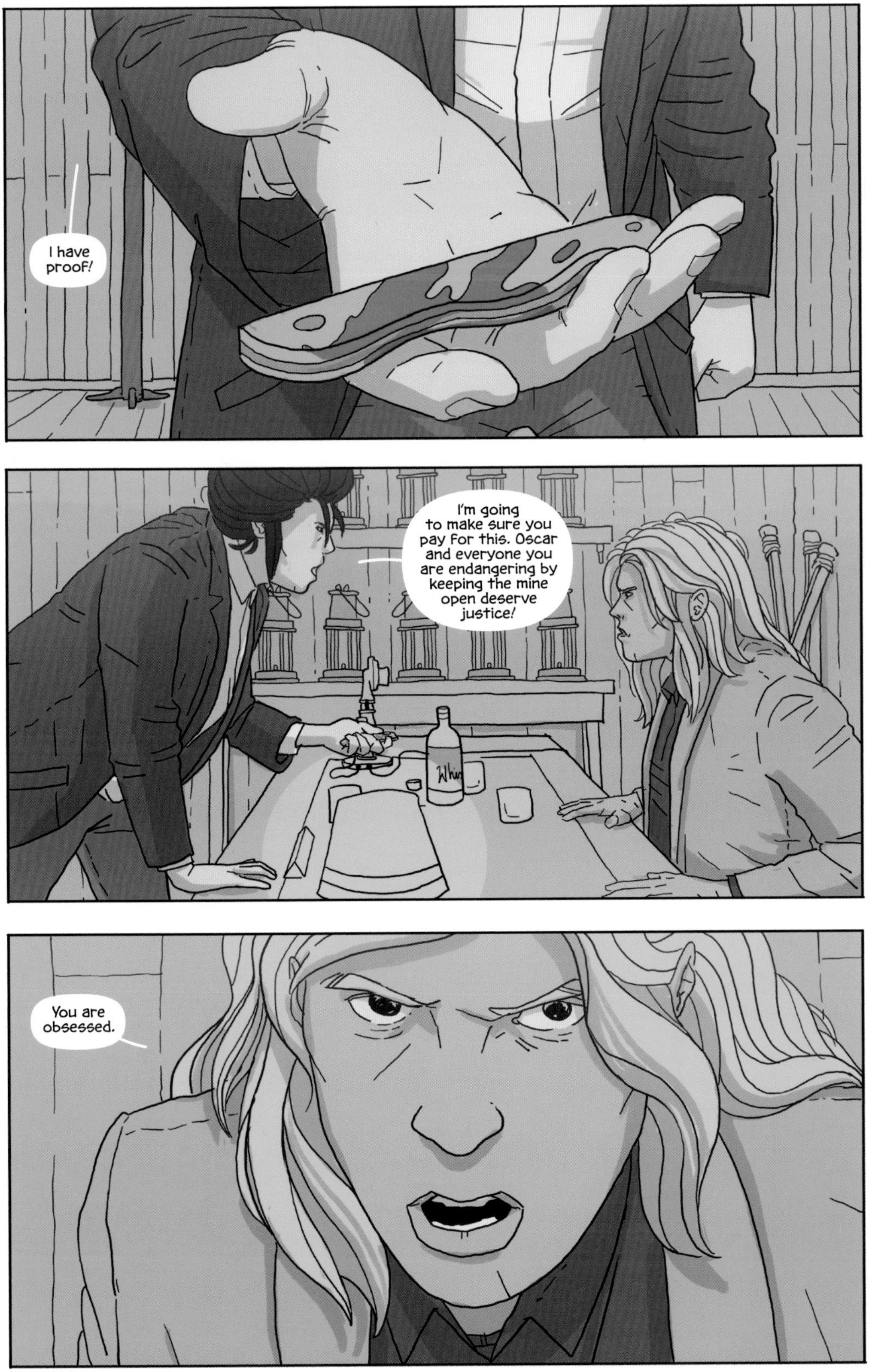
I have proof!
I'm going to make sure you pay for this. Oscar and everyone you are endangering by keeping the mine open deserve justice!
Whis
You are obsessed.

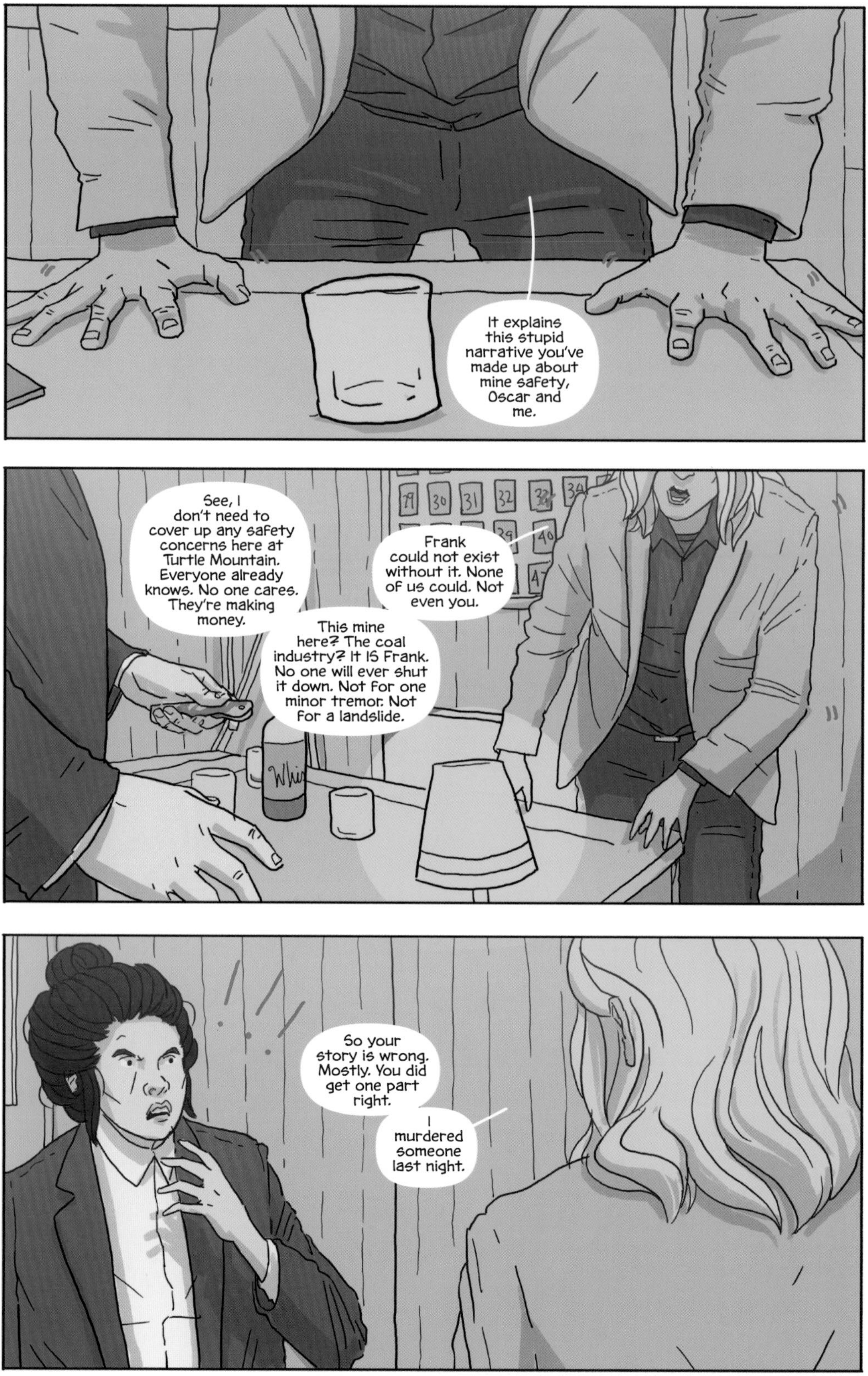
It explains this stupid narrative you've made up about mine safety, Oscar and me.
See, I don't need to cover up any safety concerns here at Turtle Mountain. Everyone already knows. No one cares. They're making money.
Frank could not exist without it. None of us could. Not even you.
This mine here? The coal industry? It IS Frank. No one will ever shut it down. Not for one minor tremor. Not for a landslide.
So your story is wrong. Mostly. You did get one part right.
I murdered someone last night.

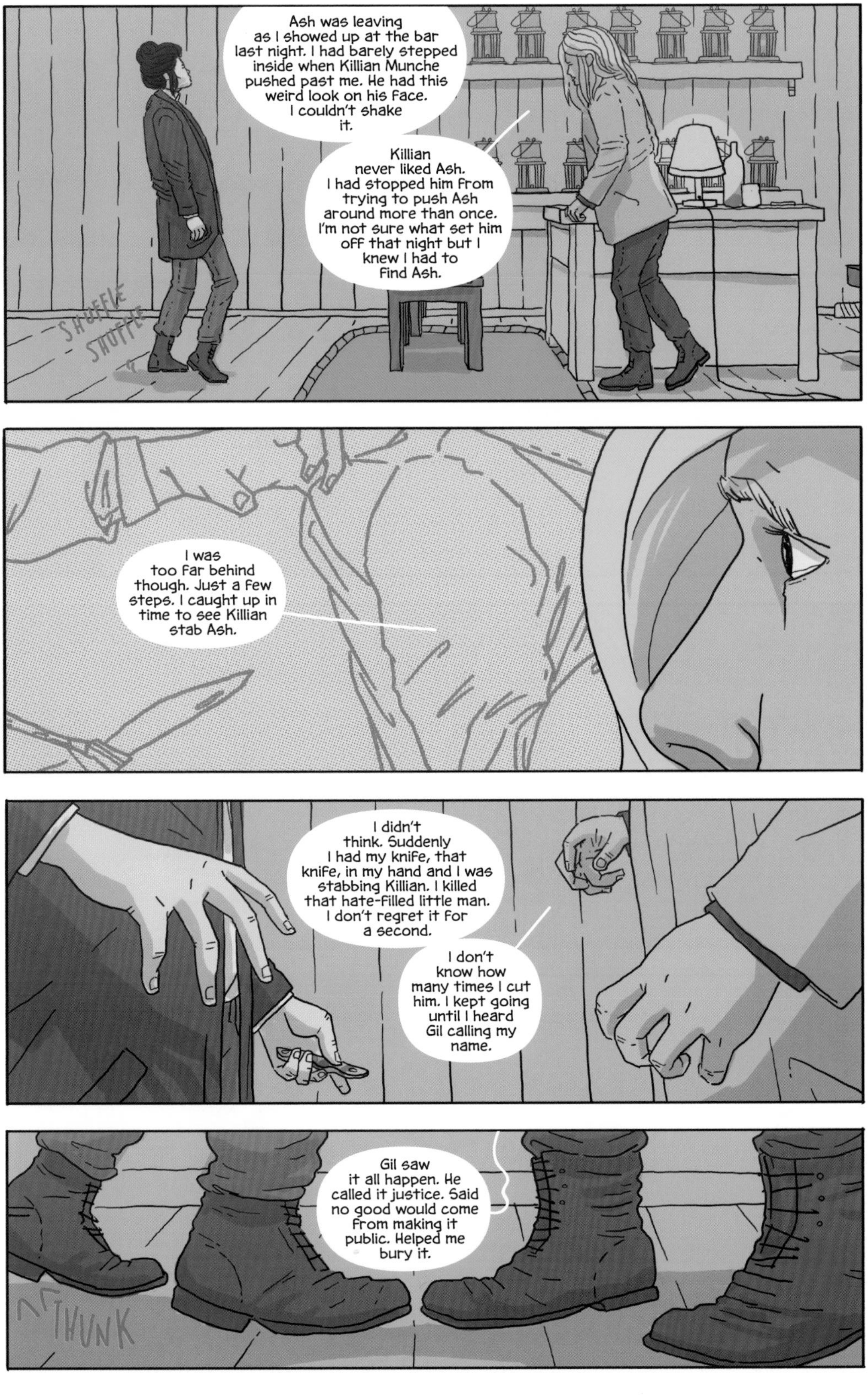
Ash was leaving as I showed up at the bar last night. I had barely stepped inside when Killian Munche pushed past me. He had this weird look on his face. I couldn't shake it.
Killian never liked Ash. I had stopped him from trying to push Ash around more than once. I'm not sure what set him off that night but I knew I had to find Ash.
SHUFFLE SHUFFLE
I was too far behind though. Just a few steps. I caught up in time to see Killian stab Ash.
I didn't think. Suddenly I had my knife, that knife, in my hand and I was stabbing Killian. I killed that hate-filled little man. I don't regret it for a second.
I don't know how many times I cut him. I kept going until I heard Gil calling my name.
Gil saw it all happen. He called it justice. Said no good would come from making it public. Helped me bury it.
THUNK

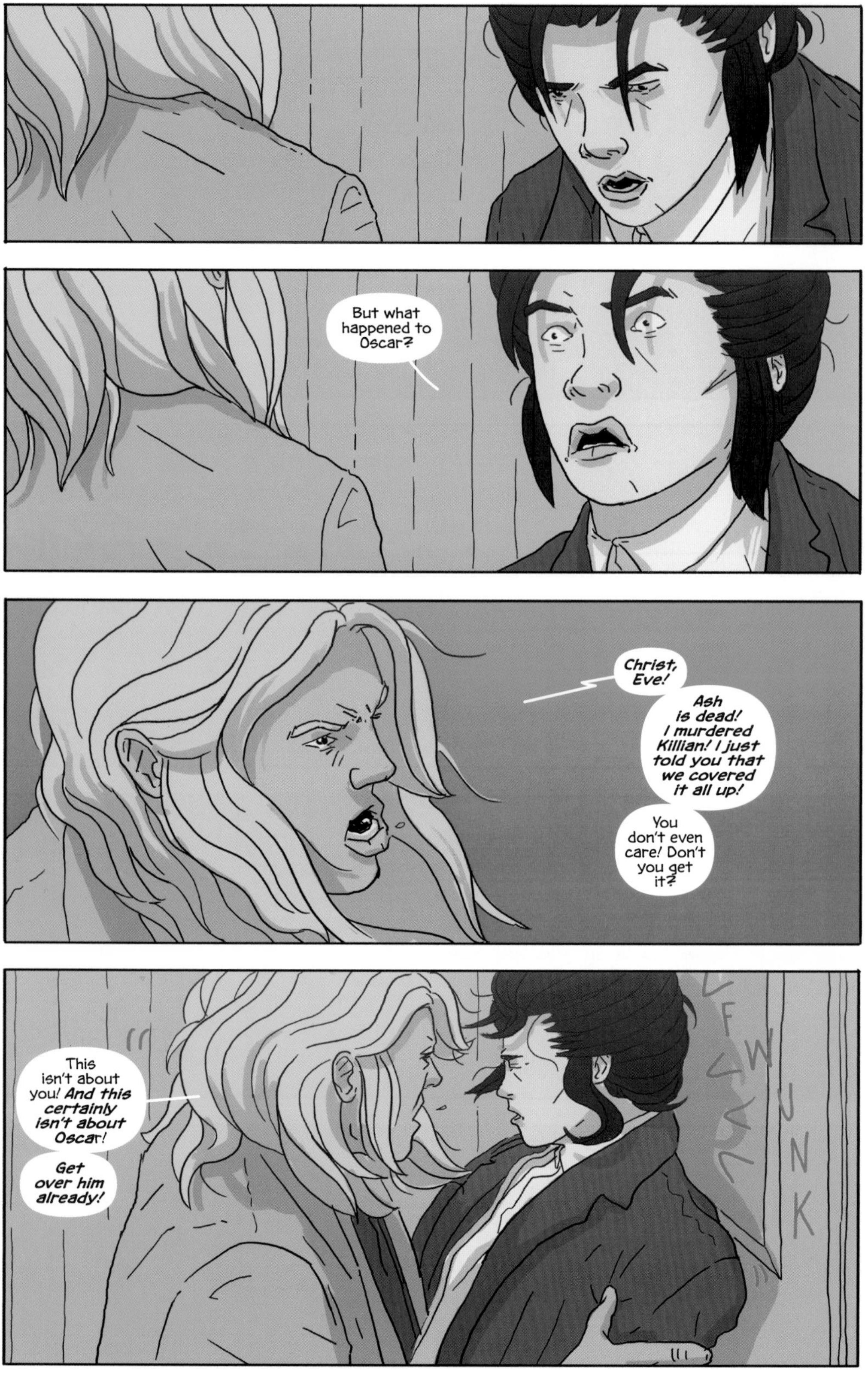

But what happened to Oscar?
Christ, Eve!
Ash is dead! I murdered Killian! I just told you that we covered it all up!
You don't even care! Don't you get it?
FWUNK
This isn't about you! And this certainly isn't about Oscar!
Get over him already!

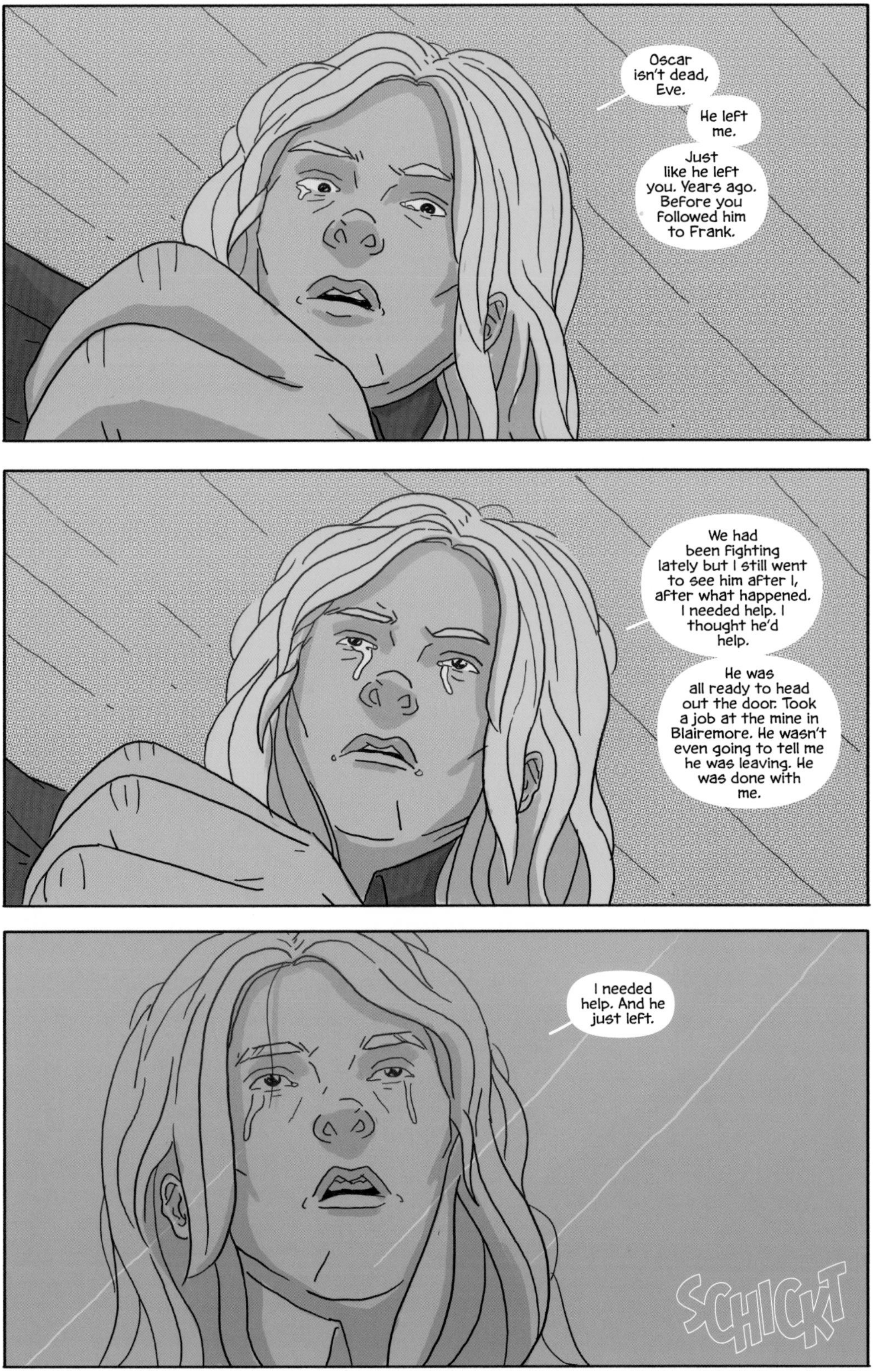
Oscar isn't dead, Eve.
He left me.
Just like he left you. Years ago. Before you followed him to Frank.
We had been fighting lately but I still went to see him after I, after what happened. I needed help. I thought he'd help.
He was all ready to head out the door. Took a job at the mine in Blairemore. He wasn't even going to tell me he was leaving. He was done with me.
I needed help. And he just left.
SCHICKT

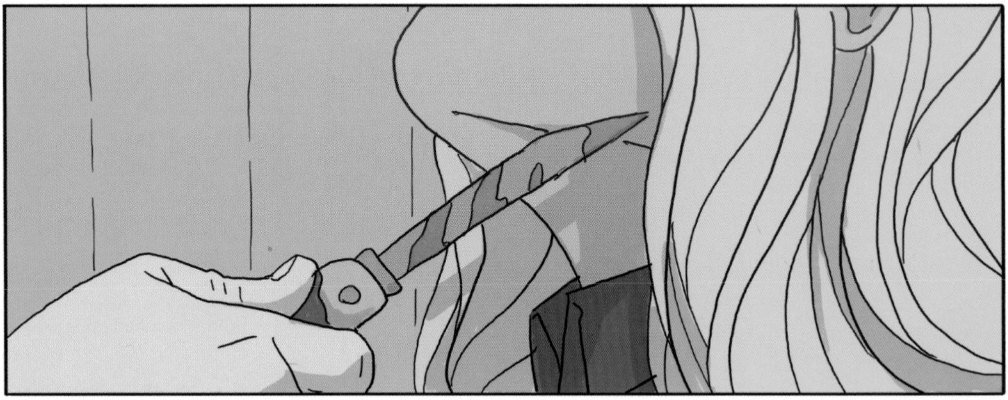

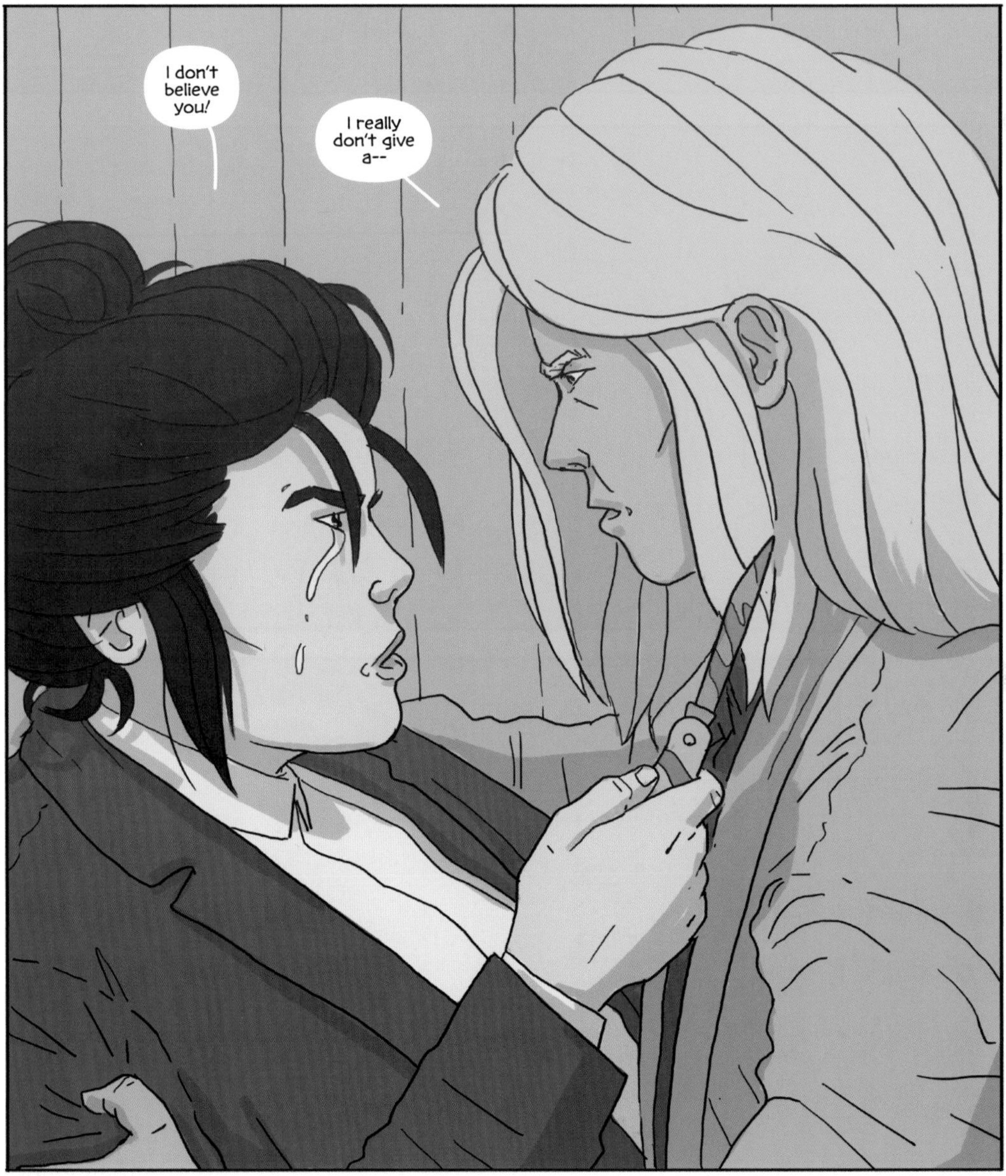
I don't believe you!
I really don't give a--

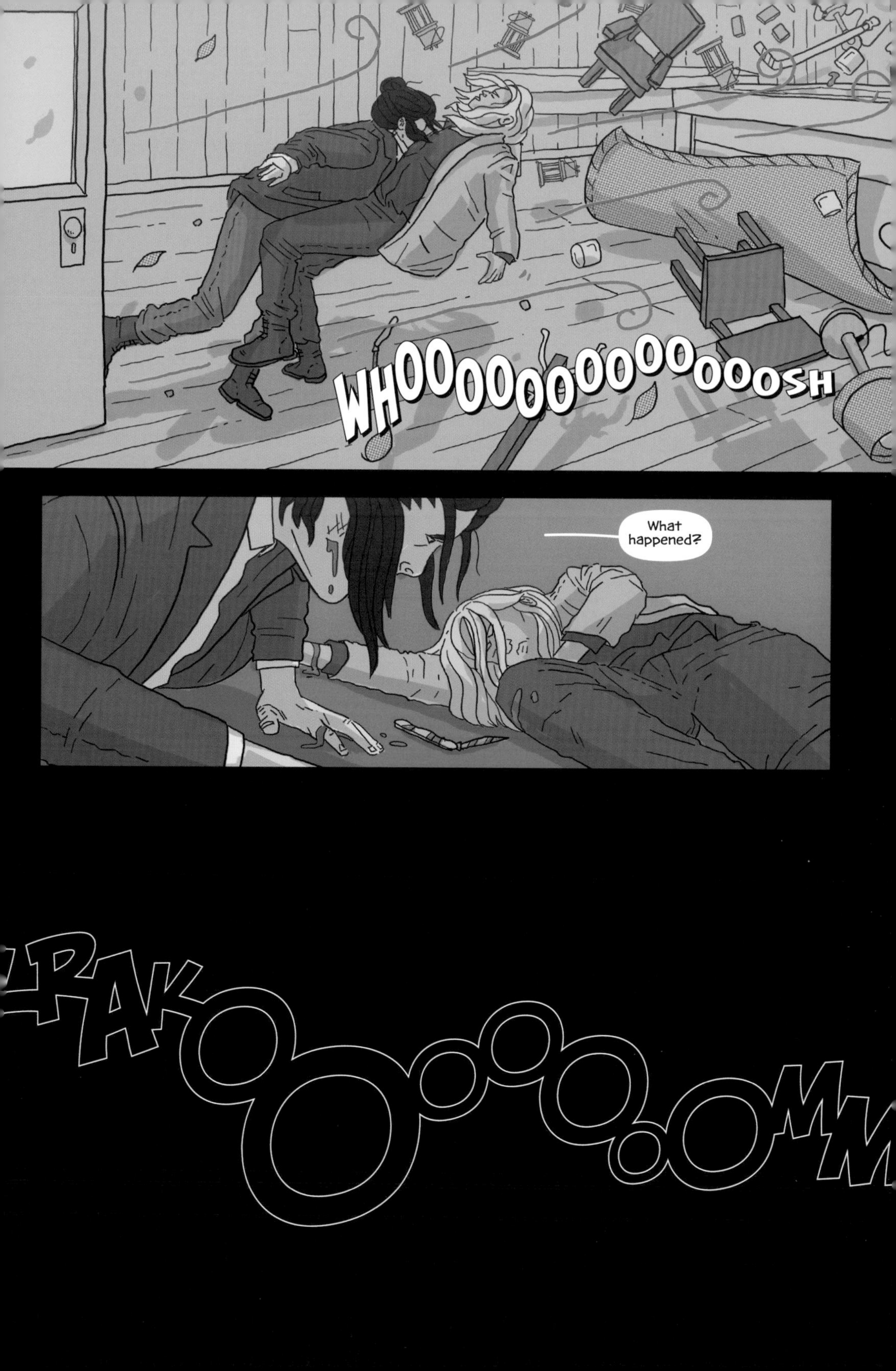
WHOOOOOOOOOOOOOSH
What happened?
RAKOOOOOOMM

Eve?!

Eve, can
you hear
me?!

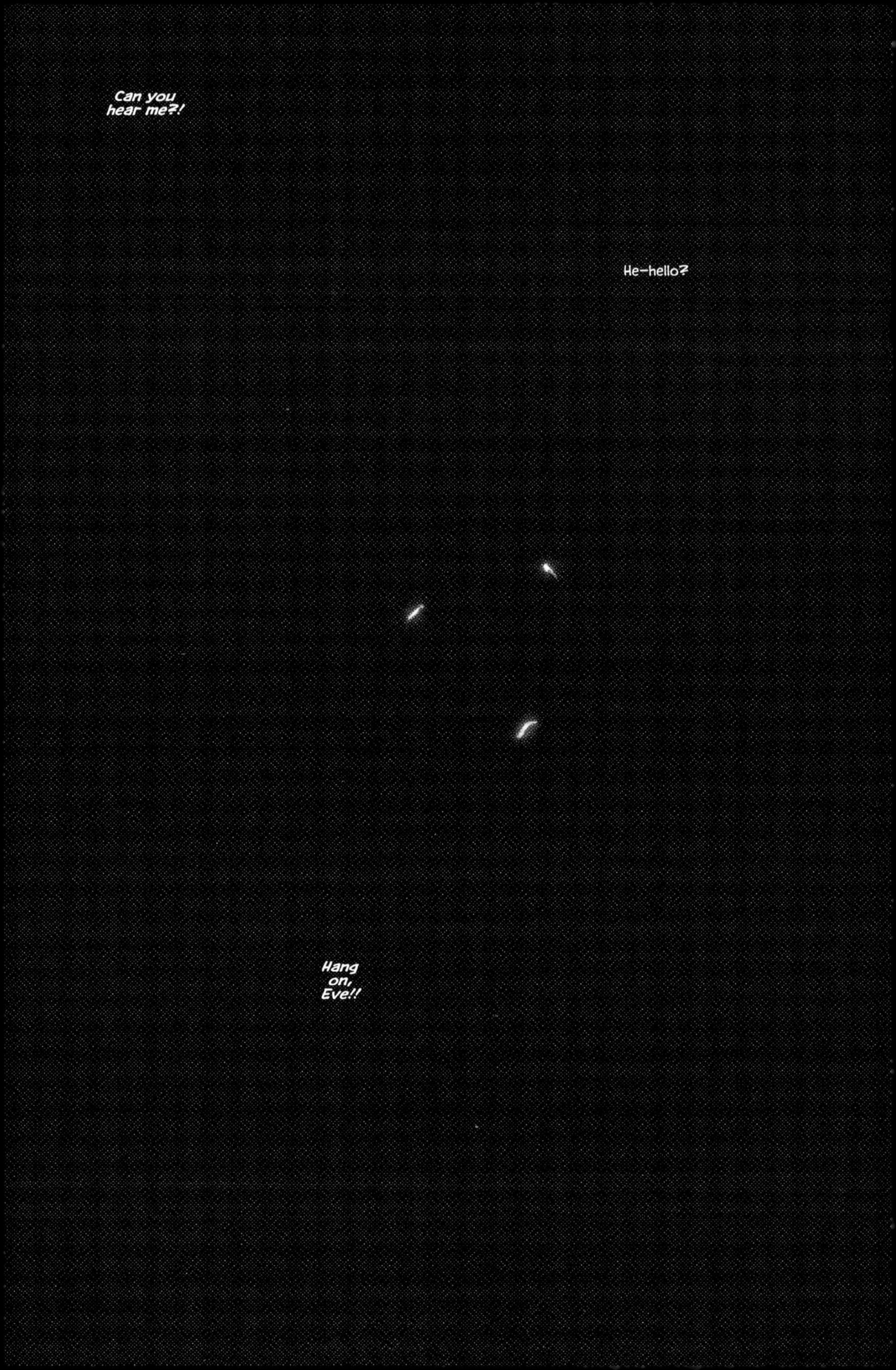
Can you hear me?!
He-hello?
Hang on, Eve!!

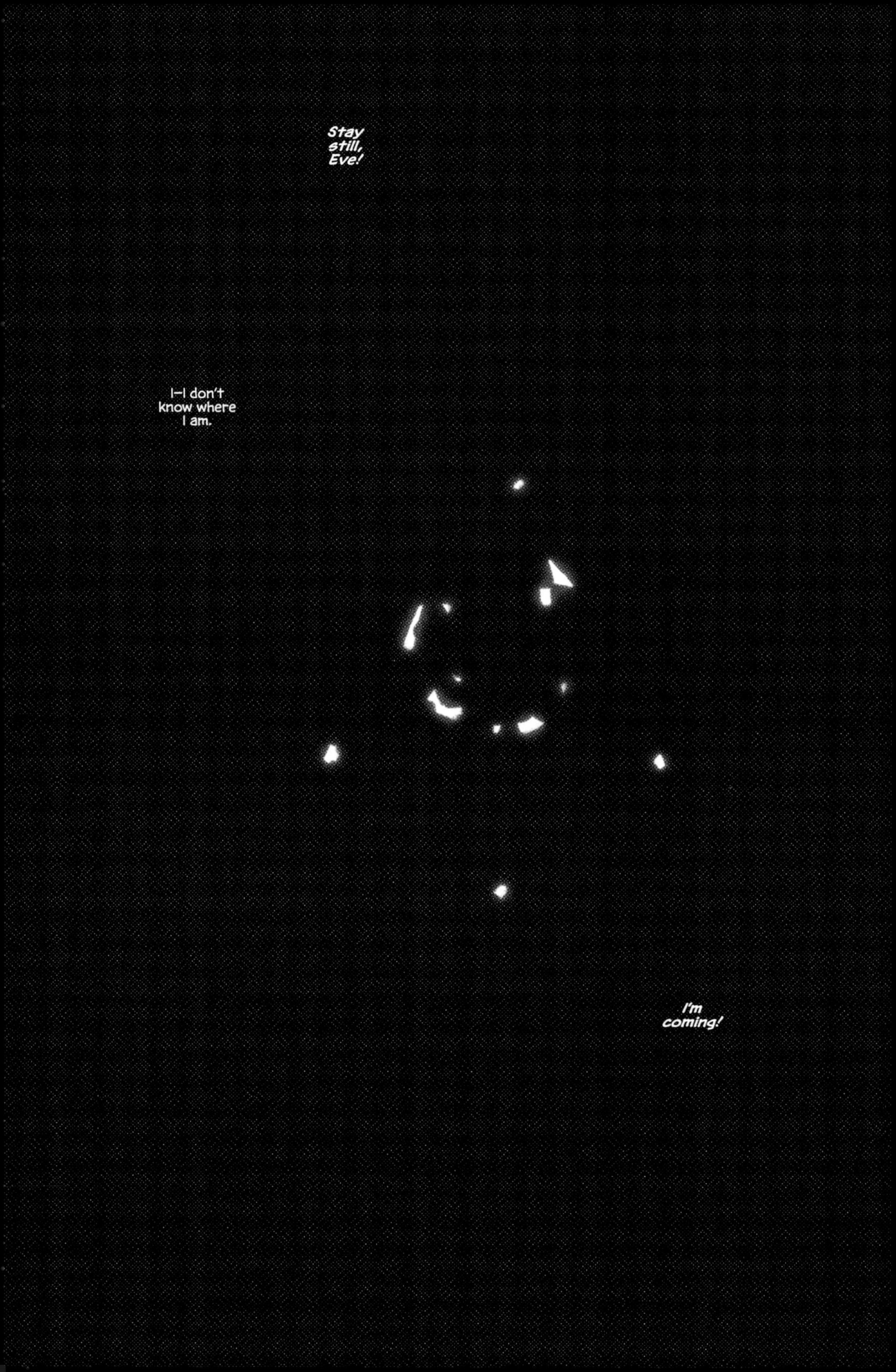
Stay still, Eve!
I–I don't know where I am.
I'm coming!

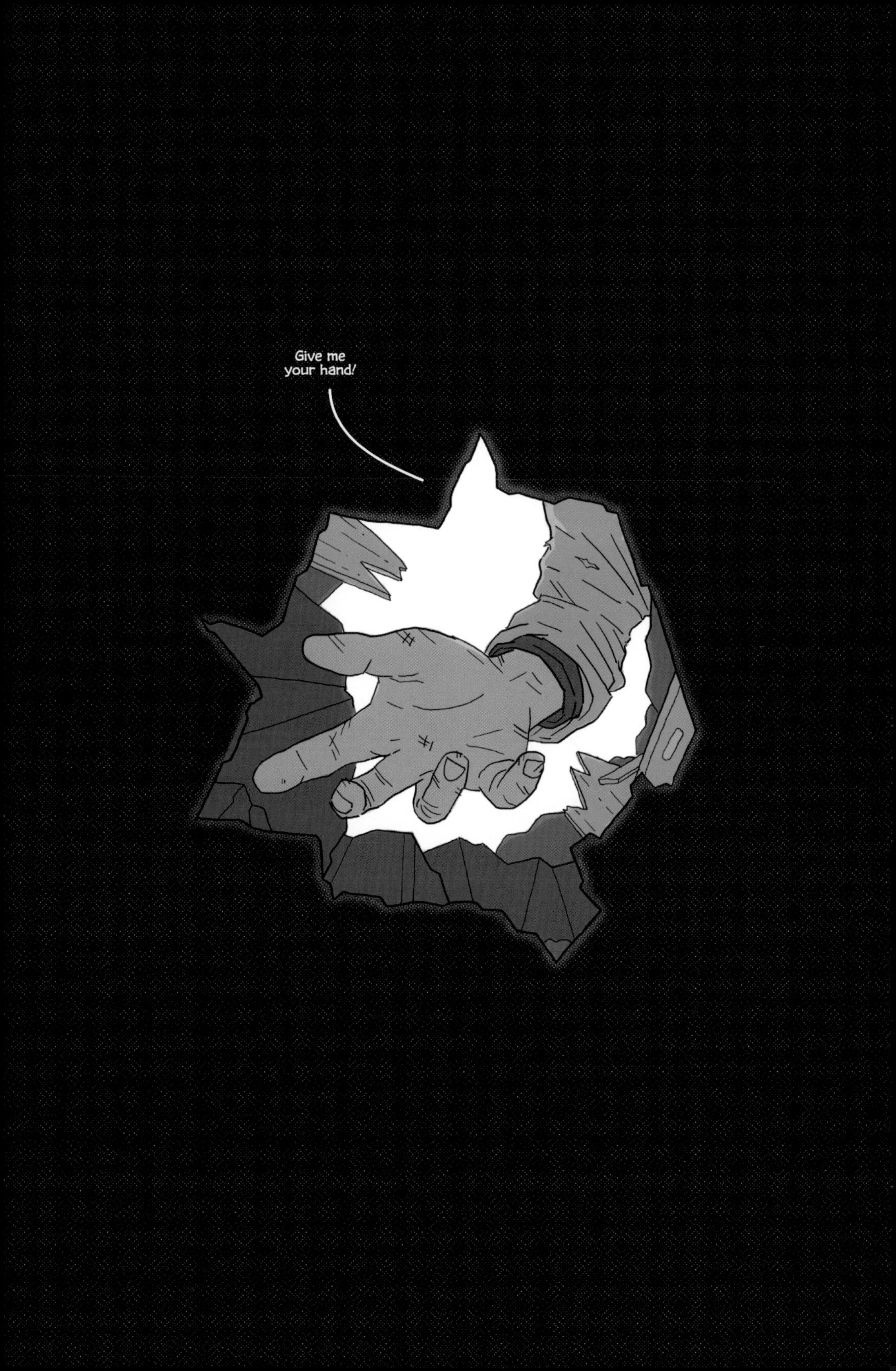
Give me
your hand!

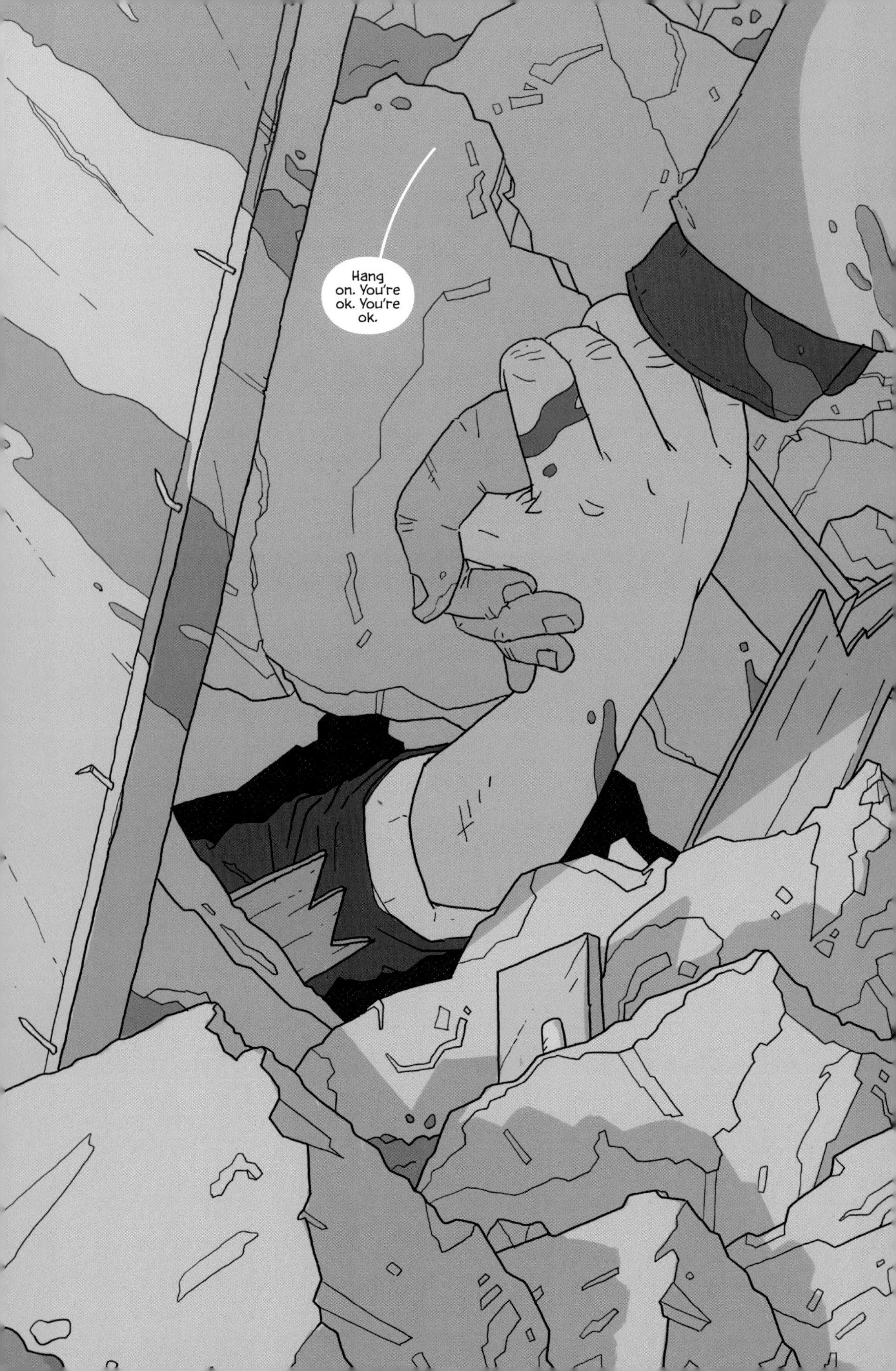
Hang on. You're ok. You're ok.

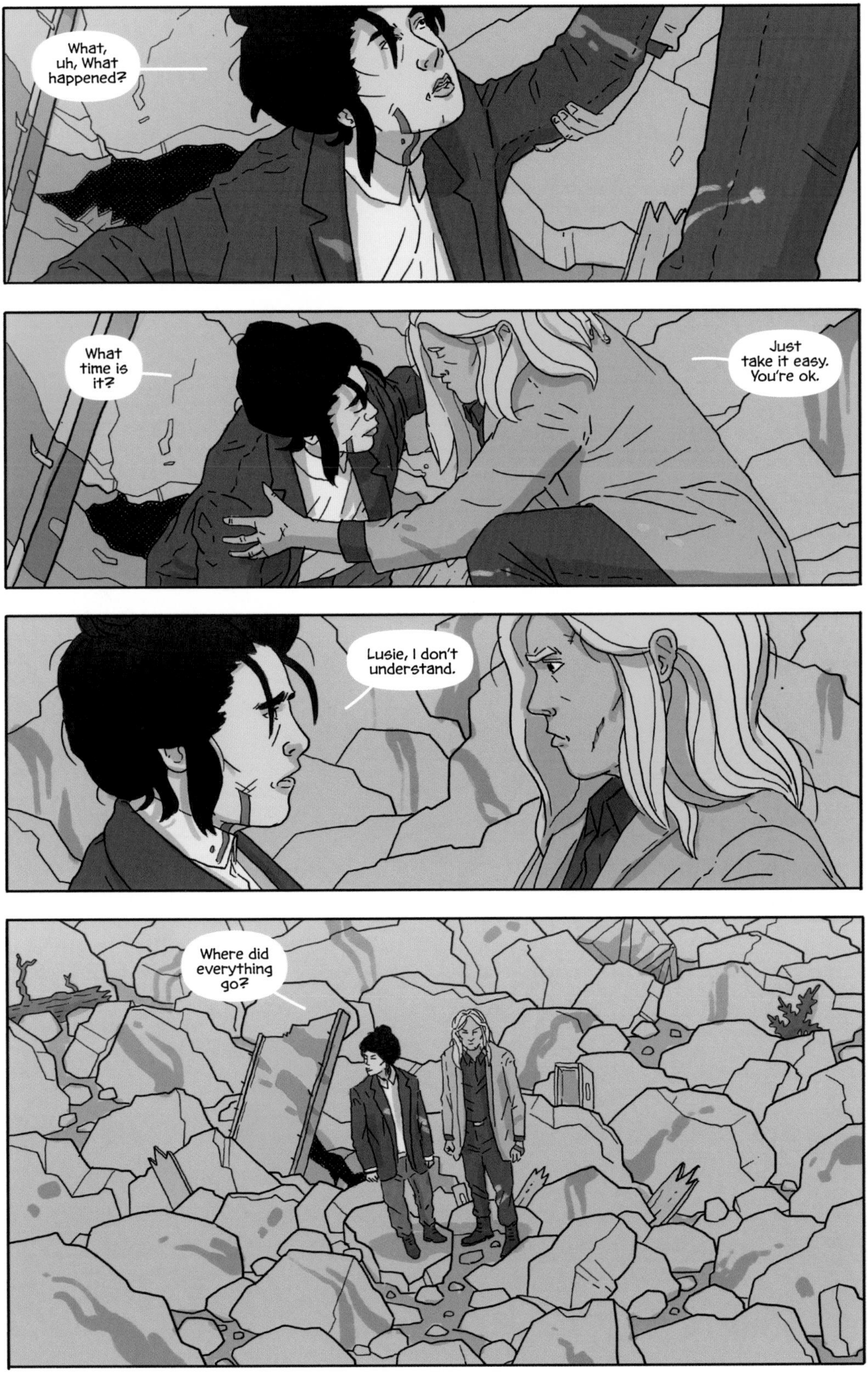
What, uh, What happened?
What time is it?
Just take it easy. You're ok.
Lusie, I don't understand.
Where did everything go?

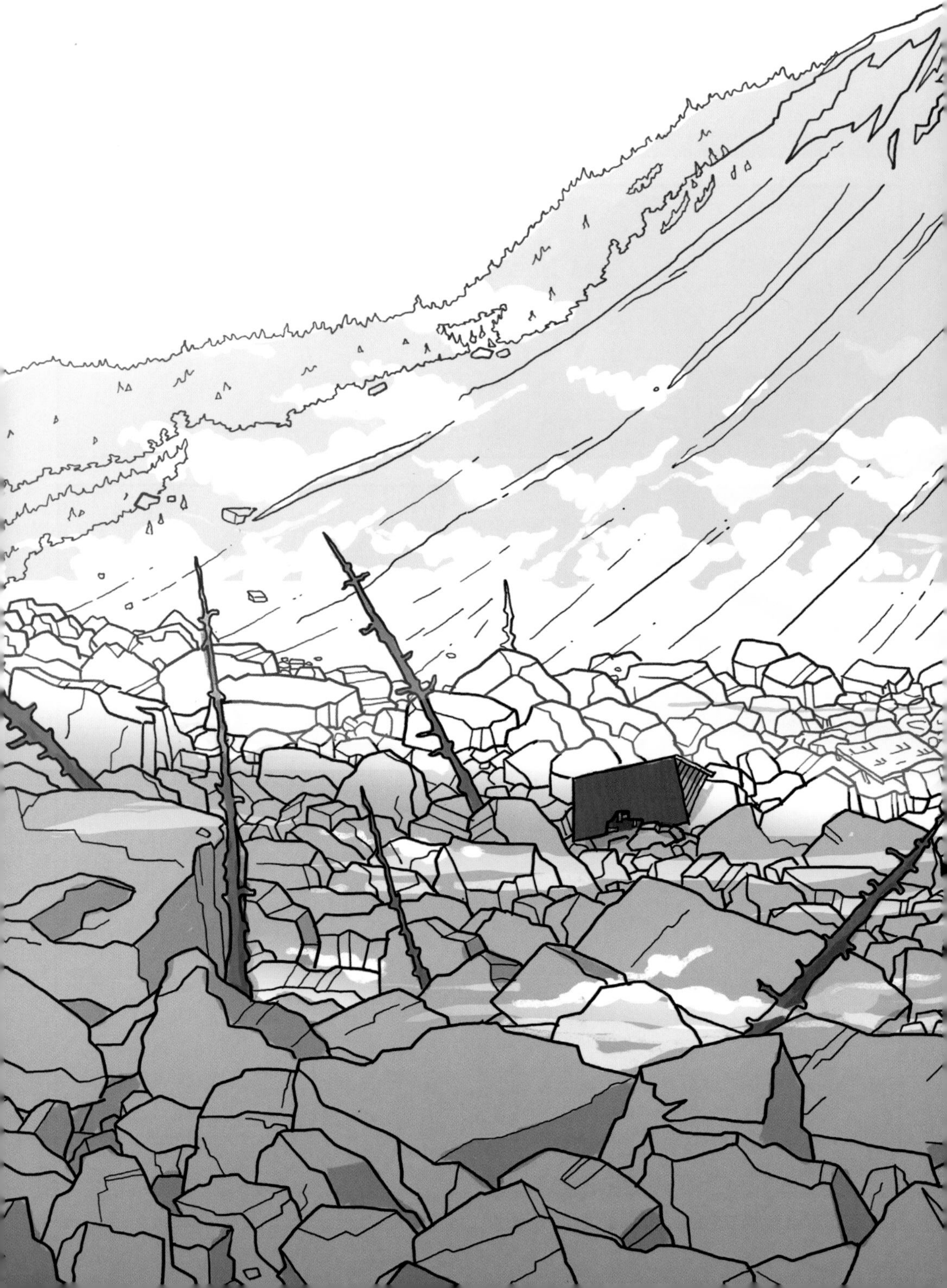

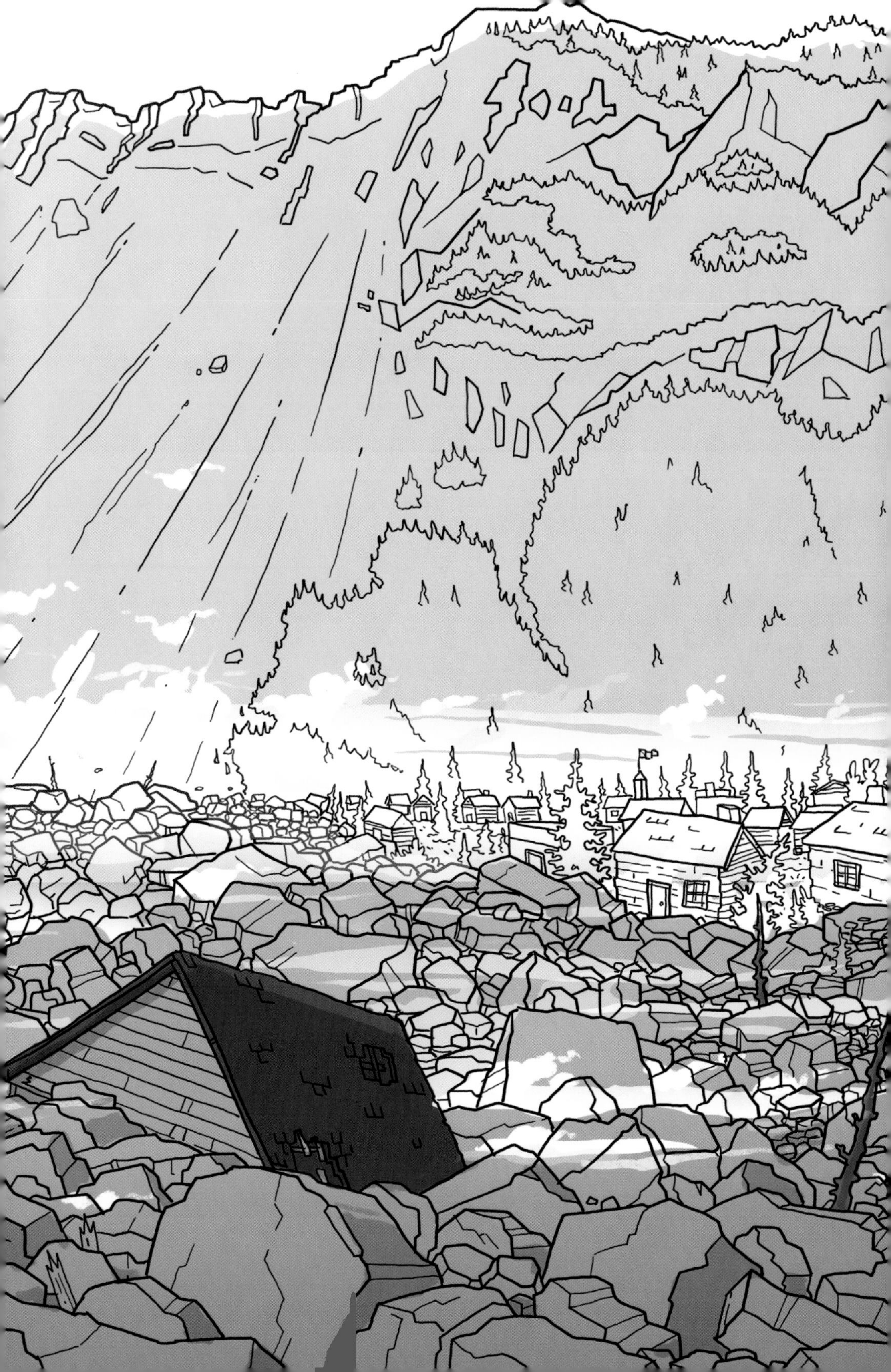

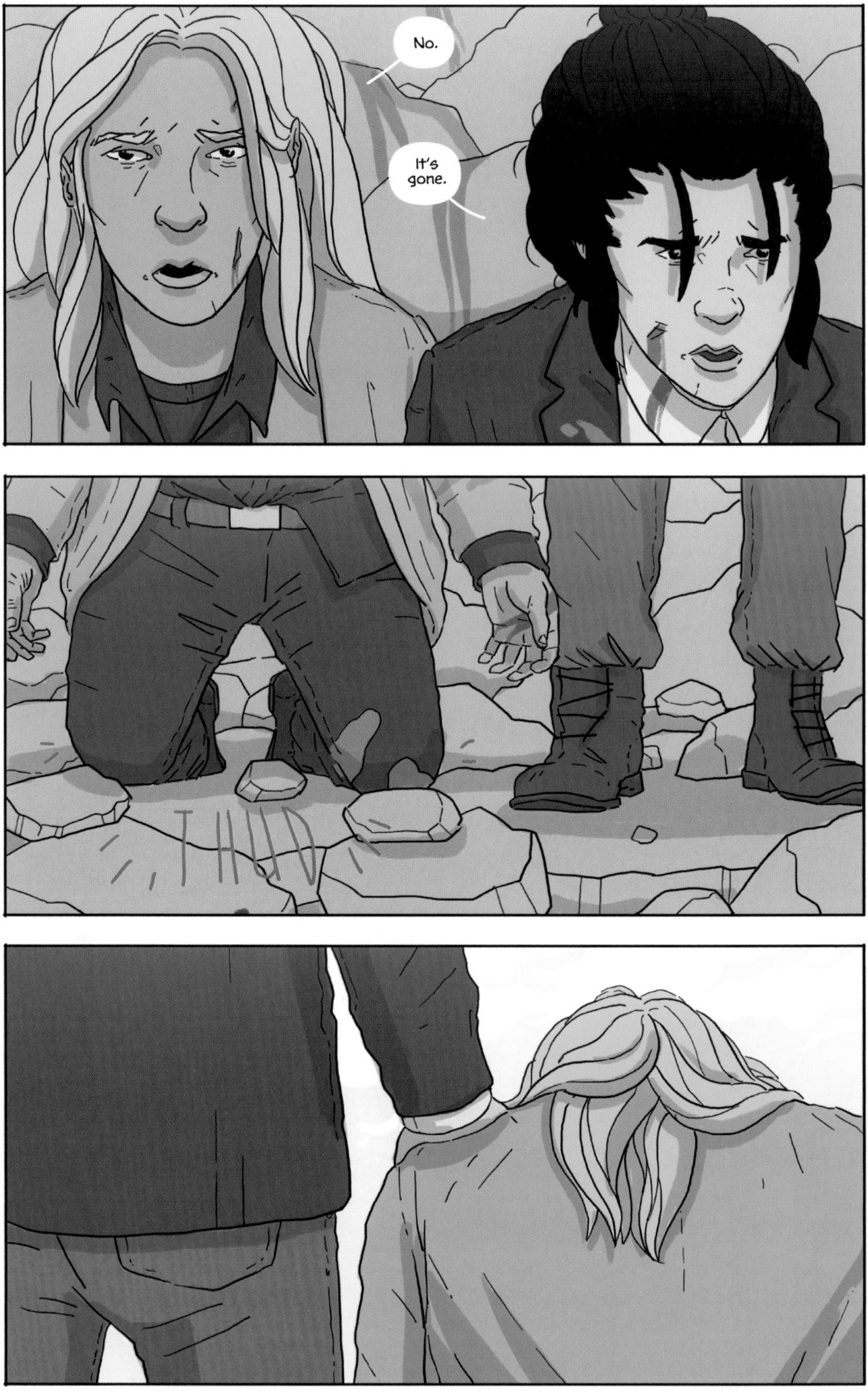
No.
It's gone.
THUD

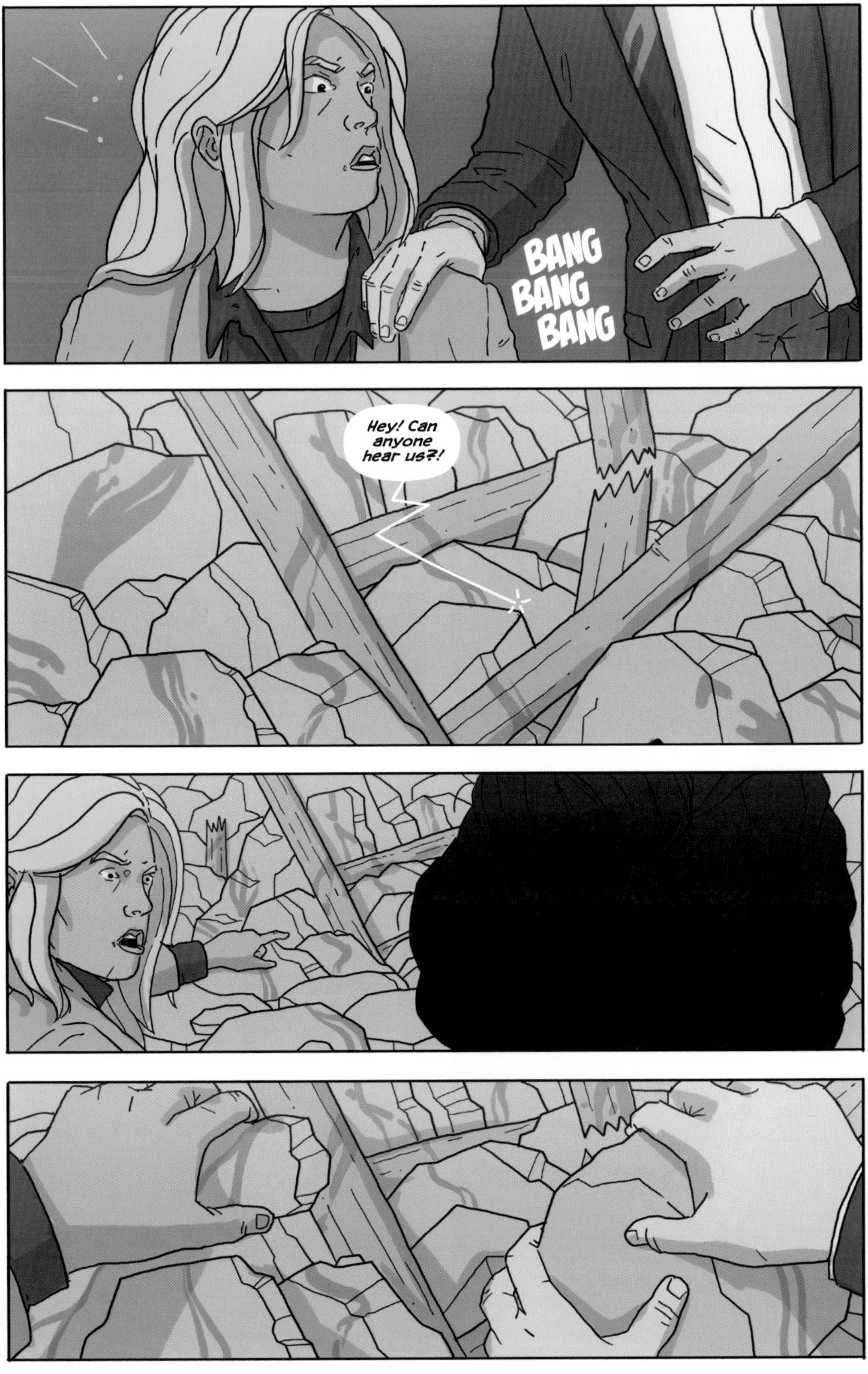
BANG
BANG
BANG
Hey! Can anyone hear us?!

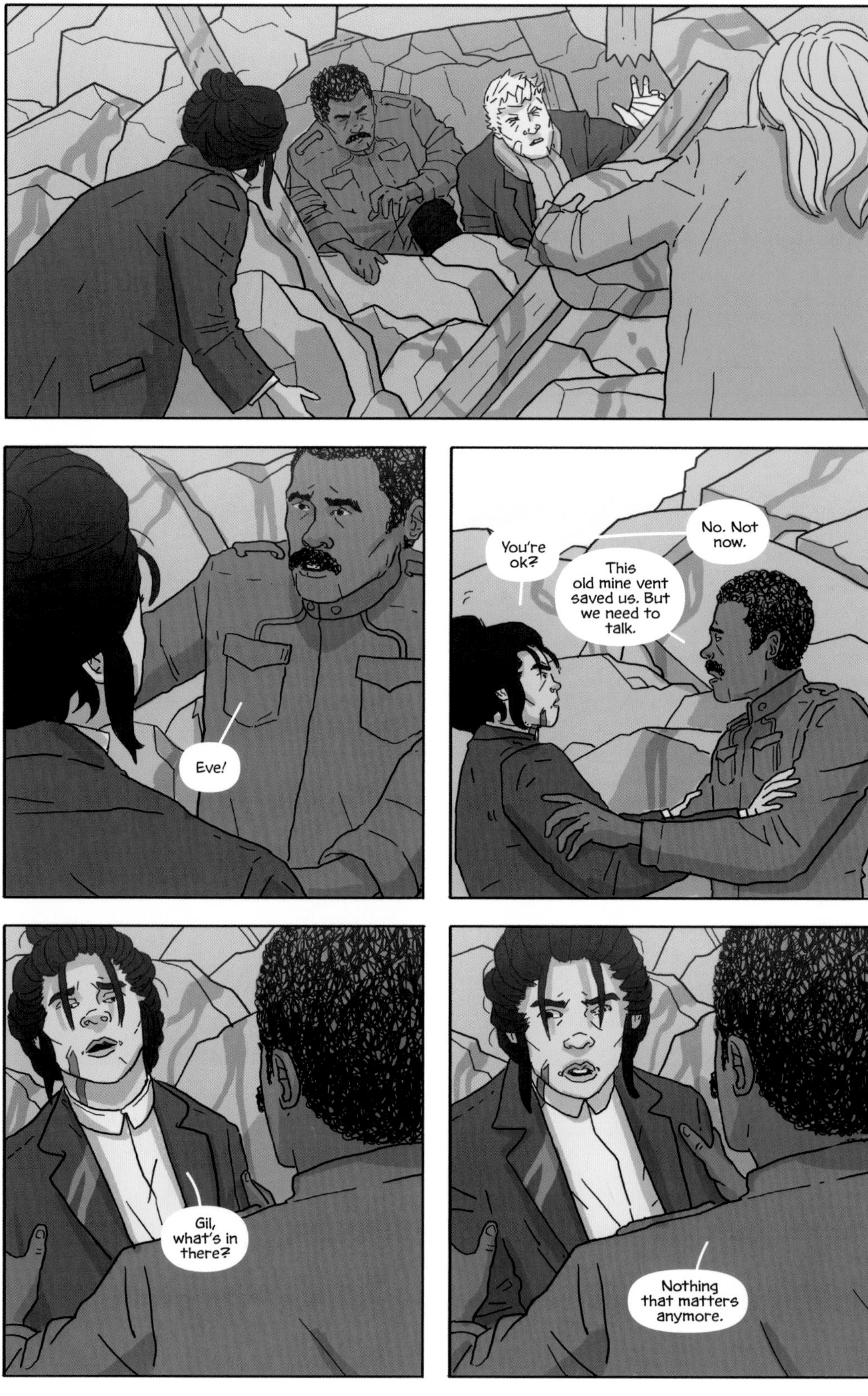
Eve!
You're ok?
No. Not now.
This old mine vent saved us. But we need to talk.
Gil, what's in there?
Nothing that matters anymore.

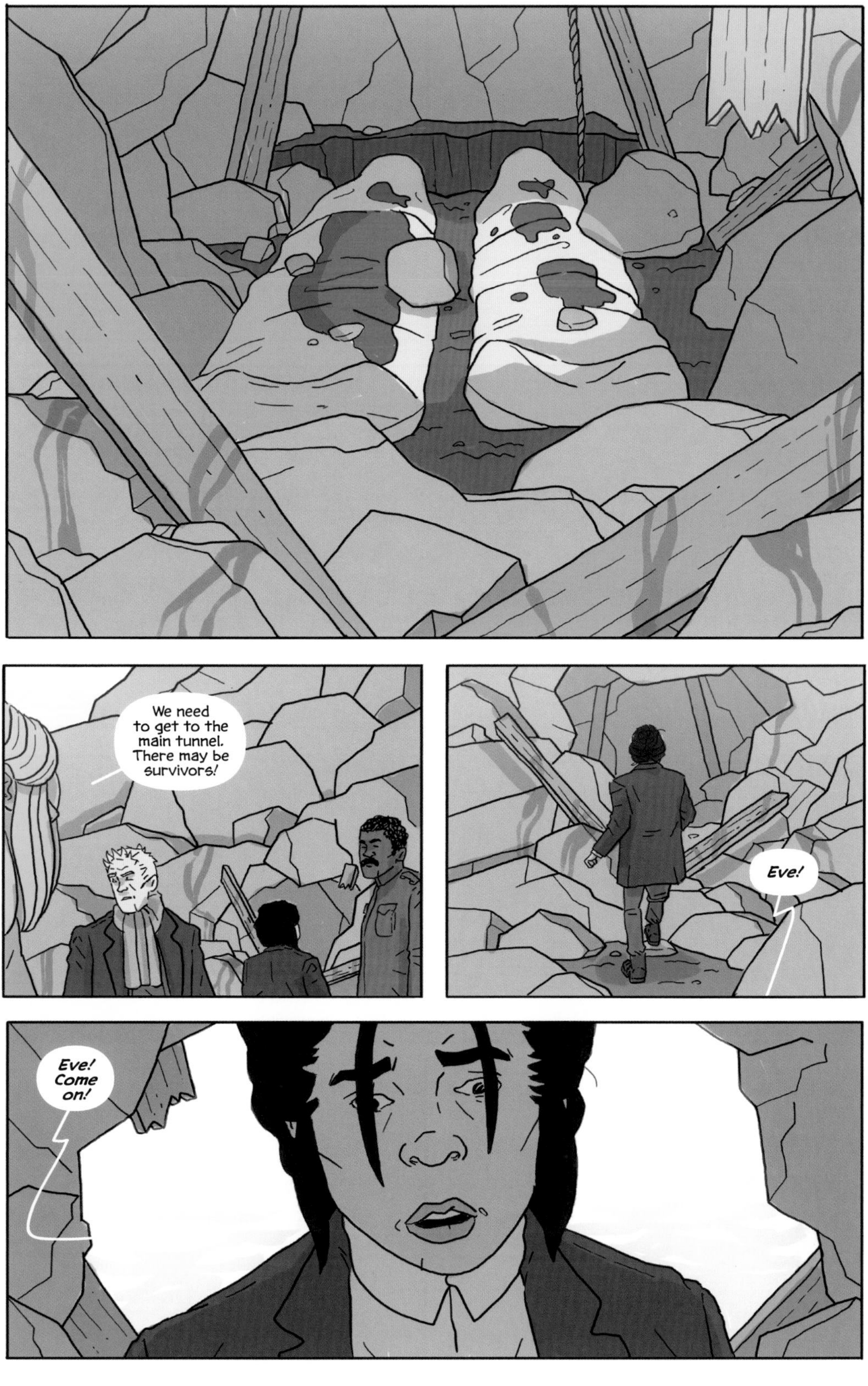
We need to get to the main tunnel. There may be survivors!
Eve!
Eve! Come on!

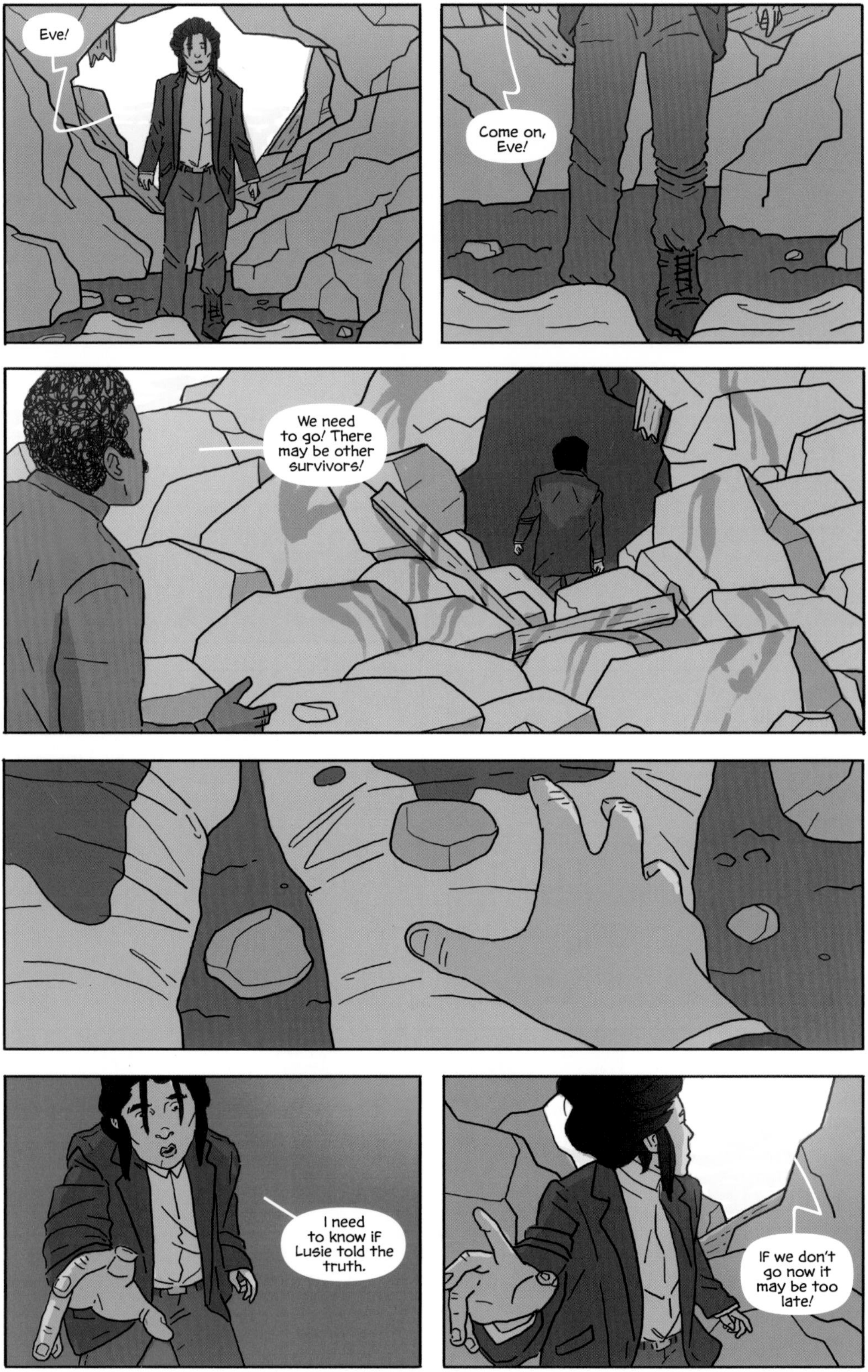
Eve!
Come on, Eve!
We need to go! There may be other survivors!
I need to know if Lusie told the truth.
If we don't go now it may be too late!

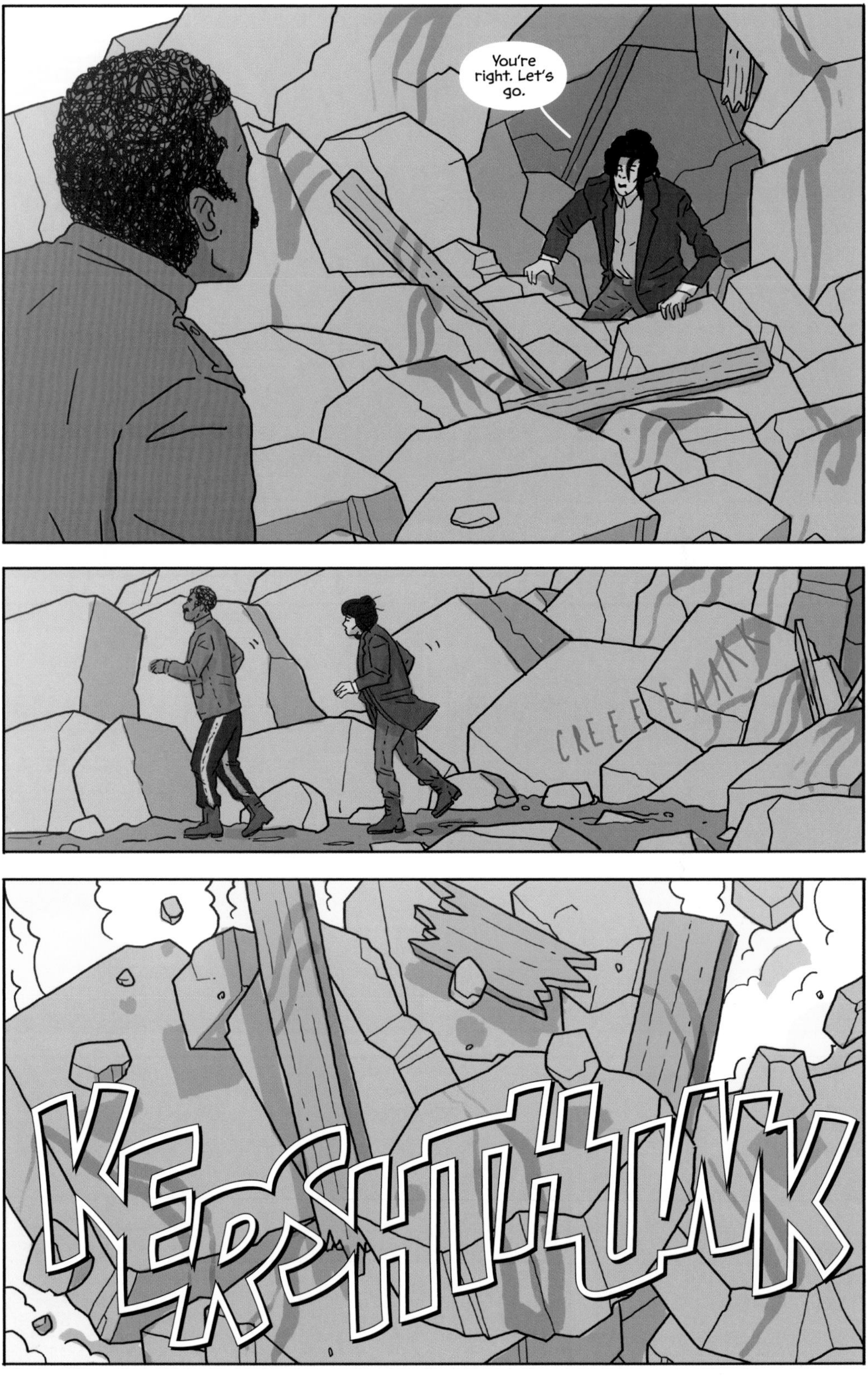
You're right. Let's go.
CREEEEAAKK
KERSHTHUNK

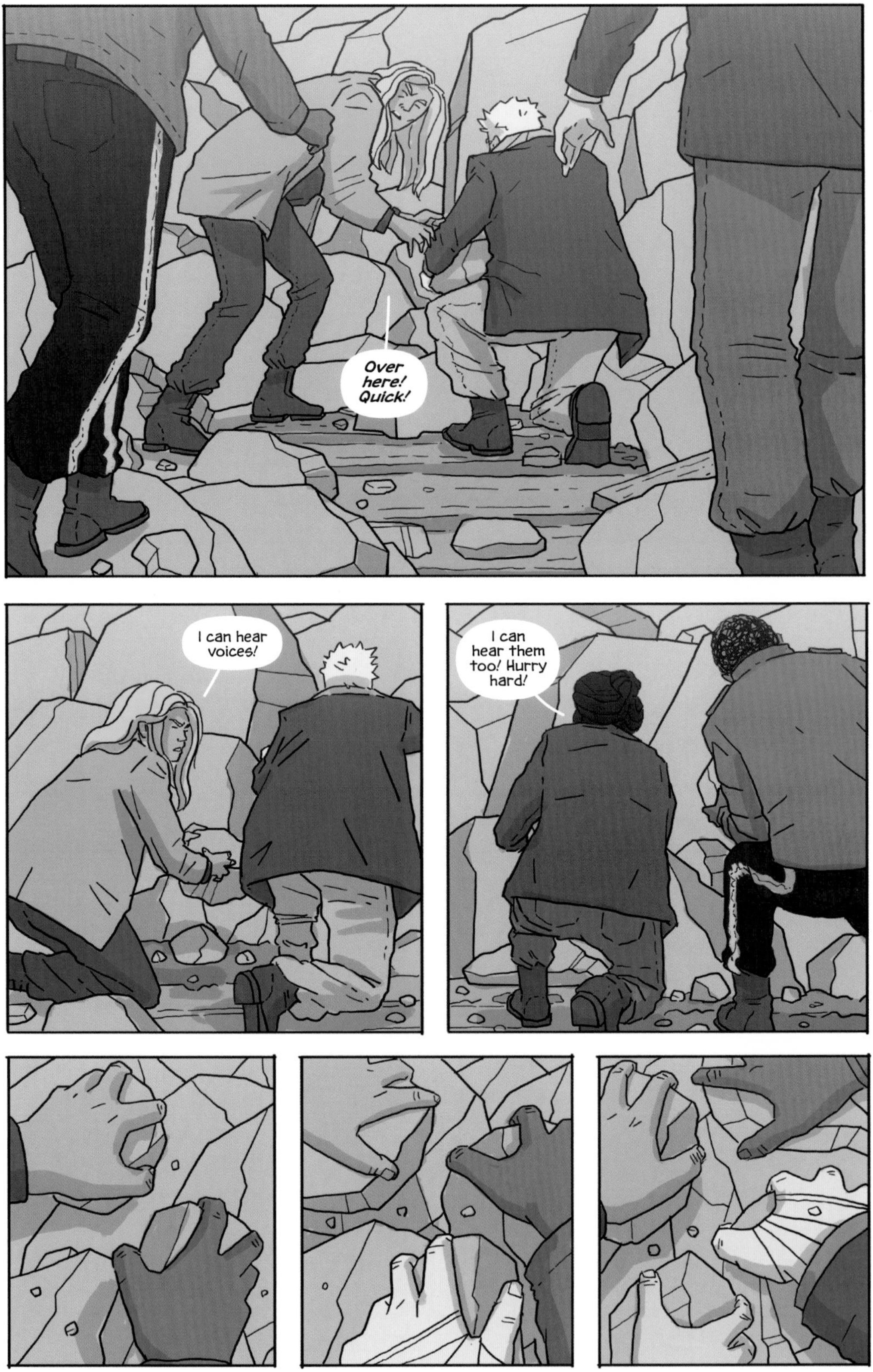
Over here! Quick!
I can hear voices!
I can hear them too! Hurry hard!

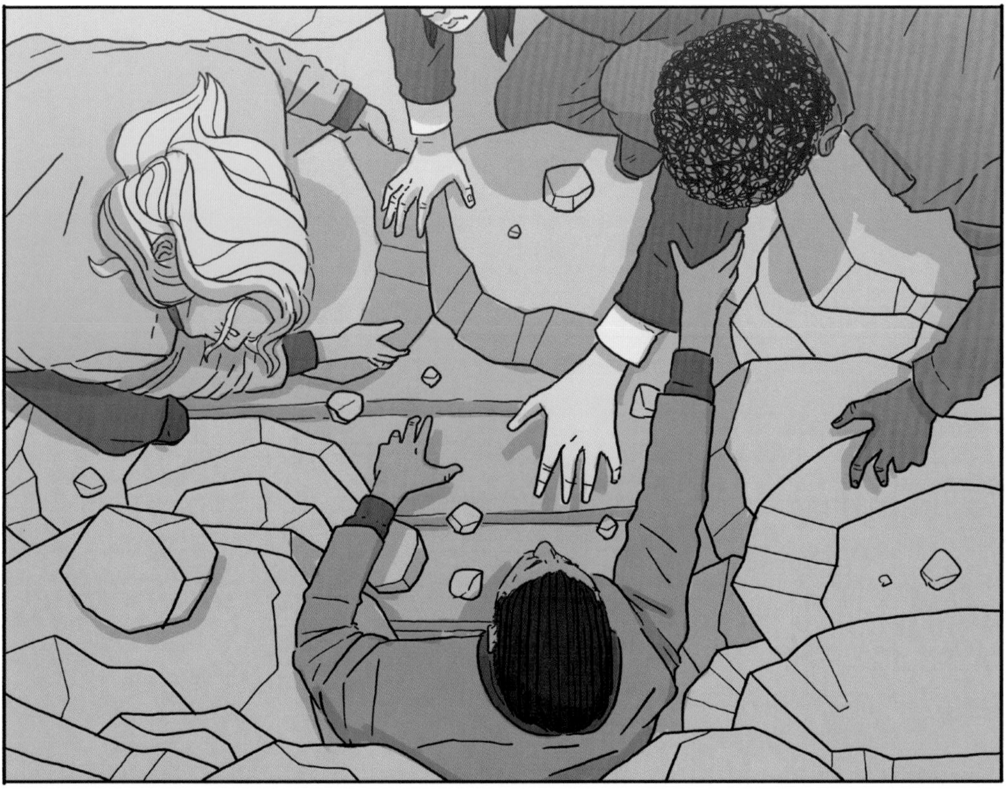
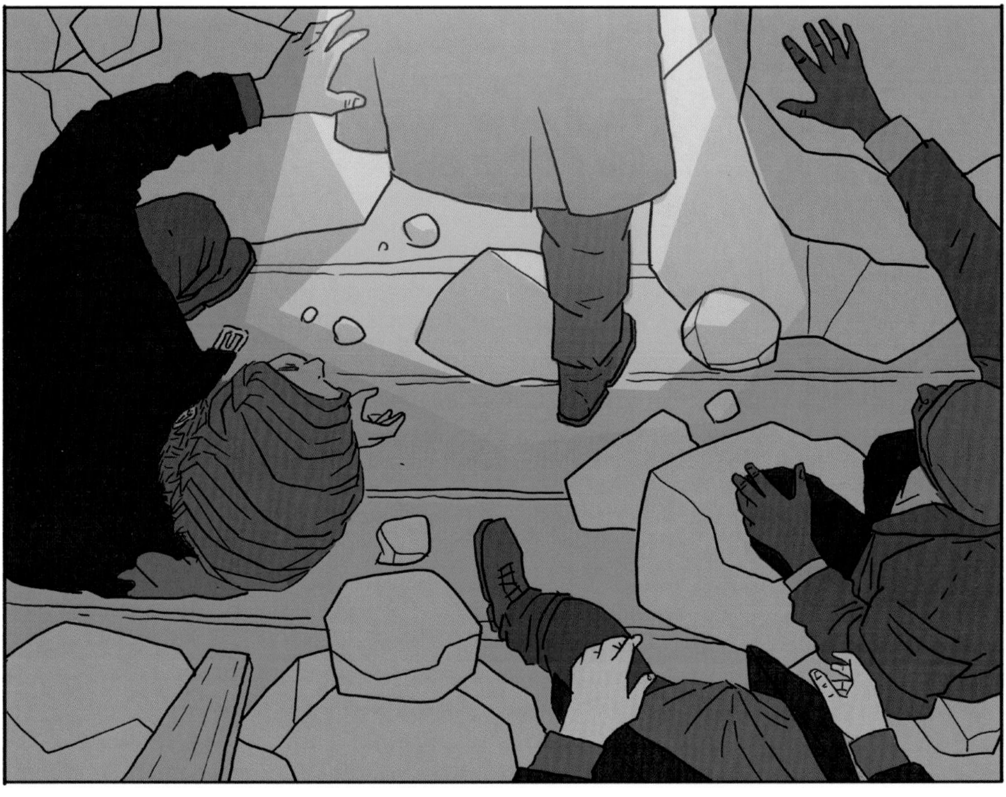

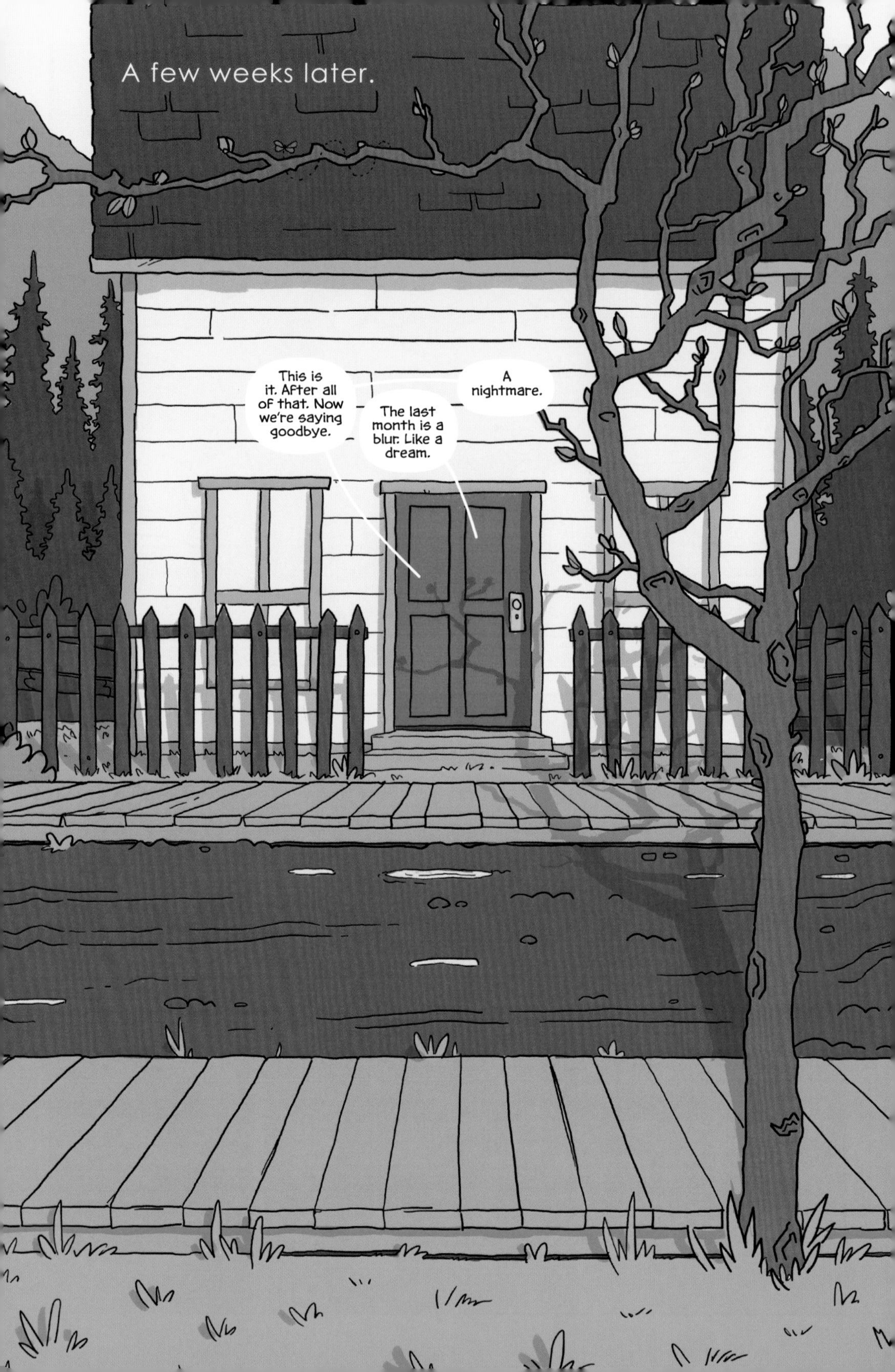
A few weeks later.
This is it. After all of that. Now we're saying goodbye.
A nightmare.
The last month is a blur. Like a dream.

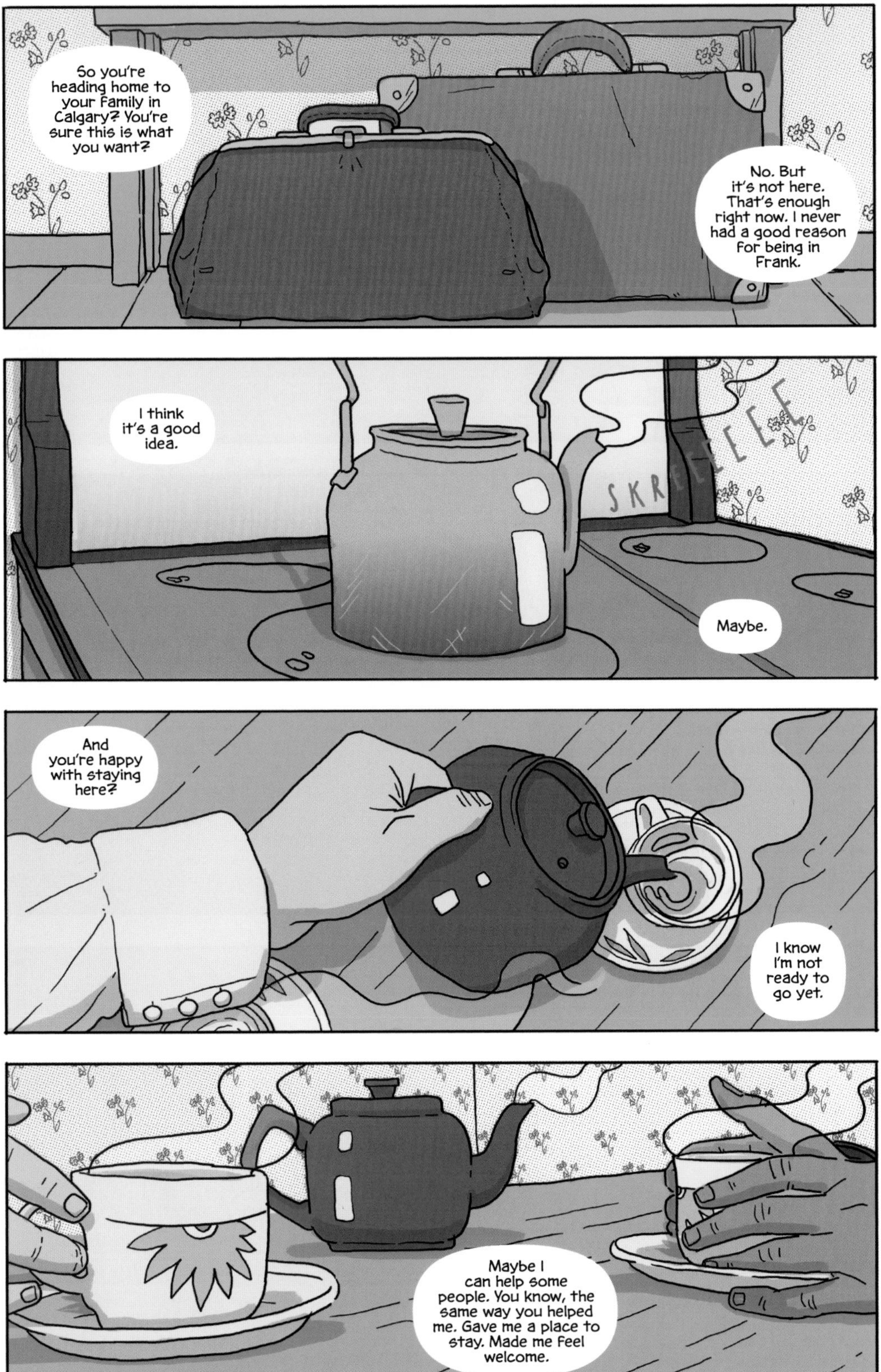

So you're heading home to your family in Calgary? You're sure this is what you want?
No. But it's not here. That's enough right now. I never had a good reason for being in Frank.
I think it's a good idea.
SKREEEEEE
Maybe.
And you're happy with staying here?
I know I'm not ready to go yet.
Maybe I can help some people. You know, the same way you helped me. Gave me a place to stay. Made me feel welcome.

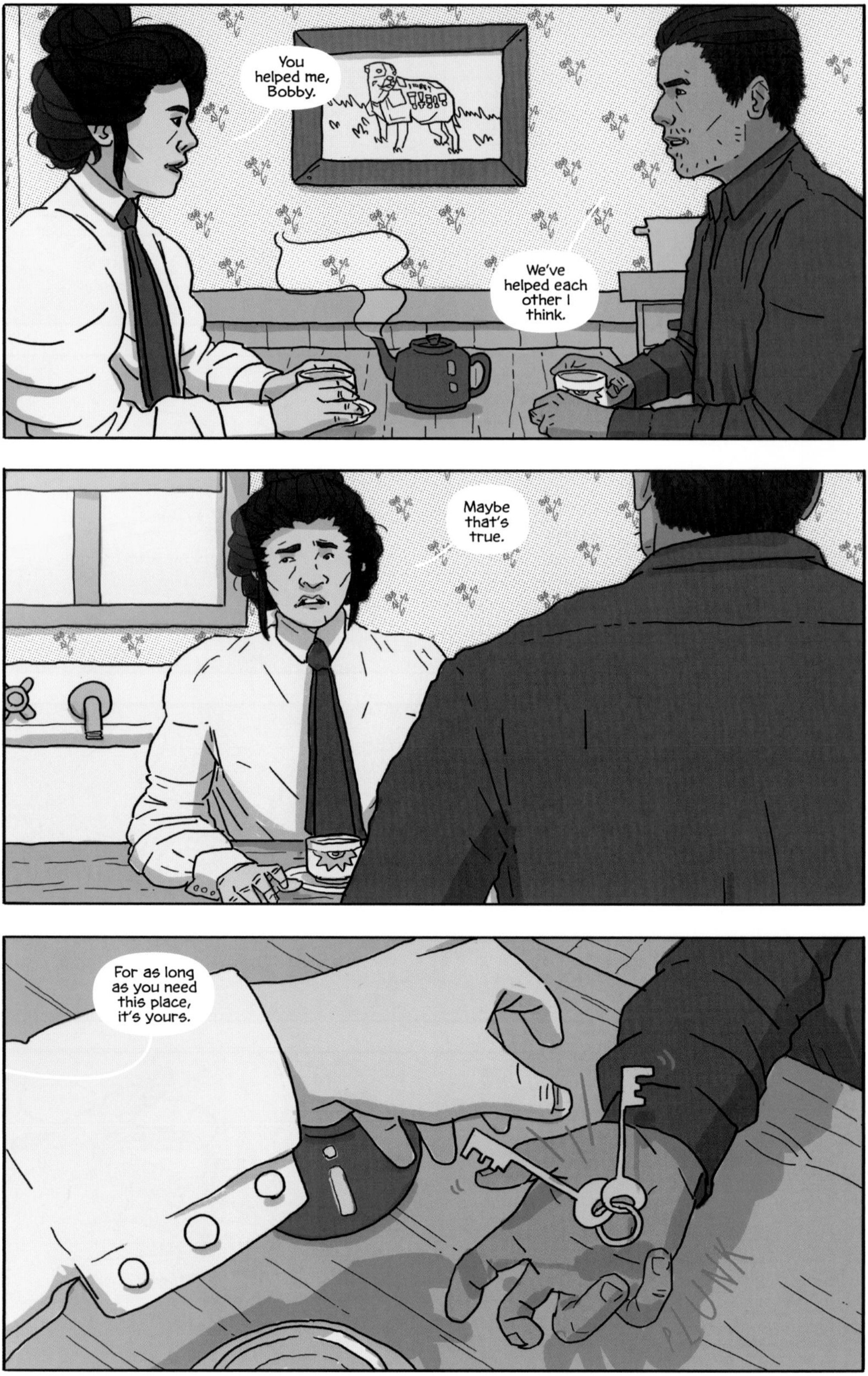
You helped me, Bobby.
We've helped each other I think.
Maybe that's true.
For as long as you need this place, it's yours.
PLUNK

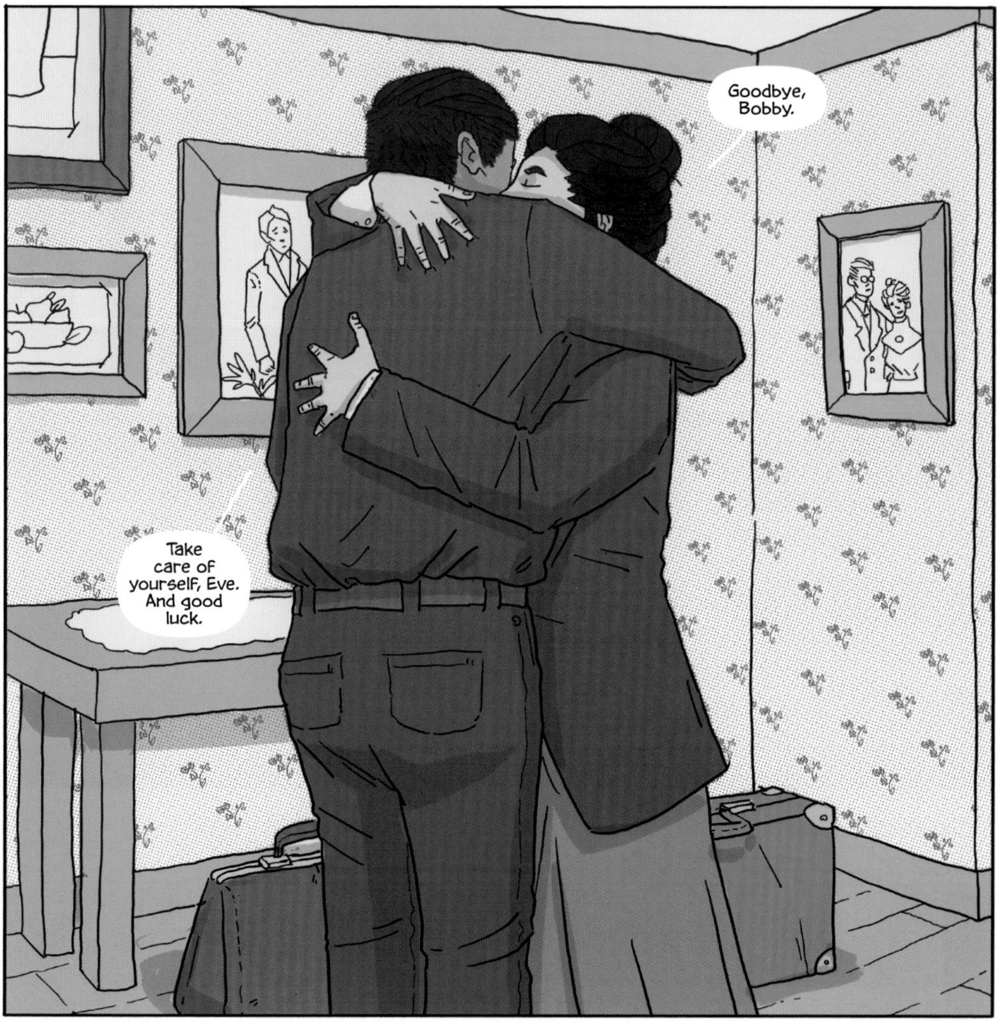
Goodbye, Bobby.
Take care of yourself, Eve. And good luck.

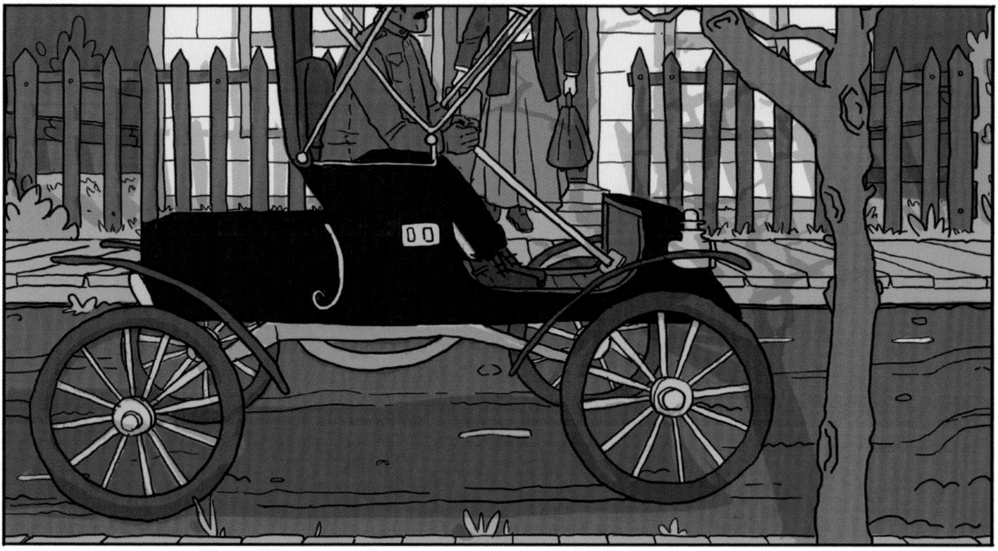

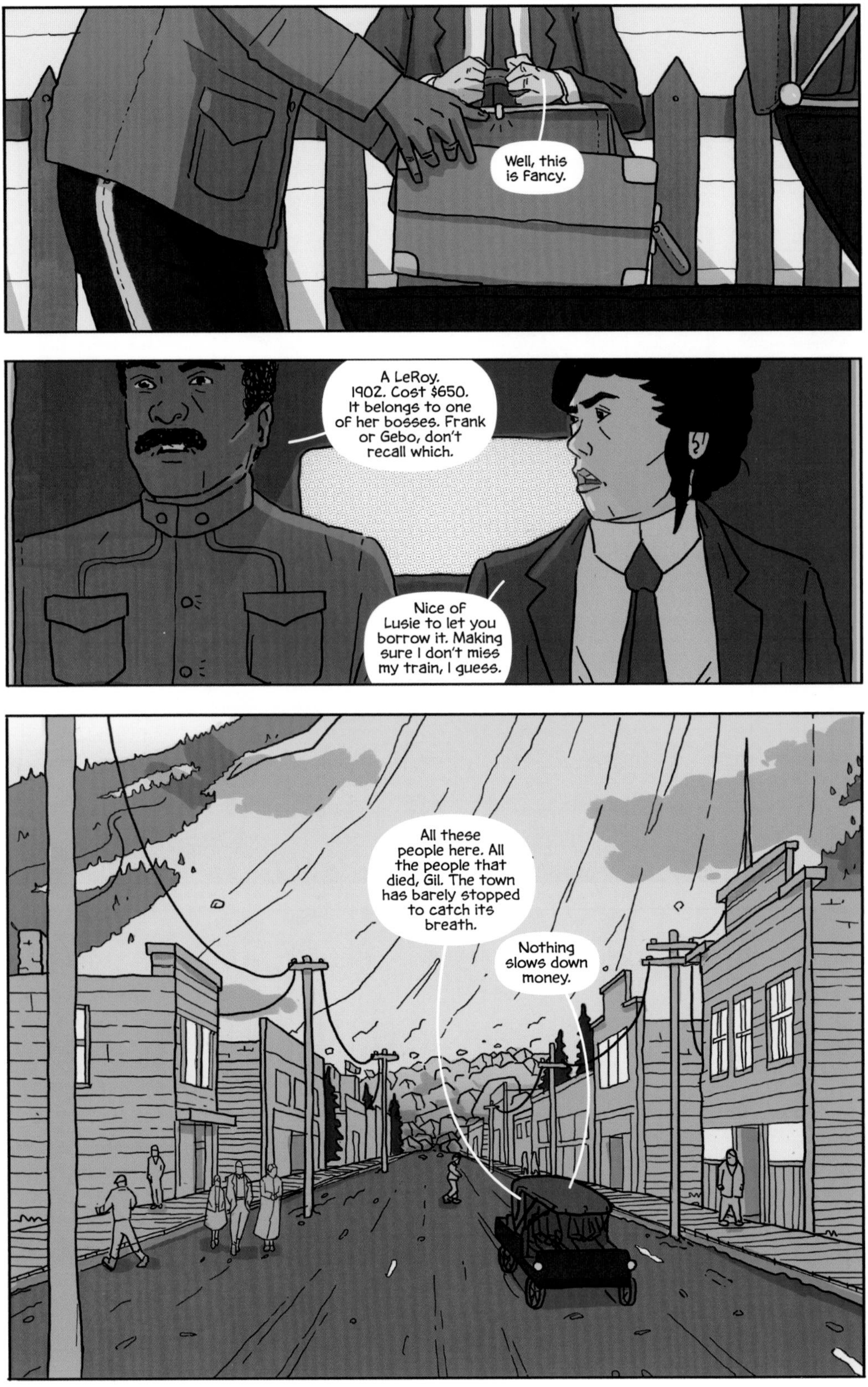
Well, this is fancy.
A LeRoy. 1902. Cost $650. It belongs to one of her bosses. Frank or Gebo, don't recall which.
Nice of Lusie to let you borrow it. Making sure I don't miss my train, I guess.
All these people here. All the people that died, Gil. The town has barely stopped to catch its breath.
Nothing slows down money.

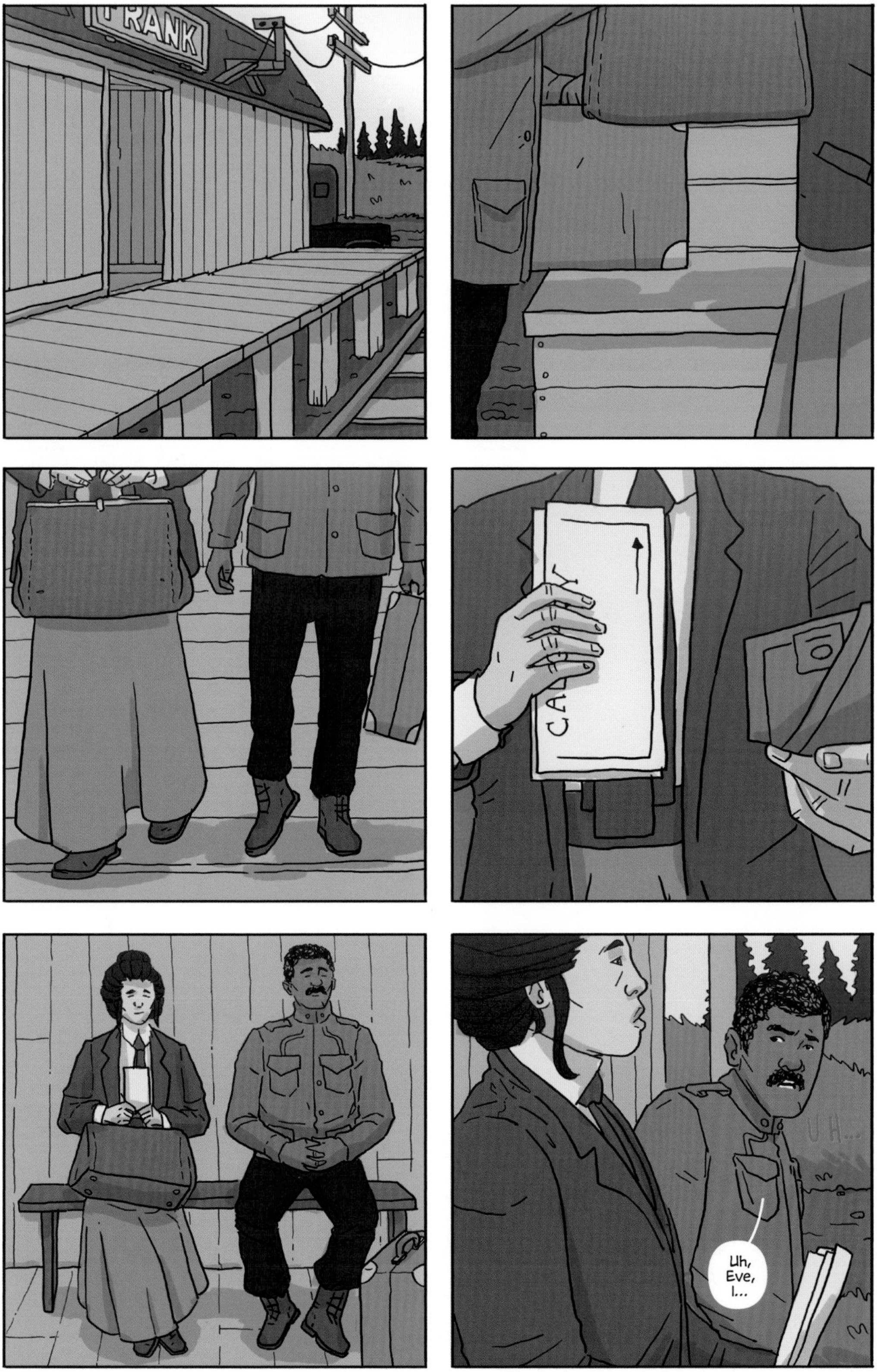
FRANK
UH...
Uh, Eve, I...

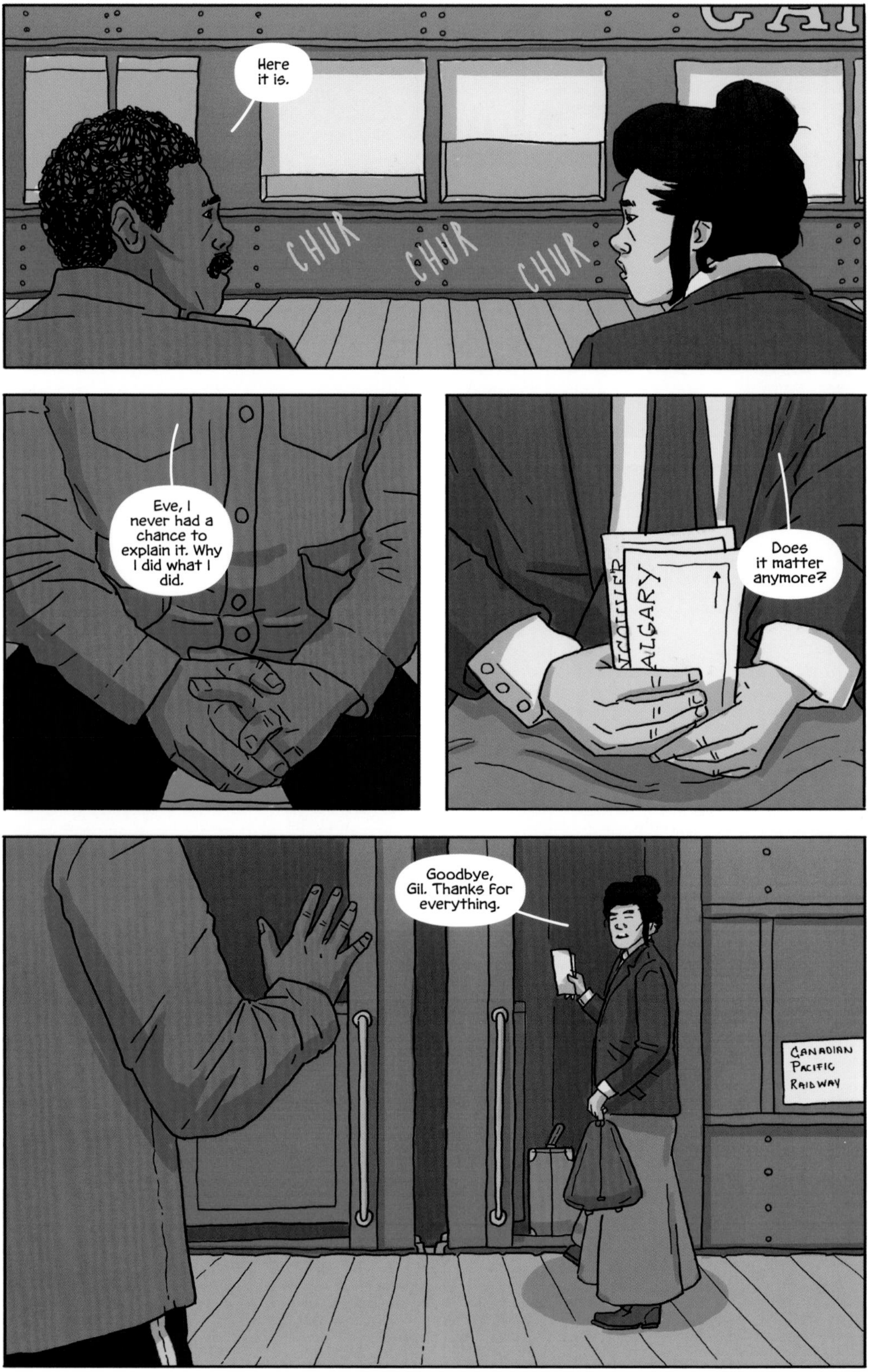
Here it is.
CHUR
CHUR
CHUR
Eve, I never had a chance to explain it. Why I did what I did.
Does it matter anymore?
Goodbye, Gil. Thanks for everything.
CANADIAN PACIFIC RAILWAY

CHUR
CHUR
CHUR
CHUR
CHUR
CHUR
CHUR
CHUR

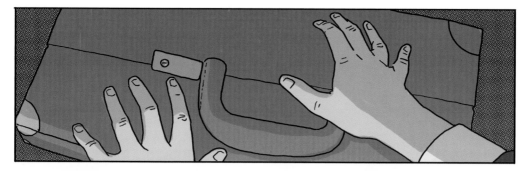

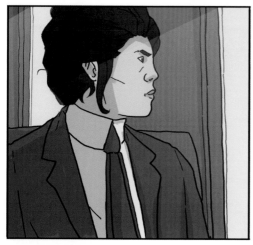

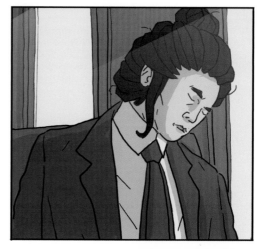

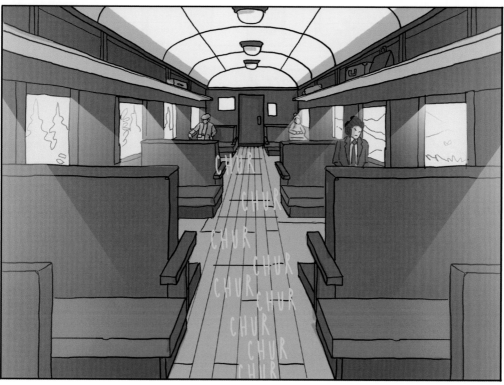

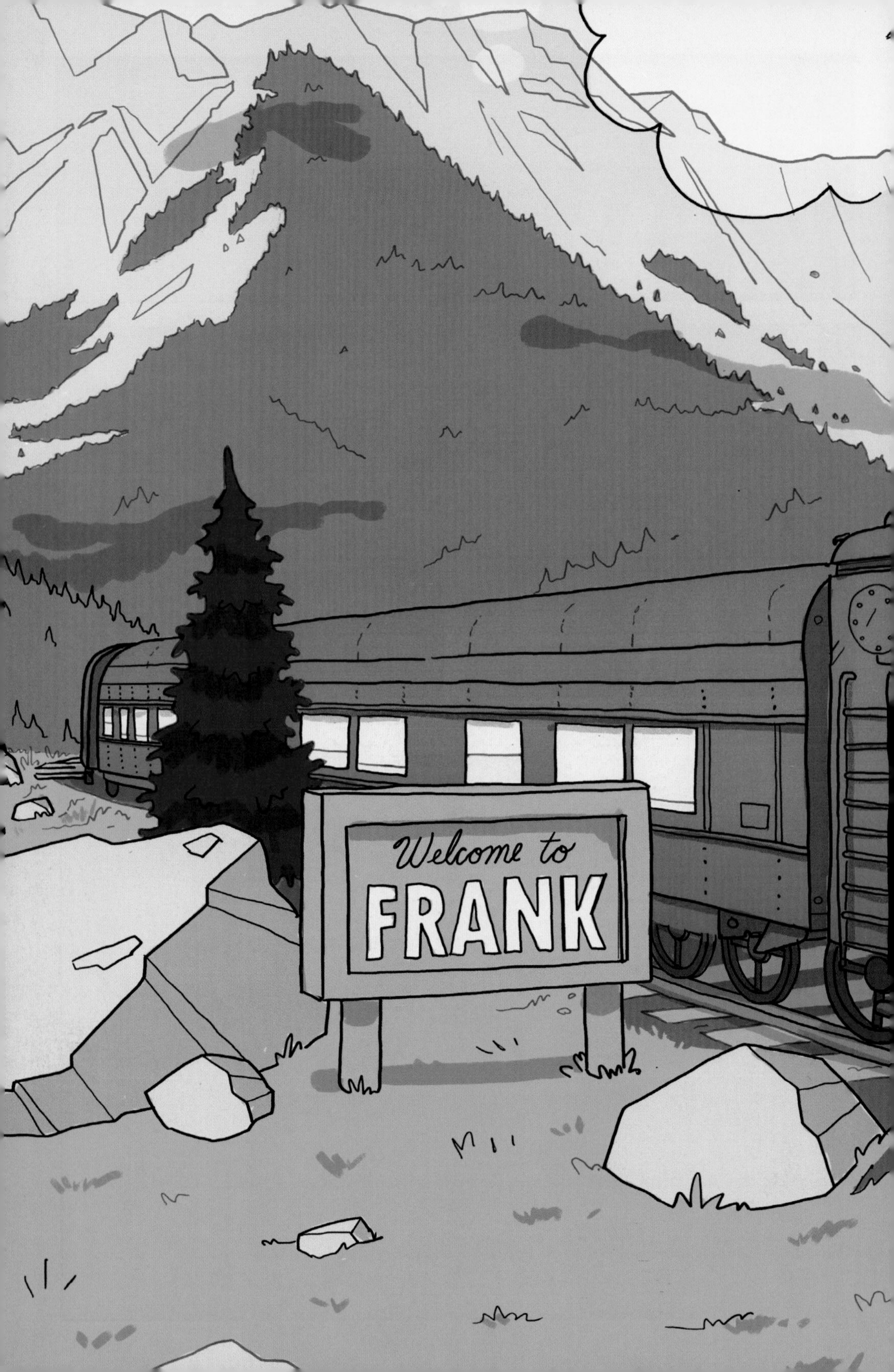
Welcome to
FRANK

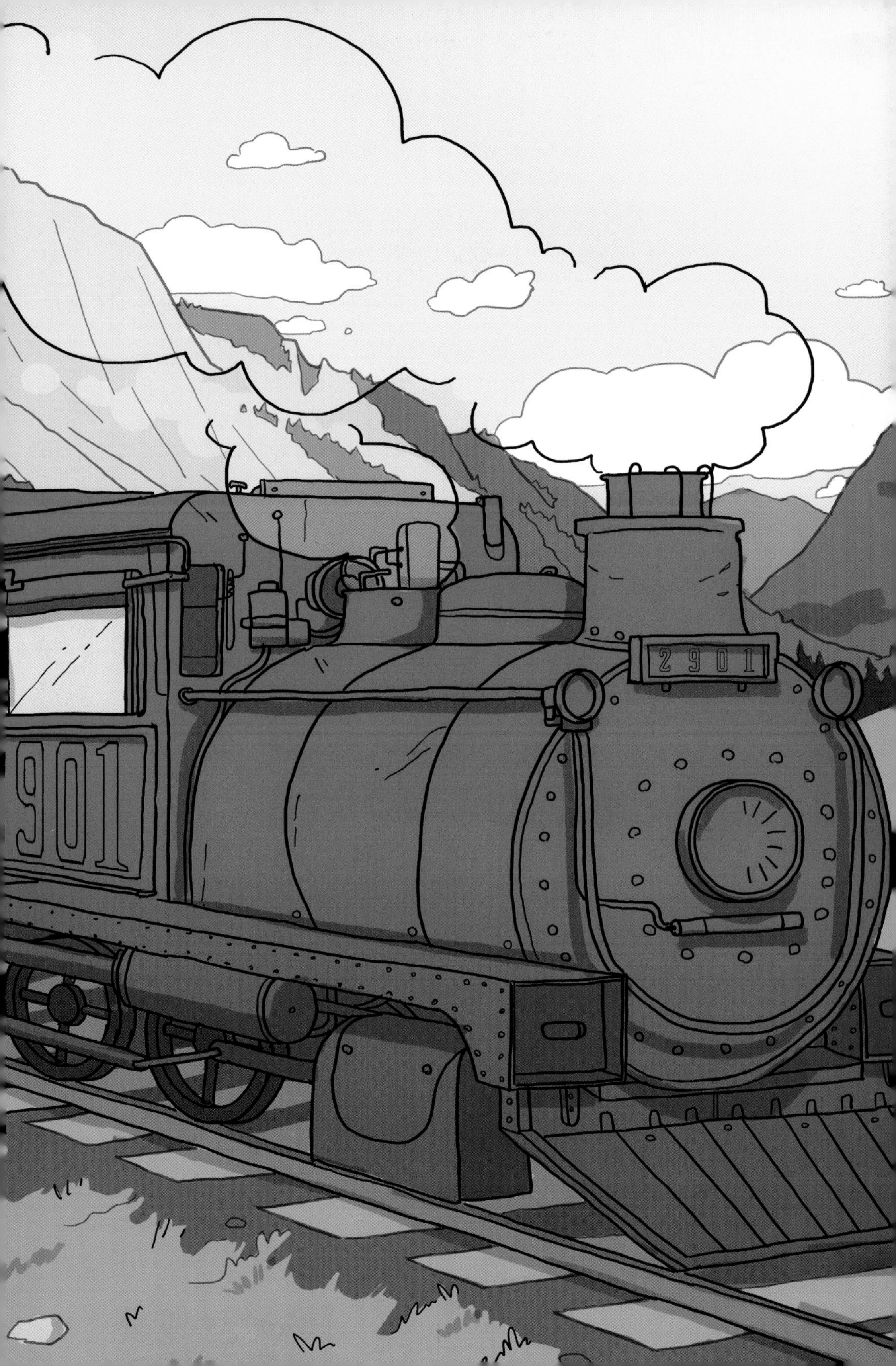
2901
901

ABOUT FRANK

FRANK, as you've probably realized now, isn't completely historical.

The town known as Frank is real (was real, its unincorporated now) and the devastating landslide depicted really did happen. But my Frank is a fiction. One inspired by my childhood memories of driving through Crowsnest Pass with my parents and 5 siblings, stuffed into the back of a Mercury Topaz. The never-ending, titanic rocks were mesmerizing and I'd spend the rest of our drive to Creston wondering just what had happened and beyond that, what could have happened. This was a place where stories grew.

The stories we get to consume as Canadians and as Albertans are often shaped and set by events and locations far beyond our range. My hope is that this simple story, like the Town of Frank for me, will inspire someone else to look around their home. To find right next door what I found as a kid, a fertile soil in which to plant the seed of a story.

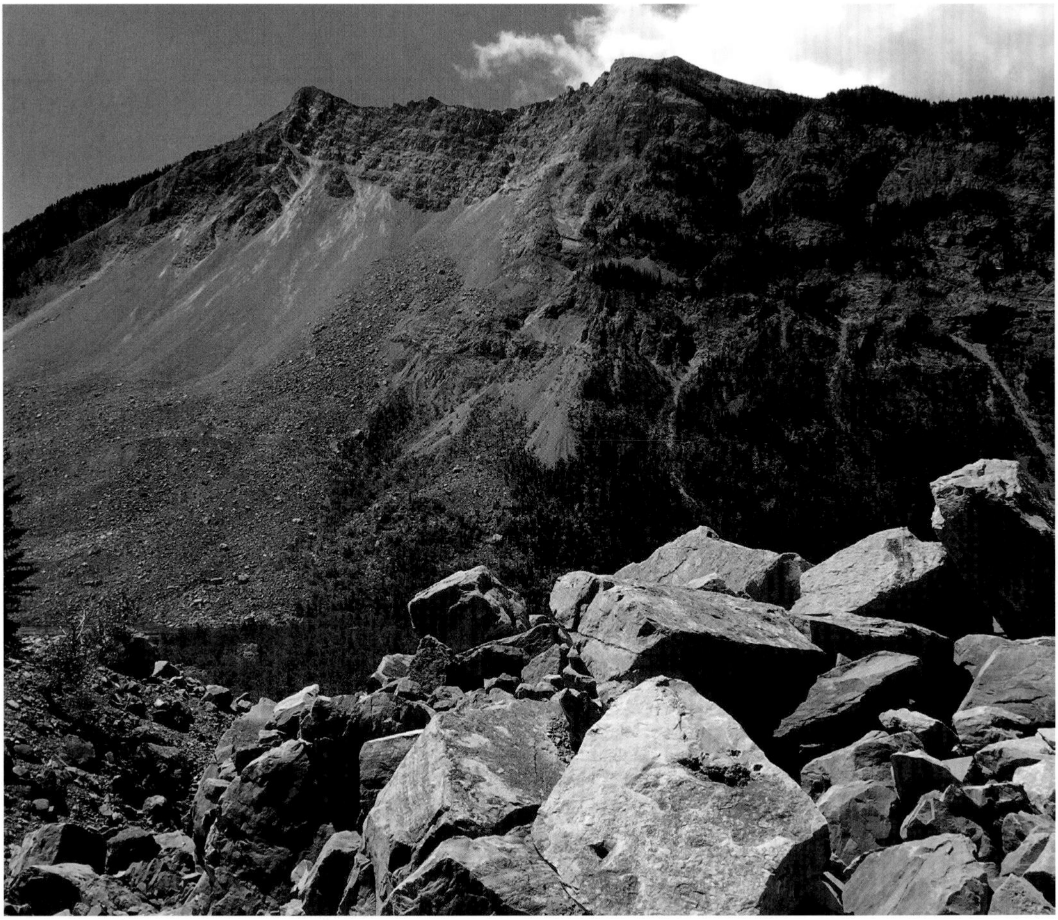

Ben Rankel is a cartoonist and this is his first original graphic novel. His other comics credits include Rat Queens shorts: GARY (Image Comics) and The Absent King (Comixology), as well as Faulty Pump (Fight! Comics/Comixology).

His comics, illustration and design work were nominated for a Western Canadian Music Award. He has also had comics work appear in Avenue Magazine, GrainsWest Magazine, and has been shown at the Roq La Rue gallery in Seattle.

Ben lives in Calgary, Alberta with his partner Fiona and their cat, Kupo.

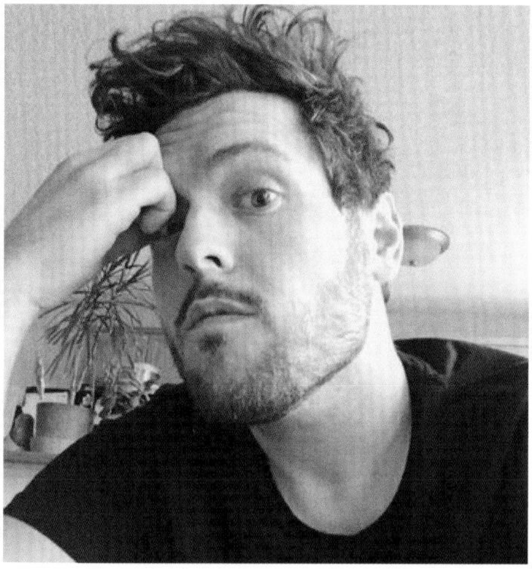

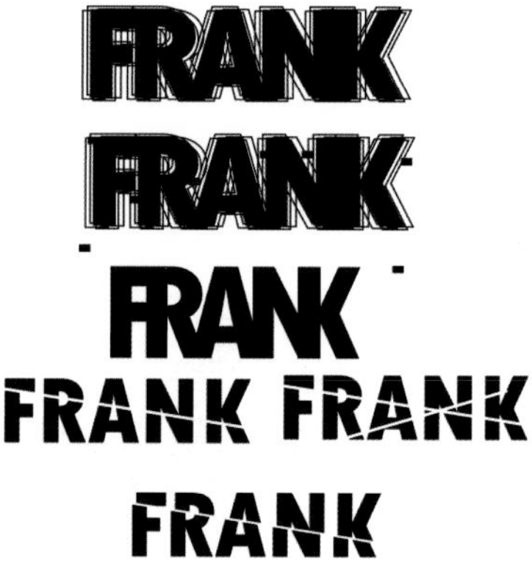
FRANK
FRANK
FRANK
FRANK FRANK
FRANK

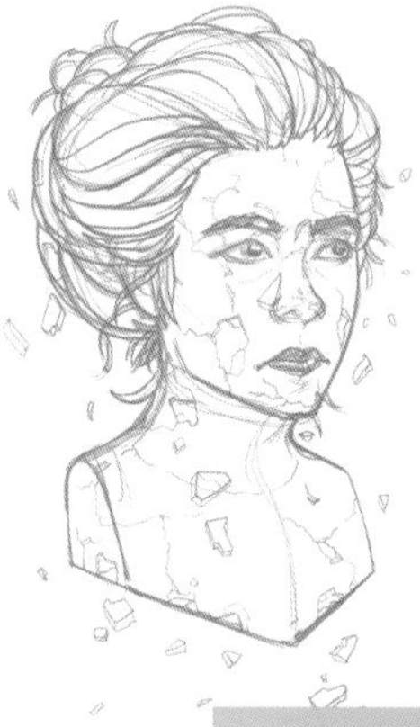

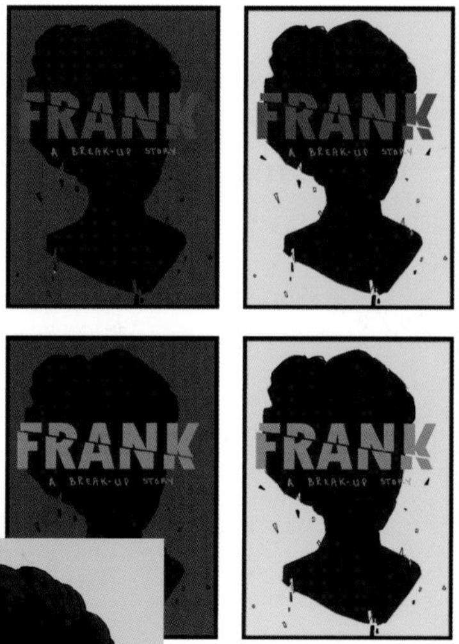
FRANK
A BREAK-UP STORY
FRANK
A BREAK-UP STORY
FRANK
A BREAK-UP STORY
FRANK
A BREAK-UP STORY

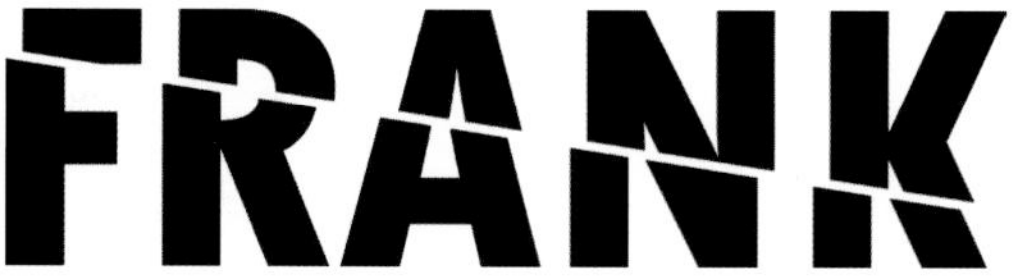
FRANK

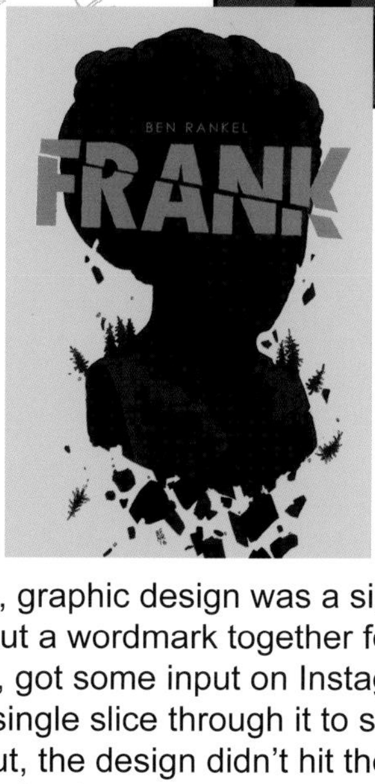
BEN RANKEL
FRANK

Before leaving my day job to work on FRANK, graphic design was a significant portion of my day to day life. So, when it came time to put a wordmark together for FRANK I wanted to take a swing at it. I did a few quick designs, got some input on Instagram and ended up choosing the bold, all caps version with a single slice through it to suggest the rock slide that the town of Frank was known for. But, the design didn't hit the sweet spot until our amazing letterer (and accomplished comic book writer) Ryan Ferrier put his stamp on it, adding the rough edges to the text and adjusting the spacing.

My process for writing the script was a little weird.

I created an outline, got it approved by my publisher/editor, then wrote one line of text for each page I thought the book should have. Following that I thumbnailed the book in its entirety. This is where the real story telling work happened for me, before I ever opened a Word document and wrote “Page One, Panel One”.

Please excuse the notes and doodles in the margins; they helped me focus.

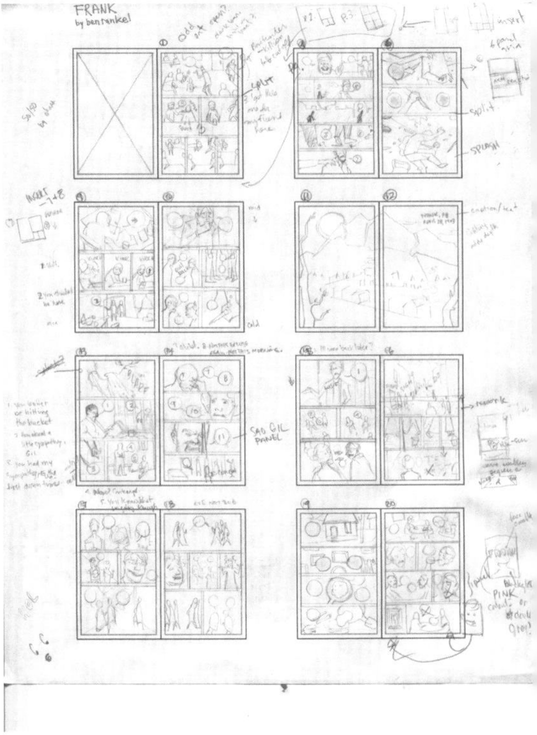
FRANK
SPLASH
SAD GIL PANEL

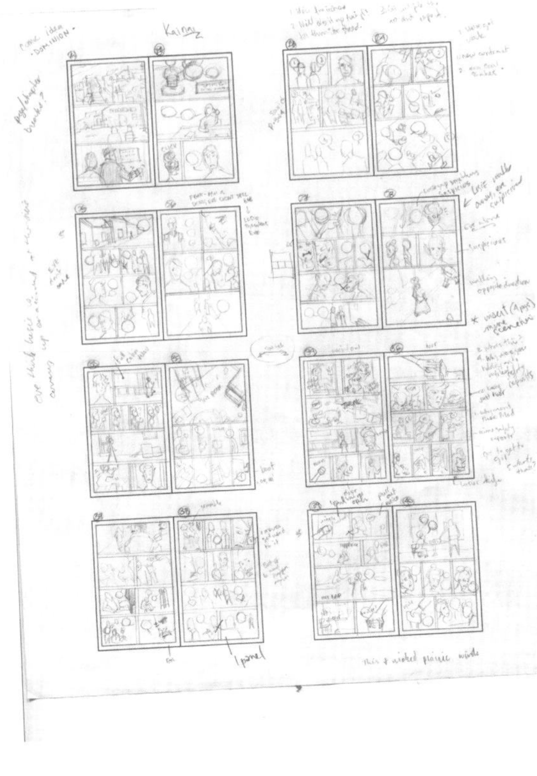

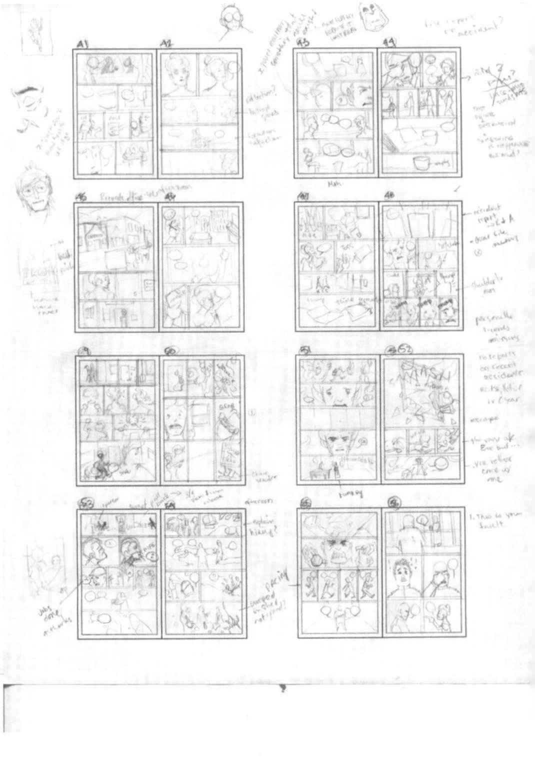

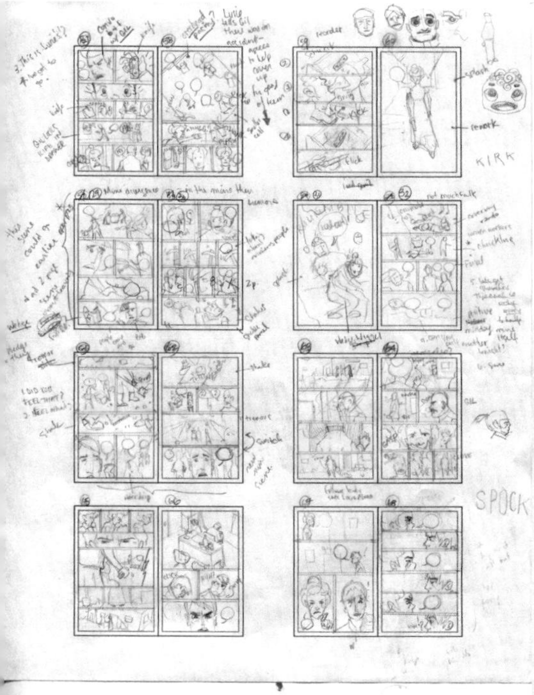
KIRK
SPOCK

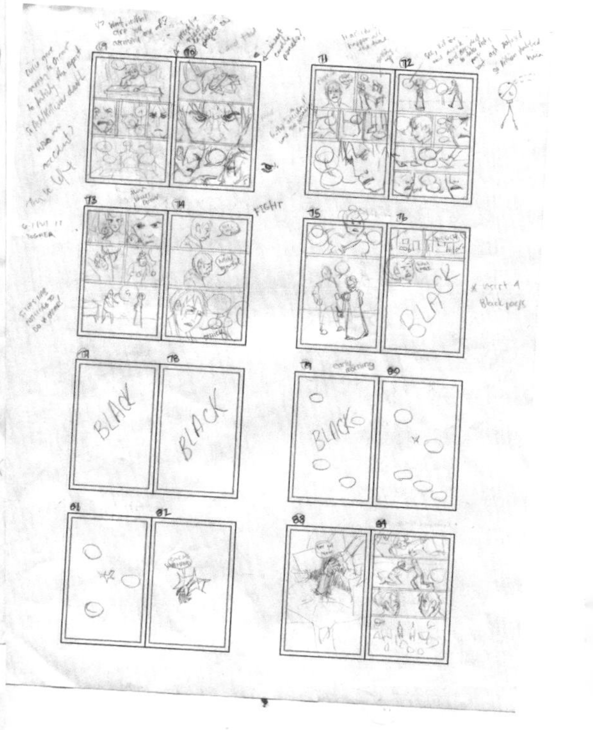
FIGHT
BLACK
BLACK
BLACK
BLACK
BLACK

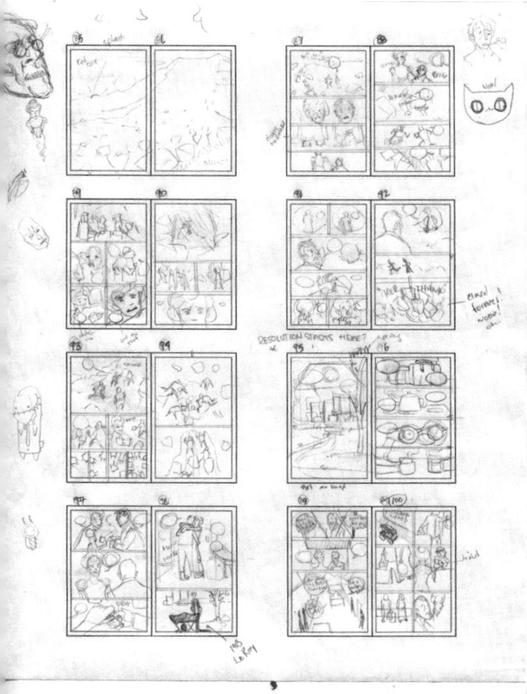
RESOLUTION STARTS HERE?

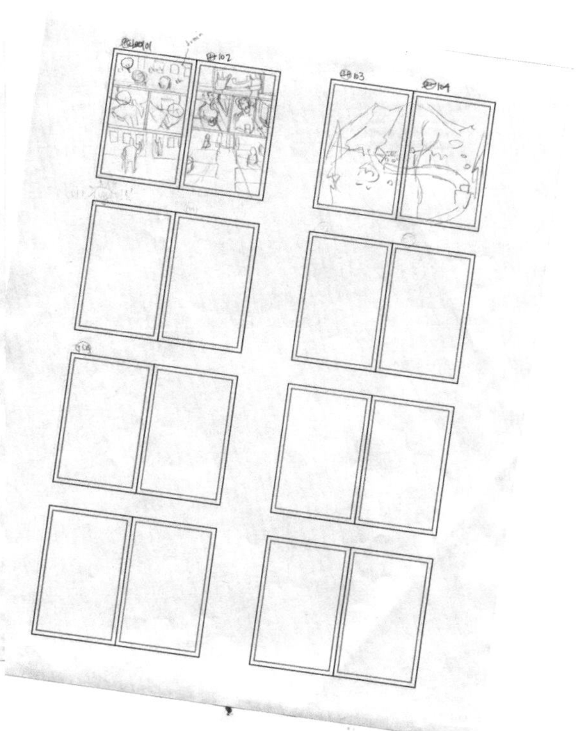

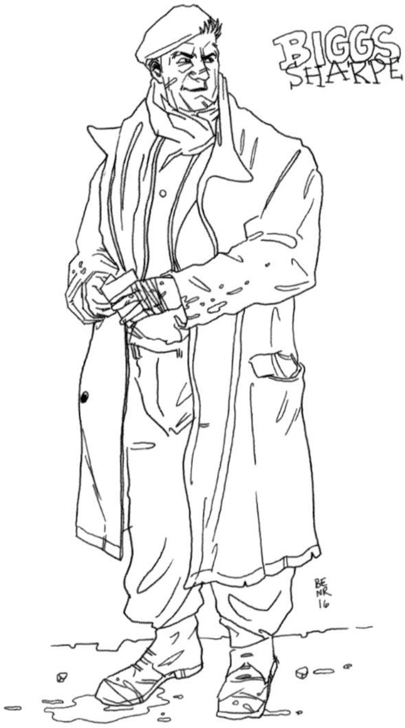
BIGGS
SHARPE

Art style & colour

Right from the beginning I knew I wanted to approach the drawing in FRANK with a style that was friendly and easy to read. I decided to ditch line weight and blacks in favour of a tech pen-like look and bright, acidic colours.

Some of those colours ended up becoming more muted to suit the story but the basic look of the book was defined here in this early sketch of one of the supporting characters.

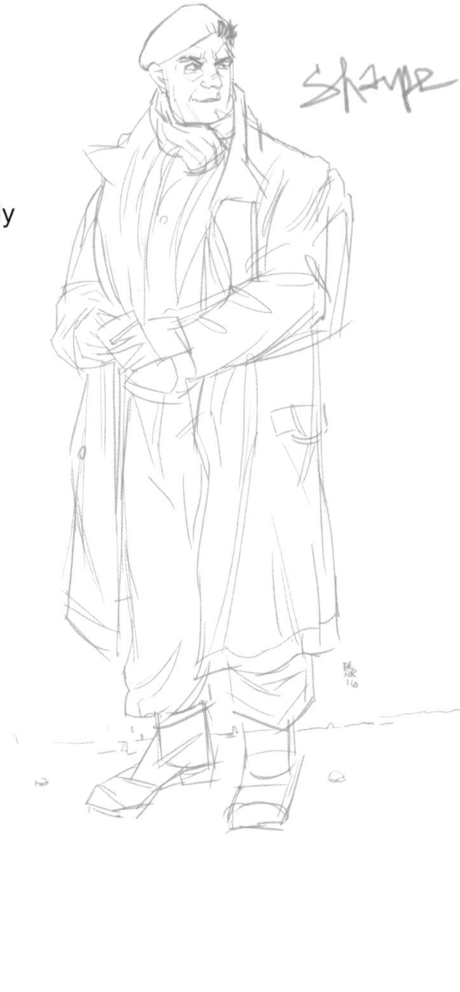
Sharpe

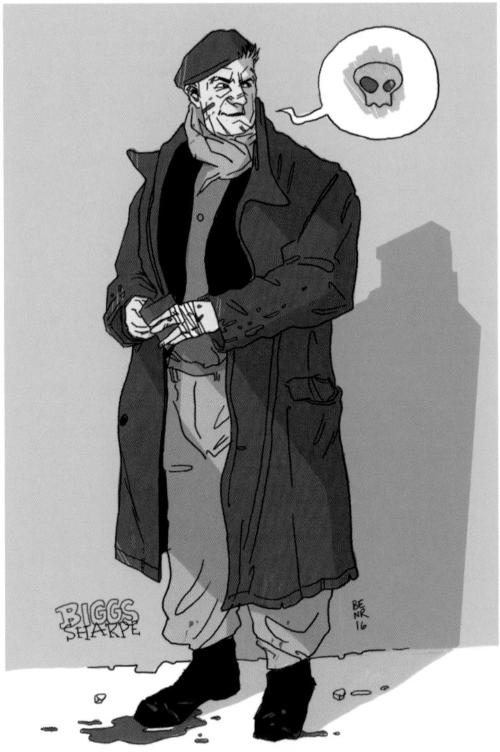
BIGGS
SHARPE